THE MIRACLES OF FRIENDSHIP

The Miracles Of Friendship

Maha Devi Li Ra La

Book 2 of the

Within The Ocean Of Eternal Love

Series

An Ananda Bliss Consciousness Book

Ananda Bliss Consciousness Inc

www.anandablissconsciousness.com
www.mahadevi-lirala.com

Book and Cover Design Copyright © 2015 Gabriele Brigitte Klonek

Book and Cover Design by Maha Devi Li Ra La

All rights reserved

ISBN: 978-1-910518-10-6

Printed and Copyrighted in the United States of America

British Library Cataloguing in Publication Data

Maha Devi Li Ra La

The Miracles Of Friendship

Book 2 of the

'Within The Ocean Of Eternal Love' Series

First Edition 2015

Dedicated to all

who unconditionally love and serve,

for they create a better world.

PREFACE

This is a spiritual fantasy novel about the power of true love and the Divine qualities it conjures from the depths of our souls. The story is fictional and loosely based on historical facts. By no means does the authoress claim historical accuracy. Nevertheless, an attempt was made to draw on the historical facts of the time period around 270 B.C. to support the storyline and characters of this novel. The story originates in Magna Graecia, Greek colonies located on the Italian Peninsula, and evolves through defining scenes taking place in additional locations and cultures, including Ancient Greece, Macedonia, and the Roman and Phoenician Empires, as well as the World Oceans.

The 'Within The Ocean Of Eternal Love' book series is a vibrant epic tale that resurrects many of Ancient Greece's most powerful and enigmatic Gods and Goddesses to either support or wreak havoc on mankind, depending on their unique traits and inclinations. Underwater Realms of exotic beauty and sunken marvels of a glorious past from long ago invite the reader to explore the oceanic depths alongside the protagonists, to rejoice in pleasant mer-folk company and sweat under the pressures of larger-than-life challenges that test the heroes and heroines to the core.

Fairies and elves enlivening the mystical forests add to the fairy tale and fantasy character of the novel; enchanting scenes of great spiritual meaning open the reader's mind to higher truths and realities. This is not a story that can easily be categorized; it is an epic tale of the kind that will still be read and appreciated a hundred years from now, for it is timeless in its message, and transforming and uplifting in its wonderfully deep impact on our souls. Let yourself be entertained by the absorbing, suspenseful adventures the heroes and heroines go through, and come out the winner in the end, as true epics always reward you with a satisfying ending that is equal to the protagonists' persistence and investment in their own self-transformation and personal growth.

CHAPTER 1

On their way back, neither Eurylochos nor Indirali feels like talking much; the revelations of the Oracle aimed at deep soul levels and need to now be reflected on and integrated. Eurylochos feverishly racks his brain as to how he can win the upper hand over his priesthood, now that he still has the advantage of knowing about their decadent and treacherous ways before they begin to suspect they are found out. The Oracle suggested initiating as many citizens into meditation as possible in order to soften the collective atmosphere of stress, anger, and fear, but for that to happen, he needs to get his hands on the many sacred texts the priests have stored away from his awareness and access. He knows he needs to be diplomatic about his approach, but right now all he feels is anger and frustration that he allowed himself to be fooled by them for so long and to such a large extent. He feels little mercy for these traitors who misled his people into believing they are the chosen spiritual elite, all the while sitting on a treasure big enough to solve every citizen's financial problems. In light of this profound betrayal, Poseidon's wrath seems almost justified, for Eurylochos' ignorance and gullibility as the King of Lucania has certainly contributed to the hardship of his people, and of course, he now wishes nothing more than to remedy the situation in accordance with divine law and mercy. Nevertheless, he sees no other choice than to march into the temple with his guards and take control of the hidden library, a wealth of knowledge he can under no circumstances risk forever losing into the hands of disloyalists who won't use it for the benefit of all of society.

Indirali, also, is immersed in her thoughts on how to proceed on her path, now that she was made aware of the potential pitfalls and dangers that might await her and Hedna on their long journey, crossing the volatile ocean to get to their final destination, Mount Olympos, the seat of the Gods. With anxious anticipation, she tries to think of a beautiful melody she wants to use to attract Zephyros to her cause, but then she remembers the Oracle's words to not let her intellect dominate her attempt to please him but to rather allow the tunes to stream from her heart and soul, the places deep within that are most intimately connected with the Divine Source, and which alone is able to inspire and provide the most touching, elevating, and ravishing melodies possible for any human to express. And so Indirali decides to let the courage and trust in a good outcome that she feels deeply within her heart take over her thoughts and feelings, and not worry about what is to come, for she knows that her infinite love for Loriolan is the best guidepost she could ever have, one that will unfailingly guide her to her lofty goal.

And so the both of them walk side by side, the sun setting and darkness starting to spread, with the sickle moon thankfully lighting their way to some extent, both silently aware of the fact that their ways are about to part, and that the pain of separation and the fear of the unknown need to stay repressed if they want to be able to let go of each other with a smile of support and encouragement for each other's destinies. Indirali notices how her inner restlessness seems to exclude the fairy kingdom from her awareness, unlike during their walk this early afternoon when her good mood and open mind allowed her to perceive the ethereal figures of the beautiful meadow and forest spirits, who laughingly and playfully interacted with her at times in telepathic ways, prompting her to laugh with them about the many cheerful things they undertook and sometimes demonstrated for her delight. She understands that it takes a cheerful attitude to be able to see these delicate, uplifting spirits and that her present somber attitude eclipses their reality from hers. But as she centers herself into a peaceful state, she begins to see several of the forest spirits again, who seem to be getting ready to fall asleep with the sunset. Indirali waves them good-night, and they dreamily respond with a wave back, wishing her well on her further journey, thankfully nodding at her for her open heart and mind that allow her to perceive them.

The two wanderers arrive late at night at the farmhouse, with several servants still awake to hurry out and welcome them back. After a hearty meal, the two tired souls retire to bed to find well-deserved sleep before their big trip begins in the morning.

Great excitement hangs in the air the next morning, as everyone gets ready to leave. Eurylochos gives his last advice to his daughter, hoping she will heed it and no misfortune will befall her on her long journey; otherwise his heart might break if she wouldn't return home safely. The Princess's garments were exchanged for some rugged men's wear, and, per Indirali's request, both Hedna and she were dressed up to look like stable boys, their hair pinned up and under a wig, all to avoid unwanted attention and to minimize being attacked by robbers and other scum. Everyone admires their looks and has to admit that they make a fine couple of lads, handsome to look at and sure to turn some women's heads around if they are not careful. Several guards jokingly try to teach the girls how to behave and walk as a man, somewhat exaggerating the differences between a woman's and a man's gait and posture. Everyone has a good laugh as the girls try to imitate the men. They agree they will have to practice quite a lot in order to pass as members of the male gender.

Finally, the moment of departure arrives, and with one last big, heartfelt hug, Indirali takes her farewell from her father. With tears in her eyes, she mounts the carriage her father brought along for her and Hedna, a royal carriage they had turned into a casual looking transport vehicle, with the royal emblem removed, and some wear and tear added to it for more authenticity. And even though Eurylochos wanted to have at least two guards accompany his daughter, he relented in the end, allowing just one guard to go along for her protection, because Indirali thought it wise to stay even more under the radar by not looking too wealthy to anyone who might make it their business to check them out. And so with a heavy heart, he waves good-bye to his daughter, watching her carriage leave and turn the corner to vanish from his sight. With a tear in his eye, he turns towards his own carriage, mounts it, and begins his own journey home, home to his beloved wife who awaits him with her sad heart, for their daughter has left, and all they are left with are their prayers for her success and safe return.

Indirali and Hedna look at each other, their eyes full of trepidation and curiosity as to what comes next. Then they smile and turn their heads to look out at the beautiful mountainous nature their carriage bumpily drives through, and soon the heaviness of departure yields to a feeling of newfound freedom and high hopes. They begin to joke at their new and changed looks, coming up with all sorts of funny gestures and behaviors they think a man would express, and which — compared to their graceful, feminine movements — seem relatively coarse and uninspiring. They each think of a male name to identify themselves with from now on, with Indirali's being Apollinaris, according to the handsome God Apollo, and Hedna's being Leonidas, for she thinks it wise to identify with the power of a lion in order to conjure the inner strength to meet any upcoming challenges adequately. The names make them feel even manlier and trigger all sorts of funny reactions from them, like trying to express each other's names with as low a voice as possible, or singing old folk songs with a man's voice, songs that allow them to express themselves as rambunctiously as their hearts desire. And so they have a blast laughing at each other's attempts to come across as manly and boastfully as possible without being too exaggerated and ridiculous in their efforts. Sometimes Eusebios, their coachman, joins their laughter, as the girls' laughter sounds rather joyous and infectious to his ears, and he likes nothing more than to hear the Princess being silly and playful, having a good start into her adventure he has the special privilege to be a part of. His job is to bring her and her maidservant safely to the Eastern shore, to the harbor city of Brundisium, in the country of Calabria. For that, they will have to travel south through the mountain range of Mount Alburnus along the Tanager River, then turn eastward towards the little town of Grumentum, find the River Aciris, and follow it to the coastal town of Heraclea. From then on, they will move along the coast of Lucania until they enter the country of Apulia for a short period, follow its southern shoreline into Calabria, and take a rest in the town of Taras, from where they will follow the eastbound Appian Way towards their final destination of Magna Graecia, the city of Brundisium, a place of much commerce and trade, with ships going in and out of its harbor all the time, trying to reach overseas destinations to enliven the economies of several countries of Magna Graecia — at least this is what he remembers from a long time ago. He also heard that much distress has befallen the seafaring world since Poseidon cursed humanity for being so arrogant and destructive to nature and the oceans, and has, since then, begun to systematically destroy many proud ship lines and wealthy owners, leaving traders without the means to exchange their goods with each other across the sea and borders. Eusebios is curious to see how life in Brundisium looks like nowadays, and whether he can help find a reliable, friendly captain whose ship can take the Princess and her maid across the Adriatic Sea.

And so the party of three continues to bump along the dirt path through a mountain canyon, letting their spirits soar and being of good cheer, for Indirali is finally enjoying the taste of freedom and self-responsibility. At lunchtime, the travelers arrive at an inn outside of Grumentum and decide to take a break to get refreshed again for their further trip.

Eusebios wants to stay with the horses, and Indirali says she will have the waitress bring out some food to him. Then the two girls-turned-men enter the inn, ready to sit and have a good meal. But how strange it is for Indirali to step into a place without being the center of attention, and without anyone moving aside to let her through. She has to adjust to this fact, and thinks it will be easier over time. But not only does the crowd ignore the two strangers, it seems the innkeepers are completely absorbed with serving a bunch of half-drunk guests, who scream at the top of their lungs for more and more of the food, meat, and wine, drowning out any requests Indirali tries to send across the room to the hurrying waitresses and preoccupied innkeepers. Several times the two girls are pushed aside in rough and inconsiderate ways, treated as if they are a nuisance, who better leave before they get either trampled on or thrown out of the inn. Increasingly desperate with the situation, Indirali raises her voice, trying to sound as baritone as possible, commanding the innkeeper to take heed of their needs, determined to not take 'No' for an answer. That, for some reason, seems to finally get the innkeeper's attention. With sweat on his forehead, he apologizes for the hustle and bustle in his place and leads the two young men to a small table in the rear of the inn. The girls order three plates of food, asking for two of them to be without meat, and for the third to be brought out to Eusebios, their coachman. The innkeeper looks at them with puzzlement; all he understood is to have one plate brought outside and the other two brought to them. To want a meal without meat does not seem to register within his range of understanding, and so the girls deem it wise to leave the innkeeper to his reality and have him bring the kind of food he is used to. For the last thing they want is to draw unwanted and potentially dangerous attention to themselves, odd as they already must come across as such gentle-looking men. The innkeeper acknowledges their order, then turns around to take care of some ruffians who have started to complain about the delays, ready to throw some food items towards the bar to draw the attention back to them. The girls try to look the other way, for the atmosphere seems harsh and provocative, and to get involved in this debasing interaction could easily reveal their charade and turn the situation bitterly against them. Inside, however, they hope to be served some food fast so they can be out of this place as quickly as possible. Every minute in this joint feels like hell, especially since one of the inconsiderate guys begins to address them, wanting to know all about where they are from and where they are off to, all the while boasting about his prey caught today from the woods, because the group are hunters, and as such — it seems — the world belongs to them. Fortunately, Indirali and Hedna have their story straight, saying they are sons of a farmer who want to try their luck as shipmates on one of the ships leaving the harbor at Heraclea. This story seems good enough for the curious guy, and with a big belch and roar he joins in with his buddies again, who all toast each other on their big feat, escalating into a thunderous song-like roar that further emphasizes their unbreakable bond of lower-self brotherhood.

After what seems like an eternity, the girls get two platters with the most simple and coarse-looking meal they must ever have gotten served. They look at each other with hesitation, but then Hedna takes a bite, chews it carefully as if to test it out for her Mistress, then lifts her thumb as if to attest to its edibility. Gingerly, Indirali takes her first bite, then swallows the plain tasting food down as if to resign herself to her fate as a simple boy from the country who doesn't know any better and who therefore doesn't miss the refined, delicious cuisine of the palace, with all the fresh and vital fruits and vegetables that are harvested daily from the many gardens surrounding the palace. She gives herself an inner push, resolved to humbly endure any hardships that may present themselves to her along the way, knowing that it is all part of a higher testing and that pride should be the least of her problems. Both of them, however, can't force themselves to eat the meat and therefore only eat the side dishes, of which there are hardly any. The meal is quite unsatisfying for them, but all that matters is that they get something into their stomachs. And so the two girls eat quietly, aware to not draw any attention to themselves if they can help it, trying to remain as invisible and inconspicuous as possible.

After they get the innkeeper's attention long enough to pay for their food, they make their way out, glad to be released from the fangs of hell without much unwanted entanglement and confrontation. And as they walk up to the stables, they become aware of a big cart the hunters must have parked right outside the inn, with one man guarding what seems to be a big pile of bloody animal corpses, prey they must have all killed and gathered throughout their triumphant day, and which now triggers immense revolt in the girls; their stomachs turning as if to throw up, they run past the stinking nuisance to escape this sad reality that so many people participate in without much regret and awareness of the subtle interrelations they share with the animal world. All the girls can think of is to get to Eusebios and to get the heck out of this unfortunate place. The stable is big, with lots of hay stacked up and several horses munching complacently around the barn. Where is Eusebios? They begin to shout his name, hoping to see his face any moment, but receive no answer. Worried, they look in all the corners and behind all walls and haystacks for their coachman, only to come out empty-handed. Where is he? He certainly wouldn't have left them to their own fate! Eusebios is one of Indirali's father's most loyal and longstanding guards, a man of high integrity and honor. With slight panic in their face, they run out to ask the hunters' guard whether he saw their coachman, describing to him exactly how Eusebios looks, but the man just grins at them and tells them he saw nothing of the kind, and to go inside and ask any of the other men whether they saw their man. Clueless, the girls look around. They know that Eusebios did not enter the inn; he therefore must be around somewhere out here. And so they thank the guard for his attention, then continue looking in the farther vicinity of the inn, searching in ever-larger circles around the perimeter only to find nothing, no trace of him whatsoever. They decide to ask the innkeeper whether Eusebios received any food, but the innkeeper can't even remember the girls ordering the extra plate. The girls are close to collapsing. What vicious game are these people playing on them? Is the world already completely against them before they even had the opportunity to get anywhere far or to a location of any real significance? Trying to repress their tears, as any man would do, they keep searching for their coachman, because until they know of his fate, Indirali doesn't feel comfortable to continue on with her journey. He might be hurt and injured for that matter, and to leave him to such questionable, unknown fate is beyond her sense of urgency to get on with her journey as quickly as possible.

Persistently, the girls keep looking, reaching farther and farther off the beaten path, and finally after several hours of painstaking search, they come across what looks like a big hole carved out from the ground, with Eusebios moaning quietly when he hears them shouting his name. Aghast, they find him lying in that hole, cramped up with pain, because someone must have beaten him up thoroughly from the looks of it, his face bleeding and many bruises showing all over his body. Feverishly, they look around to find a stick long enough for Eusebios to hold on to and be pulled up by them. They encourage him to hold on while they get ready to pull him out, but it turns out Eusebios is unable to stand on his feet because his right knee is twisted out of its socket. Anxiously, the girls want to know who did this to him, but he is unable to speak coherently at this point, the pain showing starkly on his face. Indirali jumps into the hole to help prop him up and do her best to push him up while Hedna holds the long branch as strongly and unwaveringly as she can. Finally, after many excruciating attempts, Eusebios is out, and all collapse on the ground to take a breather from the ordeal. Slowly, Eusebios comes to his senses enough to convey how three masked men took him by surprise while he was brushing the horses, gagged him, threw him into the carriage, harnessed the horses to it, and began to race wildly into the forest with him, where after a while they stopped, being far enough from the inn, to beat him up severely and throw him into this big hole they must have either known about or shoveled out themselves for exactly this kind of purpose. Eusebios is distraught that the carriage and horses are lost, and his leg is injured to the extent that he can hardly walk by himself anymore. He feels a broken man who regrets deeply to have let the Princess and his King down in such an embarrassing and unfortunate way. But Indirali doesn't want to hear of it. With words of encouragement and compassion, she tries to lift his spirits, telling him that he has served her father for many years unfailingly, and that this misfortune that just happened should not find her father's ears, for it would surely make her parents sick with worry to hear that such calamity has befallen their daughter so early in her journey. Eusebios sees the wisdom in her words and gratefully accepts her suggestion. But the task he received from his King, namely to deliver her safely to an agreeable captain, still rests on his shoulders, even though he has no idea how to stand up at this point and walk.

Indirali needs to think about it all for a moment. Then she asks Hedna to help her create a stretcher from the many twigs and branches that lie all around the forest ground, so they can successfully carry Eusebios back to the inn and hopefully find out whether a doctor lives nearby. Hedna immediately gets to work, and soon the stretcher is built, and they can begin their return walk to the inn they were hoping to not ever have to see again. They just hope the hunters have left by now, for they are not in the mood to run into troubles with them at this poignant hour of emergency.

Fortunately, the bulk of misbehaving guests has already left, allowing Indirali to get more, but not all, of the innkeeper's attention, for he is busy helping his staff clean up the enormous dirt and mess his guests caused to his establishment, cussing and growling as if at odds with the whole world. When Indirali asks him whether he might have any idea who did this underhanded and mean thing to her coachman, he becomes almost irritated at her persistence, telling her to leave and not bother him with questions he can't answer. He says they should have watched their carriage better and not blame people who have nothing to do with their plight. No matter how kindly Indirali tries to get a reasonable answer out of him, he just isn't in the mood today, and maybe not ever, for he hates his ungrateful job, and he couldn't care less if he never saw any of his bullying guests ever again. Indirali realizes there is no reasoning with him and finally holds a beautiful emerald ring under his nose to get his attention. And lo and behold, his eyes start to glow, and he looks at the ring as if it was an answer from the Gods to all his problems. "What do you want?" he asks her with a changed tone of voice that is still rather unkind, for his heart is still bitter towards anyone but his own family.

"First, I would like some food for our injured and weakened friend here," she points at Eusebios who can hardly hold it together anymore. "We want to take the food with us, and we need to find a doctor for him right away. His wounds are bad, and he needs a doctor to yank his knee into place. Do you know of any doctor in this area who can help us?"

The innkeeper's wife approaches, a loaf of bread and cheese in her hand. She hands it to Hedna, then affirms that there is a doctor in town, and that it will take them about an hour to walk there. Indirali thanks her for her help and asks for directions on how to get there. The couple takes turns describing the way, and by the end of it feel better about their day, for a couple of fine young lads brought them back to their own good senses, and if they are honest with themselves, they like the idea of being able to help out and be richly rewarded for it with a ring that reminds them of royal splendor.

With all the strength and endurance they have, Indirali and Hedna set out to drag Eusebios behind on the stretcher, hoping he will be okay and the pain won't traumatize him beyond measure. With feeble words of gratitude that he keeps muttering whenever he is conscious enough, Eusebios lets himself be helped by the very girls the King entrusted into his own care.

CHAPTER 2

At nightfall they all arrive at the doctor's residence, with a gate blocking the view onto the main house. Firmly, Indirali knocks on the gate hoping someone will answer it right away. But after another several knocks, the gate still doesn't open. At a loss, the girls stare at each other, then walk along the fenced property, only to find that there is no entrance possible from any other side. But they don't want to give up and let Eusebios die from his wounds; they just have to knock harder and louder, and even shout if nothing else works. And so the girls begin to create a spectacle, shouting for the doctor at the top of their lungs, when neighbors start noticing them and begin to complain about their rude and inconsiderate behavior. At some point, someone threatens to call the authorities, when all of a sudden, the doctor's door opens, and an old maid asks them to hush up and state their business.

Indirali points at Eusebios, explaining how he got beaten up and therefore desperately needs a doctor's attention. The maid lets them in, shouting to the upset neighbors that all is well and they should just go to bed. The girls take up the stretcher again and pull Eusebios inside the gate. Now the doctor himself comes to the door and, wrapping a stola around his shoulders, meets with them.

"What do we have here?" he wonders. "Gotten in a fight with other drunkards, have we?"

Indirali doesn't like his tone of voice, nor does she like his insinuation. "He is a royal guard whom we found bleeding in the ditch. His horse was stolen, and the robbers left him there to die. Will you please help him?"

The doctor looks at her startled: "Royal guard? Are you sure you're not inventing some incredible story just so you get me to help your friend here for free?"

"Why would I want to do that, and what would we gain from such a lie?" she retorts, getting almost angry with him. It is one thing for a lowlife robber to beat someone to death, but another thing altogether for a doctor to ask all sorts of degrading questions. But then she realizes the doctor doesn't know who she truly is, and that he might have a history with people lying to him. And so she tries to stay patient, even though Hedna and she are quite exhausted from the haul and pretty frustrated with the situation. "He is a royal guard, whether you believe it or not, and what does it matter in the end anyway?" she asks with a hint of frustration. "Are you not a doctor and, as such, bound by the oath of Hippocrates that states you serve any patient with all the skill and goodwill you can muster, no matter what his station in life?"

The doctor looks at the lad in front of him a bit closer. Who is this guy to remind him of the oath of his profession, and how does this uneducated looking farm boy know anything about his craft anyway!

A moan from Eusebios, however, reminds him of his duty, and with a commanding voice, he calls on two servants from the house to carry the wounded man in and prepare him for the treatment. Indirali and Hedna follow the doctor into the house, and since nobody orders them to stay outside the treatment room, they mingle with the rest, trying to be of further help. But mostly they watch the doctor take care of Eusebios, with a maid trickling some fluid into his mouth to ease the pain and help him relax. After carefully cleaning his biggest wounds, the doctor rubs some bitter herbs between his hands to sprinkle on them, to help stop the bleeding and numb the pain even more. Then he takes a look at the hurt leg, and indicates for his servants to hold the man's arms so he won't jeopardize the resetting of his knee. A piece of leather-bound wood is put into his mouth, and then the doctor pulls Eusebios' lower leg, all the while turning his knee, until a pop is heard and the leg is reset. Eusebios screams out with pain, and then collapses into a comatose sleep.

The doctor looks somewhat tired and a bit stressed out. "So what did you say your relationship with this man was?"

"No relation!" Indirali explains. "We traveled along the forest road, when all of a sudden, we heard a heartwrenching moan from someone below the earth. When we came closer, we detected this unfortunate man, who had been robbed by some underhanded thieves and thrown into a deep hole that could have easily become his grave, would fortune not have sent us to find him."

"Well, he was fortunate indeed to have been found by you, for he would have surely died from his bleeding if you would not have brought him to me as quickly as you did. A couple of rare individuals you both are," he looks at Indirali and Hedna with a frown on his forehead, "to drag a man's body for such a long distance without even knowing him. In all my lifelong practice, I have not encountered such a selfless act as you have demonstrated." He tips his finger to his head as if to salute their braveness and kindness.

Indirali lowers her gaze. "He would have surely done the same for us!" she mutters quietly, uncertain as to how to keep up this game of pretense much longer. Because the truth of the matter is that Eusebios would have given his life for hers, a code of honor any soldier of her father's proudly and honorably lives by.

"Anyway, Sophos," he extends his hand for a greeting, "my name is Sophos, and I'm sorry for not answering the door right away."

Indirali takes his hand and shakes it like a man. "Apollinaris! I'm just glad you helped this man out!"

Hedna shakes his hand as well, and introduces herself as Leonidas.

"You have no idea how many rude people come to the doctor's door at night," the old maid informs them as if to defend the doctor, "disturbing his much-needed sleep, all because they like hanging out in the company of drunkards and criminals who, by the end of their nightly orgies, strip them of all they have, beat them up, and leave them in the gutter, like the poor man you guys just picked up."

Indirali is appalled to hear this. She can't believe what she is hearing. How could she have lived a life of blissful ignorance and relative carefreeness within the protective walls of her parents' palace when, just outside the gates, such mean and desperate behavior is going on, with victimizers and victims rendering the streets unsafe, leaving many homes broken and joyless. Her heart feels heavy from the thought, and gratefully she accepts Sophos' invitation to stay the night, since night has fallen, and no good citizen should be on the streets anymore.

The old maid stays with Eusebios, tucking him in to make sure he gets a good night's sleep. The rest of the group rejoins in the big dining hall, where food sits on a richly decorated table, with plates of half-eaten food indicating the group had interrupted their meal to come to their aid. Two empty seats are shown to the guests, and soon the two young men are able to dig in to some great-tasting salad and sandwiches to satisfy their pent-up hunger, and finally come to their deeper senses again.

Sophos asks them a few questions as to their home and destination, which they answer according to the story they laid out for themselves, carefully watching their words to not betray their true identity and plans. Then he confides to them some rather delicate facts about his profession, for he felt a bit challenged before by Apollinaris pointing out to him the oath of the physician Hippocrates, prompting him now to straighten a few facts out for the two young men, who — for some inexplicable reason — seem wise and sensitive beyond their years. Strangely drawn to pour his heart out to Apollinaris, Sophos begins to describe how he used to be a very idealistic young man who wanted nothing more than to heal people of any and all ailments, to be a servant unto the Divine and good to all of his patients, and to live by the highest code of honor and service a doctor can live by. He then continues to say that time has taught him otherwise, and that he has come across a majority of patients who — as far as he can tell — seem so ignorant and lower-self-oriented as to keep attracting the evil and the diseases they suffer under, and that even if he gives it his absolute best, most of the patients go out after he healed them with all the healing power he was able to apply, only to find that they continue to sin and often come back with the same ailment, or with another one that is even stronger and more defeating than the first. He has learned, much to his dismay, that most people cannot be helped in the long run, and just want a quick cure without being interested in changing their ways of life and their ways of eating, thus continuing to create diseases for themselves, not only on the physical level, but also on the emotional and mental levels. He says that he feels completely overwhelmed by the graveness of ailments people attract on a constant basis, because hardly any of his patients are interested in helping themselves and relinquishing from their daily diets and lifestyles what makes them sick and ill in the end. And instead, they come to him with the attitude of a consumer, and if he refuses to help them because they seem to not want to change their ways, then they gang up with others of like negative mind, accusing him of being a bad doctor and spreading bad rumors about him to jeopardize his practice to prove to themselves that he must be wrong, for they want to stay right. Instead, those idiots run to a bunch of fake doctors, who seem to pop up faster on the healing market than a meadow of dandelions in spring, all catering to the tastes of the decadent and lazy, selling to the eager-to-hear many health-deteriorating potions that only aim at short-term relief, but because of their inferior quality or randomly composed — and therefore toxic — mixtures, they leave much long-term health damage behind, which Sophos has to eventually clean up when the most sick and desperate finally come to his door again, having lost all hope for health. And with the Goddess of Death knocking at their door, they therefore find themselves finally desperate and ready enough to undertake the dietary and lifestyle changes he suggested to them earlier, and without which healing is and stays just a cheap act of scamming. And what gets him the most, he says, is the fact that these quack doctors give out death sentences to their patients after they are done with them and the patients have nothing more to give, thus accelerating a gullible patient's actual death, for their non-belief in their patients' health is often the last trigger for a desperate person to give up on himself and slip into a premature and often unwarranted death rather than believing in his own self-healing powers and getting well again.

He pauses to examine the effect of his speech on his listeners. After a moment of reflection, he adds that only the very poor come to him readily for treatments, those who cannot afford any of the relatively expensive potions the quack doctors advertise and sell as the ultimate quick solutions to any ailments one can think of. And thus his practice has become known as the place the very desperate go to, the ones that either are healthwise ready to die but still harbor enough of a spark of hope against all negative predictions of their fake doctors that they are able to find their way to him, or the ones that are so destitute that no one else will help them.

Indirali shakes her head in disbelief. She has been following every word he said with much attention and puzzlement, wondering how contradictory people can be when it comes to their own wellbeing. To think that it would be more important to hold on to self-destructive attitudes and behaviors rather than heeding the advice of a seasoned doctor, who has proven his healing abilities to many of his patients over time, is beyond her. But this journey will probably continue to stretch her capacity for being able to integrate all kinds of paradoxical and opposing views, including the fact that people create their own misfortune, no matter how much they attest to the fact that they want fortune, health, wealth, and happiness in their lives.

With words of understanding and agreement, Indirali supports the doctor's outlook on his profession, which, in her eyes, seems to be just one facet of an underlying problem that has started to usurp the whole world around them in a cloud of darkness and distortion, faster than any sensible person would ever want it to spread. Inspired by his honesty and candidness, she begins to describe their stop at the inn earlier in the day, how bad and arrogantly the group of hunters behaved, how they drove the innkeepers crazy with their bullying shouts, and how alienated she and Leonidas felt for not being understood in their need for a meat-free diet.

This report gets Sophos going even more passionately for some reason, and everyone at the table for that matter. Everyone has stories to tell of how this inn seems to be a place that many such ruffians like to stop at along their way through the canyon and woods, that they like to hide behind each other's backs, appearing in groups of several badly behaving jerks, thus tyrannizing their surroundings, and threatening anyone with their violence who dares to stand in their way. They like to hunt and kill, and their murderous instincts often don't stop when it comes to humans. The innkeepers have learned to turn a blind eye towards the many suspicious and violent incidents that befall the more innocent travelers that happen to stop by their place. What happened to Eusebios seems to be not at all unusual for this whole area, and the doctor says that this trend unfortunately is spreading to other areas as well, as the authorities feel completely overwhelmed with the increasing crime wave and so have become almost resigned to a state of paralysis and incompetence, leaving the citizens to fend for themselves and thus nurturing the cycle of crime even more. He says that many town guards have become corrupt as well, and thus live the life of a hypocrite, and often even as criminals themselves. He says that if he wouldn't have his family, he would not want to live in today's world, for it seems cruel and unjust to the kind and just at heart, and it seems not many causes are left worth believing in and fighting for. He admits that his compassionate heart as a healer has long been taxed to the maximum, as victimized, seriously wounded bodies and souls are often left at his doorstep to take care of when no one else will help. He says he sees charlatan sales people and their minions, the quack doctors, using cheap, often toxic side-effects-producing medicinal preparations that actually destroy health over time rather than cure the patients, quacksters who pose as healers and who accumulate more wealth than he, Sophos, would ever care to make, by telling paying patients what they want to hear rather than what they should hear in order to recover and get well. By the time most of their patients are so run down in their health that they are about to die, these so-called doctors have amassed such incredible wealth that they can afford the luxuries of several lifetimes at the expense of all the gullible patients they carelessly drive into incurable disease and death.

Indirali is shocked to hear such harrowing information. How come she never heard of this sad and bitter truth? Her parents and palatial environment protected her from such merciless happenings, and now she feels stunned and speechless at the extent of illusion she lived under, having Lucania's people live in such miserable conditions, and letting the goodness of life deteriorate with the speed it obviously does! She touches her forehead, as if to wipe off some sweat. Sophos notices her unease and begins to apologize for such negative talk, but young Apollinaris dismisses his effort, conveying to him that he just speaks the truth of his/her own heart, and that he/she wishes she could change things around for everyone, putting the virtuous at heart into positions of power and running the scum out of the country, to live in exile from the very people they violated with their base natures and behaviors.

Sophos agrees this would be a great gesture, but deep within, he doubts that any such radical change could ever come about, at least not in his lifetime. And so the group continues to chat about less important things, slowly wrapping the evening up, until at some point the hosts show their guests to their rooms to spend the night. With words of appreciation, the two young men bid them good night and retire to bed.

It takes the two lady-gentlemen some time to unwind from the stress of the day. The conversation during dinner still sits like an indigestible rock in Indirali's stomach. Her sense of responsibility makes her crumble with a bad conscience, for she sees it her parents' failure to have allowed conditions to deteriorate to the extent they have, and being their daughter triggers her own guilt and shame in regard to this failure. On top of that, she also feels guilty about not heeding her father's words and agreeing to take at least one more guard along, one who might have been able to prevent the disaster Eusebios had to go through. Indirali's chest feels tight from this guilt, and she almost has trouble breathing. Sophos' frustration with his profession showed her again the wisdom of the Oracle's words when she suggested that a profound collective change in consciousness has to take place for many of today's problems to disappear; otherwise, the ignorance makes people not only repeat their mistakes but also gang up with the ignorant masses and try to squash whatever little higher intelligence and unconditional love is still left in their world. Outer change has to begin with inner change, and any true and lasting change is based on the individual's self-transformation, on his ability to transcend and overcome his limitations that otherwise create a reality of more negative connotations, caught in the vicious cycles of victimization. Indirali needs some fresh air and decides to go out into the garden, hoping to be able to clear her head, and have an easier time to fall asleep. And so she adjusts her wig again, and walks outside.

A wave of beautiful smelling scents greets her warmly, immediately lifting her spirits up as if awakening from a bad dream. Indirali takes a few steps into the moonlit dark, when her eyes fall on a beautiful maiden, clad in a white, long garment, standing dreamily beside a big tree, her hair and garment flowing softly in the wind as she looks up into the sky to gaze at the stars. Indirali's first impulse is to turn in the other direction and leave the girl to her dreams, but her move caused a soft rustle that prompts the beauty to turn her head and behold Apollinaris, the good-looking young lad she earlier got a glimpse of when she walked past the dining room in which her parents finished their dinner.

"Hi!" Apollinaris waves his hand at the beautiful girl. She answers with a smile: "Hi!"

"It's nice, fresh, and beautifully smelling out here, isn't it?" Apollinaris tries to break the awkwardness of the situation.

"Yes it is! Are you from around here?" she asks gently.

Apollinaris/Indirali takes a few steps towards her, and she turns around to come closer as well.

"Not from Grumentum, but from a few miles outside of it. Our parents own a farmhouse. Are you Sophos' daughter?" Apollinaris inquires.

The girl nods, and then the two of them have an odd moment in which Apollinaris feels the girl's loving attention resting on him in ways he can't respond to. But an inner sensation of gentle compassion with the girl's crush on him emerges, prompting him to find a way to break the ice in ways that stay innocent and good-willed. After a few more nice words, Apollinaris wants to say goodnight to her, only to find that she tries to bind him in a web of romantic feelings. Feeling increasingly awkward and at unease with the situation, Apollinaris tries to disentangle himself in a manner that doesn't harm her innocent feelings for him, only to find that it seems to arouse even more of her love interest. Quite desperate at some point, he clumsily bids good night to her and leaves her standing by herself, puzzled and dismayed with his sudden retreat and odd, emotionally charged behavior.

He must feel the same for her as she does for him, Sophos' daughter reasons. He probably doesn't want to betray her father's hospitality by flirting around with his daughter. Little does he know that her father doesn't need to know about their feelings, and if he does learn about them one day, he very likely won't mind since she is his pride and love, and he loves nothing more than to satisfy her wants.

Indirali is already tucked into bed when, out of nowhere, the doctor's daughter stands before him, kneeling down to whisper into his ears that it is okay and they might only have this night to celebrate their love for each other. But when she gets ready to slip under his blanket and cuddle with him, Apollinaris reacts strongly, asking her to please leave and not involve him in something he doesn't feel ready for. So convincing is his argument, and so loudly and persuasively expressed, that Leonidas awakes and loudly begins to laugh at the situation. Offended and hurt, the doctor's daughter collects the garment she dropped to the floor and slowly begins to retreat to the door.

"I thought you felt the same way!" she explains, tears welling up in her eyes.

"Don't get me wrong," Apollinaris tells her. "You are a most beautiful girl, and any man who will have you as his lover one day will be extraordinarily fortunate, for you know how to enchant a man's heart with your wit and beauty. But my brother and I will leave as soon as we know the wounded man is able to travel again, never to return, and I just don't see a future for us both right now." His eyes sparkle with a subtle sense of pleasure.

The girl still looks offended and, with an air of aloofness, storms out the door, not to be seen or heard from again.

"A nice and supportive lover you are!" Hedna teases her Mistress, for the incident woke her up with a laugh and has her still reeling with laughter and giggles that only seem to subside slowly throughout the next hour of the night.

Indirali, however, thinks about Loriolan, about how much she misses his noble, loving self, and how much she hopes this girl will find a love as pure and elevating as she has the fortune of having found in her life. With a deep desire to help all the good and deserving people in her parents' kingdom, she resolves to give it her utmost best on her ascent to the heavenly realms and to return as a ray of hope, ready to disperse her inner-found riches for the benefit of all the loving people who are able to appreciate the spiritual and material wealth she is eager to share.

CHAPTER 3

The next morning, the girls are woken by the excited voices of many different people, and an unusually high traffic of them in the house. Sounds of various kinds and occasional subdued cries begin to rattle the girls' nerves, making it impossible to continue staying in the dream world they felt so comfortable in. With a big yawn, they get up and take a look outside the window. Several patients stand around the garden, immersed in conversations, some approaching the house, others leaving it. It seems the doctor is in full business, and his team must have all hands full with keeping up.

Quickly, the girls get dressed, gather their few belongings, and step into the hallway. A male servant catches them on his way into the treatment room. "Your friend is doing much better this morning. I think he will be able to travel pretty soon. The doctor said to tell you he wants a word with you before you leave. Breakfast is served, and he will join you for a moment as soon as he can." He points to the dining room and, without awaiting their reaction, turns towards the treatment room. "I'll let him know you are awake!"

A bit confused as to how to proceed with Eusebios, the girls sit down to have breakfast. The doctor's daughter enters the room bringing some warm tea and deliciously smelling honey-sesame fritters for the guests. Her eyes are cast down as she sulkily serves them the food. The young men wish her a good morning and inquire about her wellbeing. The girl answers shortly with a common phrase, then quickly leaves the room.

Indirali and Hedna look at each other, wondering whether there is anything they could say to the poor girl that would ease her sense of rejection, but they can't think of anything that wouldn't betray their true identity, and so they shrug their shoulders helplessly and enjoy the good meal instead.

After a while, Sophos joins them at the table, having a cup of tea as well while conveying to them that their friend will need a few days to get to the point of being able to travel again. If what they said is true and Eusebios is, in fact, a royal guard, then Sophos would take it upon himself to keep Eusebios in his home until he is ready to travel, and would then provide him with a horse and someone to accompany him, in the hope of being compensated by the King for his services. What do the men think about this offer? Do they think the King cares about the life of one of his guards enough to pay for his treatment?

Apollinaris is quick to respond to this question with a big "yes", relaying to Sophos facts about the King that are meant to demonstrate his good heart and care for his soldiers. He also thinks it generous of Sophos to keep Eusebios in his care when, obviously, his home is teeming with patients. As a token of his appreciation, Apollinaris pulls a ruby broach from his sleeve and hands it to the perplexed doctor. "Please take this as an advance payment for your generous help you have shown to all of us. I wish the world would have more of your kind! You certainly have restored our faith in goodness ultimately winning out over evil, as the heartbroken certainly have a place in your home to come to and recuperate!"

Touched by Apollinaris' gift, Sophos stares at the broach in his hand as if trying to comprehend how such a simple-looking boy can carry such wealth around with him, and still touch him with his words as if they are coming from a higher place of mercy and goodness. He has to fight back his tears, and then shakes the men's hands to wish them a good and safe journey, assuring them he will take good care of Eusebios, and they can be at ease, able to continue their journey with a good conscience.

Seeing how people line up at his door to be helped by him, Indirali has no doubt that Eusebios is in good hands, and therefore decides to leave within the hour. She still wants to see Eusebios and make sure he is okay with the plan. The doctor shows them to his room, then takes his farewell, for he is needed urgently by his patients.

Eusebios has a weak smile on his face when he sees the Princess approaching, and as soon as he is sure no one else is listening in on their conversation, he begins to profusely apologize for his negligent and delinquent behavior, being full of regret and remorse. Indirali puts her hand over his mouth as if to silence him, then tells him to drop this point of view and concentrate on becoming better instead. She says she is counting on him to deliver a message to her father for her, one that states that she has, through a miracle, met one of the finer and more selfless individuals of his kingdom, and that it is due to the criminal attack Eusebios endured that this miracle was able to occur. She therefore asks her father to generously compensate the doctor who took care of Eusebios, for he is a savior unto many people who have nowhere else to turn in their hardship and despair. Then she hands the guard a sealed letter and asks him to deliver it directly into the King's hands.

Eusebios agrees, and with great humility, he thanks the Princess for saving his life and for being so good about it all. Indirali squeezes his hand gently for a farewell, whereas Hedna smilingly nods at him. Then the two young gentlemen bundle their packs and throw them over their shoulders, say good-bye to the woman of the house, Oechalia, the doctor's wife and mother to the beautiful daughter whose name is to remain a mystery to them, and then they leave the house, glad to be on the road again.

The air is fresh and full of scents as they pass by the many small gardens of the town's inhabitants. The two girls point various plants out to each other, marveling about the color and opulence of many beautiful flowerbeds and bushes they see along the way. The colorful varieties put them into a good mood; they keep greeting anyone they see with a cheery salute, and with a song on their lips, they wander through and out of the town, following the Aciris River along the path that leads to Heraclea.

And thus the freshness of the morning slowly subsides into the heat of the midday sun, rendering the two hikers increasingly hot and tired from the brisk walk. The cool and fresh water from the river looks more and more enticing to them, and as soon as they behold a favorable spot, they feel like throwing off their clothes and wigs to jump into the coolness of the water, and take a deep dive to shake off the heat and dust of the road.

So much fun do they have dunking their heads, resurfacing with the water trickling down from their faces, and splashing each other with much giggling and laughter, that it feels like a big, wonderful relief from the strains of their journey. The water feels refreshing and relaxing, and soon it feels like they are merging with the flowing waters, letting themselves float on top of it until they get washed ashore, only to throw themselves back into the pools to repeat the whole fun procedure. But all of a sudden, they hear a man shouting at them, his voice raised as if trying to drown out the noise of the streaming waters. Startled, the two girls look at the shore, only to behold a priest standing there with his hands formed in front of his mouth like a mouthpiece, shouting for them to come out of the water. Puzzled, the two girls swim closer to the shore, asking him to retreat behind the bushes to allow them to come out and get dressed. The man looks at them more closely and, upon recognizing them as girls, begins to express his dismay that they as girls dare to strip naked in public and enjoy this blasphemous state with no signs of a conscience or shame. Then he picks up the men's clothes and wigs he finds lying on the grass, examines them, and holds them out for them to tell him what this charade is all about. Again, Indirali asks him to look the other way, for otherwise, they will not come out. Cussing, the man finally drops the clothes and steps behind a nearby bush. The girls look at each other with bewilderment, then run out to quickly get dressed before this maniac of a priest can have a look at their half-naked bodies. They thought they were safe from any onlookers at this bend of the river, with their clothes tucked away behind a bush, but this man seems to have made it his business to seek them out in this remote and tucked away place, judging and condemning them as if they were sinners that just trespassed on the grounds of the Gods.

And as if the situation wasn't bad enough, another two priests emerge from around the corner, shouting to the priest in the bush whether he found the source of suspicious activity and exaggerated gaiety. The priest steps out from the bush to meet his buddies, affirming he just found two shameful women who bared themselves of men's clothes, only to relish their God-given state in public for anyone to behold.

With their jackets thrown on and their other belongings in their hands, Indirali signals Hedna to start running from the scene lest they be overcome by these strange priests and forced to justify their very existence to men who think of themselves as judges over the innocent. But the men are not ready to let the incidence go undealt with. Challenged in their sense of superiority, they run after the girls and catch up with them to forcefully throw them to the ground. "Want to escape like little rats, do you?" one of them shouts, agitatedly. The jackets fly open and show their breasts partially. The men stand there and stare, their mouths gaping with repressed lust, and then one of them picks up the rest of their clothes, holds them under the girls' noses, and commands them to immediately dress themselves to a decent standard if they don't want to commit the crime of enticing priests with their overtly sexual behavior.

Indirali asks them to please look the other way, but by now their sexual juices have begun to flow, and none of them possesses the strength of character to turn their heads around. Instead, they keep accusing the girls of trying to seduce them and being a public nuisance that needs to be punished and gotten rid of. Violated by their accusatory and lustful behavior, the girls begin to dress, hoping these jerks will disperse once they are fully dressed again, but to their disappointment, the men have taken a deep, sexually charged interest in them, wanting to either molest the girls or tyrannize them in other ways that would satisfy their need for dominance and control. Two of them begin to shove the girls around, calling them whores and other derogatory names, feverishly deciding in their heads whether it is safe to molest and rape them without any unwanted consequences. The third priest stands there laughing, enjoying the spectacle to the fullest.

Hedna tries to remind them of their spiritual oath of celibacy and of being a role model unto others, but the men don't care about such trivial things right now, their lust and greed written all over their faces. One of them pushes Indirali against a tree, holding her arms tight to it, when she desperately calls out Aphrodite's name in her mind, and instantly an idea pops into her mind, which she agitatedly conveys to her oppressor: "Sophos, a well-known doctor of Grumentum is our uncle, and he expected us back at his home a while ago! If we don't show up right away, he is going to send his servants out to find us, if they are not already on their way to locate us here!"

The priest's face sours, thoughts running through his mind that seem to spoil the occasion. The other priests let loose as well, weighing inside whether this satisfaction is still worth the risk. They all know the doctor from hearsay and know that he enjoys quite a reputation for as far as Atina where they just came from. To think that he might find out about their little prank, and convey it to their superiors in rank, shakes them out of their sexual fever. And so they switch gears: from being inconsiderate jerks and rapists to being overly caring, concerned priests who want to see the girls brought back home safely, lest other rapists cross their way and not be as friendly as they are. And so the group begins to travel back to Grumentum to deliver the girls safely back to their male patron and sponsor of life, without which the girls would just be like free radicals, inviting with their unencumbered and carefree nature other lustful men who might just get the better of them after all. Deep down, however, the priests want to find out for certain that these girls are indeed under another man's protection, because if they are not, the priests can still have their way with them, and then even more so, because the girls will have proven themselves to be guilty of lying and of seducing gullible men. And then nobody will care what might happen to these lying bitches. Yes, on some level the priests hope that the girls will turn out to be liars, for then they can have a sexual relief without any consequences, and without overstepping another man's territory.

On the way back to Grumentum, the atmosphere is tightly controlled by the men, who keep pretending to act in the interest and for the benefit of society, taking care of the kind of business others might deem inappropriate and undesirable to deal with. They try to lecture the girls on good and decent behavior, wanting to look all pious and self-controlled all of a sudden, arguing with the girls that they have no business in the first place to scream around lustfully in the river, and additionally pointing out the wrong of disguising themselves in manly wardrobes, pretending to be men and wanting to enjoy the privileges of a man. When Indirali dares to speak up saying they wear these kinds of clothes so men would leave them alone and not get funny ideas of trying to take advantage of them and harassing them for being young, beautiful women, the men react angrily, for they feel found out and nailed to the spot with absolutely no wiggle room left for excuses anymore, but of course they can't admit to any of it, and so they rather accuse the girls for distorting the issue and for trying to cheat and take advantage of others with their appearances.

The walk back feels endlessly long and tiresome. Every step feels like an inquisition to the girls, with the men trying to condemn the very women they feel lustfully attracted to, shamelessly projecting their weakness and viciousness onto their prey, lest they would have to look into the mirror and see their ugly faces that don't look at all like the pious priests they pretend to be. The girls resign themselves to their fate as victims, since every word they utter is taken the wrong way, twisted around and against them, and thrown into their faces as perpetuating lies that are supposed to help aggrandize the men's lower selves to the status of judges over the meek and "evil", and to spiritual guides over all the gullible people they can force and manipulate into following them.

In their minds, the girls envision meeting Sophos and his family again, hoping he will look through the nastiness of the situation and not react offended by the fact they deceived him and his family as well in regard to their identities, and that he hopefully will help them rather than sending them back into the arms of their cruel and hypocritical perpetrators. They feel quite miserable by the time they arrive in Grumentum and at the door of the doctor's house. One of the priests solemnly asks a male servant to go fetch the doctor, realizing the servant's puzzled look when he sees the girls. But instead of coming to the door himself, the doctor sends word to wait in the garden until he finds a moment to extract himself from his patients.

The priests look dissatisfied, telling the servant to make sure the doctor understands they are priests from the temple of Atina on their way to help the poor in Heraclea, priests who have an urgent question for him before they are off to continue their journey. Several minutes later, Oechalia comes to the door, inquiring how she can help the priests. Perplexed to see a woman show up at the door instead of a man, the priests hesitate for a moment to decide whether their business can be handled by a woman or not. But then one of them points at the girls, and as soon as Oechelia recognizes the girls' faces, she exclaims her surprise of seeing them again. The priest asks whether she recognizes the girls, which she affirms. Upon seeing their dismayed faces, however, she asks whether something is wrong. One priest is about to ask whether the girls are relatives of the doctor when the doctor comes to the door himself, wanting to know what the matter is. The priests drop their attention towards Oechalia and immediately turn to the doctor, explaining that they caught the women bathing nude in the river, and that they, on top of that, disguised themselves as men, trying to fool other men to treat them as their equal.

Sophos doesn't need to hear much more. The way the priests describe the situation does not sit well with him. He notices their arrogance in even taking the girls' fates into their hands and therefore tells them on the spot that the girls are under his protection, and for the priests to just leave. One priest feels offended by his tone of voice and begins to accuse the doctor of being so negligent as to allow these girls to travel the way they did instead of making sure they don't become a public nuisance. And insisting, he wants to know whether the doctor overtakes responsibility for the girls' behavior and travels, or not! He looks at the doctor as if to take him on, feisty and relentless.

"You mean, a nuisance to you!" Sophos retorts, indicating to the girls they should go inside the house, away from this abysmal influence of male arrogance and condemnation. The girls are happy to oblige, for there is no winning over this battle of male wills. They are just happy Sophos comes to their aid and does not betray them to these fanatics.

With swift words of conviction, Sophos overtakes the responsibility for the girls' behavior and further fate, thanks the men for bringing them to his house safely, aware to appease their pride and arrogance, then dismisses them from his doorstep to go back to their duties of reconciling seekers with the love, forgiveness, and mercy of the all-reigning Gods.

Slightly thrown off balance by the doctor's last remark, the three priests get on with their lives, irritated to have lost another chance of satisfying the all-consuming sexual fire of their lower selves in ways that could easily have been condoned in regard to their spiritual reputation, which certainly would have allowed them to feel good and justified about such act of rape, since the victims would have been lawbreakers and prostitutes anyway, the way they behaved and dressed. Too bad this scenario couldn't play itself out in their favor, because the Gods would have been certainly on their side on this one!

Inside the house, Sophos and Oechalia look at the girls, then at each other, and begin to laugh heartily. "You fooled not only those idiots out there, but us simple-minded folks as well!" Sophos explains their laughter.

Indirali and Hedna lower their gaze. Strange how many times over they must contend with feeling guilty over the fact that they simply want to travel unencumbered and freely, as men obviously are able to and take for granted. Instead, they have to explain and justify, feeling like criminals until proven innocent.

"We wanted to avoid running into idiots like these hypocritical priests, but I guess we let our guard down, and these vultures immediately were there to gang up against us!" Indirali explains.

"Yeah, those priests accuse us for pretending to be men," Hedna gets all excited, "but they are pretending to be of good, model-like character, pious and celibate, all the while ready to rape innocent girls they shooed out of the water so they can have a better look at their naked bodies and get all lustful and uncontrollable about it. Who wants to follow such violators anyway into the dumbed-down and hellish spheres they are creating?"

Sophos tries to calm them down, acknowledging that they have a point, and that they need to understand that not every man is as nasty as these characters are. And yes, he and Oechalia agree that the priests' pretensions and deceptions are of far greater reach, since they belong to a relatively big and influential temple and have people follow their every word and suggestion, misleading them into corrupt attitudes and behaviors that have nothing to do with true spirituality. With a sigh of frustration, Sophos sinks into a chair, telling the girls that this is yet another negative tendency his wife and he see in the world, one of moral degradation and many other harrowing implications that leave many of the good-hearted people despairing as to the bleak future ahead of them. Because as far as their eyes can see, there is no hope in sight, no man or woman strong enough to stand up to all the corruption that is trying to overtake the kingdom on any and all levels, but also primarily in the spiritual sector that forms the basis for material life.

Indirali touches his shoulder in sympathy. So strongly does she feel the urge to comfort him and his wife that she decides spontaneously to come clean, and tells them who she is and what her plan and goal are. Hedna looks at her anxiously when her Mistress begins to reveal her identity, but the Princess nods affirmatively towards her maidservant, for in her heart she knows she can trust the doctor couple's integrity and good heart. Several times now they have proven that they deserve to know the truth about the girl they offered shelter, food, and protection to. And so she reveals the whole story, of how Princess Indirali and her father, King Eurylochos, sought the advice of the Oracle of Atina, how their guard was robbed and beaten, and how they decided to travel as men in order to not only stay unrecognized, but also be able to travel as safely as possible.

Sophos and Oechalia are speechless, for they would not have guessed to have been graced with the Princess's presence herself, a royal visit they never in their lives would have anticipated to take place in such inconspicuous ways, having the honor to help her out the way they were led to do. In light of her true identity, her selfless act in bringing a wounded royal guard to their door makes her stand out even more in her selfless and unconditionally loving nature, and the couple feel all of a sudden deeply honored to have met her. With deepest reverence, the two of them sink to their knees, touching the Princess's sandals, then lead their hands to their hearts as if to indicate their indestructible love and devotion to the royal palace, to the King, and to his daughter.

With a smile, Indirali asks them to rise, thanking them for their loyalty and friendship. She assures them that her father has learned many things about the spiritual elite of the country from the Oracle, and that many good changes will come from that encounter. Then she explains in few words how she has deeply fallen in love with a noble, virtuous, and loving man, and after consulting with the

Oracle, she knows she can only be with him if she succeeds in meeting Goddess Aphrodite on Mount Olympos, master her self along the way, and thus win the favors of the Olympian Gods and Goddesses, who will hopefully support her unification with her twin soul and help restore peace, virtuousness, and affluence to the people of Lucania, and to the neighboring kingdoms, if possible. She explains how she intends to help rescind Poseidon's curse on humanity and have the Gods and Goddesses take compassion on the human world and their fate, to the degree of unleashing an outpour of abundance of every good thing so mankind can feel at ease and hopeful about its future again. She says she will not rest until good but desperate people, like the doctor and his family, are justified and well taken care of, and the negative trends are turned around so the meek and humble will inherit this ultimately wonderful world of ours. This is the reason she is on the road with only her maidservant: to withstand the onslaught of negativity, to suffer through it, overcome it, and live to tell others about her victory and realizations! And for that to happen, they need to continue their travels to Heraclea, and from there on to Macedonia, across the Adriatic Sea.

Sophos immediately proposes to help the Princess and Hedna to get to Heraclea in a more speedy and safe way. He says he has one patient who occasionally comes from Heraclea to seek him out, because he and his family have learned over the years to trust Sophos with their health issues. As fate wills it, this man is just in town, staying in the 'Golden Harp' Inn, ready to leave town to go back to Heraclea after he has had his lunch. He just left the doctor's practice a few minutes ago, so the girls should still be able to catch him. Sophos will send one of his servants along with them to ask the businessman whether he would do the doctor the favor of delivering the girls safely to Heraclea. Sophos thinks the man will certainly do this, for he is a good man and feels quite indebted to the doctor for helping him cure several of his most critical ailments over time.

The girls are quite happy to hear the good news; it seems their ordeal has had a higher purpose and meaning after all. Thankfully they accept the doctor's help and get ready to leave again, when all of a sudden, the doctor's daughter enters the room and, upon seeing the girls without their wigs, begins to laugh out loud. "Apollinaris, ha!" she reels with laughter. "A fine lad you are! No wonder you didn't want anything to do with me!" It feels like a weight has fallen off her shoulder, and she seems quite amused with the situation. She looks at Hedna: "Leonidas, ha?" And another round of laughter escapes her cheery mouth, intent on not letting this one go past her again.

Indirali steps up to her and gives her a hug. "I wanted to do that yesterday already," she confides, making the girl's parents look up and take heed, for they don't really understand what the Princess is referring to. "But I was afraid you might further misconstrue my attempts to make you feel good, without making you feel more than just good. You know what I mean, don't you?"

"Well, yeah, now I do. Thanks for coming back and clearing that one up for me. I felt a bit lousy from what happened yesterday. Because usually I'm not so straightforward with just any man either, you know!" She winks at Indirali. "But you certainly make a cute guy!"

"Zosime, this is the Princess of Lucania!" her mother reprimands her. "You can't talk to her like that!"

But Indirali begins to laugh herself, while Zosime claps her hands in front of her mouth, blushing with embarrassment.

"Nice to finally know your name!" Indirali looks at Zosime with caring eyes. "And again, I hope you will soon meet the man of your dreams, and let those be high and wondrous dreams, for the man who deserves you must be of strong and enduring character, ready to give it his all to win your blessed heart, and ready to undergo the deepest self-transformation in order to secure your love for all eternity! Don't settle for less, Zosime, lest you be trapped in an unfulfilling relationship, forced to do the biddings of a man who cannot control himself and therefore has nothing of higher value to offer to mankind and to the delicate and loving nature of your heart!"

Zosime stares at the Princess, her mind spinning from what she just heard, trying to string these pearls of wisdom together in her memory to form a holistic picture of her encounter with the Princess of Lucania, an event she intends to never forget and to never lose sight of in her future dealings, not if she wants to gain the happiness the Princess just described as desirable and possible.

Then the parents inform Zosime about the Princess's travel plans, reminding everyone the two girls have to leave pretty right away if they want to catch Menelaus' carriage. Indirali takes another quick look at Eusebios, who is doing much better already, informing him that she chose to reveal her true identity to the family and asking him to let her father know she is in good hands, as they are about to get a lift from one of Sophos' cherished clients. Eusebios is happy to hear the Princess has found a ride, for this issue has been weighing on his soul, and with tears in his eyes, he waves the Princess good-bye, hoping to see her soon again, well, and successful with everything she has been setting out to accomplish. She smiles at him once more, then leaves the room.

Indirali and Hedna thank the doctor's family for their extraordinary kindness and hospitality, then they all hug, and the family wishes the girls a safe and pleasant trip from hereon out. They express their hopes of someday soon seeing the Princess again and hearing all about her journey and success. Indirali promises to return soon with the good news. Then the girls leave, accompanied by Nikandros, the servant.

CHAPTER 4

Somewhere between realities, Loriolan and Chekilian dream about being reunited with everyone they love: Torilander, their families and friends, and their beloveds, for Loriolan his Indirali, and for Chekilian his Thallo, the sweet maiden he met at Rhode's pleasure palace. Mile upon mile they surrender to the dolphins' strength and wisdom, hanging on to their back fins as if holding on to life itself, occasionally changing gears in pace as the strongest members of the herd take turns in carrying the two melancholic travelers towards the Northern Seas. Many miles have been covered already, with the group now swimming quite some distance away from the coast of Gaul (France), up and up to soon pass by the island of Lernis (Ireland). The water is gradually turning colder, and the dolphins say that at some point it will be too cold for them to continue, but there is still a great distance they can accompany their friends.

There is always a leading dolphin at the tip of the triangular-shaped, arrow-like formation of dolphins, one who does not carry a merman and who echolocates the terrain in front of them, navigating everyone safely around large obstructing rocks or sea mountains and along any currents spurring them on towards the North. The mermen need to occasionally switch arms in order to not risk letting go of the fins out of tiredness and exhaustion. Sometimes, other dolphins swim beside them, mentally conveying stories of their ancestors who roamed the Atlantic Ocean during times of certain volcanic activities, land mass displacements, and human shipwrecking, times of greater numbers and greater varieties of their kind, and of all oceanic living creatures for that matter, and also conveying how certain underwater sites have changed over time, what they have begun to miss, and what they still love. Their recounts are colorful and interesting, and the mermen find themselves marveling, smiling, and sometimes even laughing with them, as the dolphins' intent is to heal their wounded hearts and to instill hope and conviction in them that have the power to break through the negative karma, help them transform, and come out as winners! And for this alchemical transformational process to unfold, the two mermen use the brush of water they constantly run up against, to catapult and lift them into a transcendental state of inner awe and unification with the grand Ocean of Life. So serenely beautiful is their experience that they begin to feel that even Torilander's kidnapping might fit into the grander scheme of things and will, very likely, in the end have served a purpose of lofty character, for all will be reunited, and all will be well, and everyone will have lots of adventuresome stories to tell about their separate journeys they undertook in the name of ultimate unification.

A pod of sperm whales has been eying the dolphin group for a while from the distance, and have now decided to approach and take a better look, for they wonder why two mermen are hanging on the dolphins' fins, especially for such a long time. They are curious as to what is going on and want to inquire about this phenomenon. The dolphins slow down their speed to allow the whales some proximity and communication. Whalla, the leading mother whale, addresses the dolphins, wondering why they all seem in such a hurry, swimming with enormous speed for such a long distance, causing the whales to wonder whether some deep sea monster is after them. The dolphins laugh out loud, for the whales have somehow hit the nail on the head with their remark, because even though no monster is pursuing them right now, not long ago the human creatures were after their brothers, the mermen, taking one of them and leaving the other two heartbroken over their loss. And so the dolphins fill the whales in on what happened; how Torilander gave up his freedom in exchange for freeing one of their dolphin babies, and how Loriolan and Chekilian decided to continue their journey to the North despite feeling much anguish and pain in their hearts for losing their brother to the human race, but that getting to the core of the Earth seems to hold the promise for them to bring everyone's fate to the highest possible outcome and loving reunification.

This account of the mermen's fate seems to leave the whales speechless for a while, reflecting on and contemplating the issue. Then Whalla has an idea she wants to suggest: How about trying to check in on the ship Torilander is being transported on to the city of Carthage? The whales could signal a request to some of their family members who might still linger in that area before retreating to the poles for their summer feeding phase. Would this be of any value to the mermen, she wants to know.

"This would be fantastic!" Loriolan exclaims. "Any help you and your family members can give us in possibly retrieving our brother is deeply appreciated!" A newfound spark of hope lights up in his eyes, and Chekilian joins his exclamations of appreciation and gratitude for this selfless offer. Can it be that it is safe to hope again, he asks himself, his vulnerable eyes resting in Whalla's generously loving eyes.

Then, followed by one of her calves, Whalla retreats to some distance to spare everyone in the group the enormous impact of her thundering voice, and begins to send out a series of loud clicking sounds, first her signature codas to introduce herself to her species members, and after receiving a signal back after a while, she begins to communicate the mermen's heartfelt request, asking whoever is able to hear to relay the message to one of their peers present on location where the royal trade ship of the King of Carthage is expected to enter port, carrying an unwarranted prey, a merman, and brother to two travelers, who desire nothing more than for the violently captured merman to be freed and released back into the waters that constitute his natural habitat. Whalla asks her peers to lend their help, if possible, and to report back whether such undertaking can be executed at this time.

After a while, the calf returns to the dolphin and mermen group that had come to a standstill, and relays a message from Whalla. A group of sperm whales swimming in the Atlantic Ocean just west of the Straits of Gibraltar has been answering, promising to relay the request to their peers further east in the Tyrrhenian Sea, hoping to still find one or several of their family members close enough to the scene that such requested liberation could possibly have a chance of being successfully executed for the vindication of all sea creatures. The mermen lower their gaze in gratitude upon hearing the news, trying to hide their rekindled hope and lingering pain from plain sight. The calf bids them farewell and returns to his mother, followed by the rest of the whale pod. And so both groups linger in the waters at some distance from each other, waiting for another signal of hope and confirmation. Suspense nags on the mermen's nerves, as all kinds of hopeful scenarios run through their minds, making them wish they would receive news rather sooner than later. After a while the calf returns, conveying to them the message that a small group of sperm whales find themselves close enough to examine the situation and will call back on them once they've made a decision as to whether an attempt of freeing the merman would be wise and doable at this time and under the circumstances. The calf says that Whalla asks everyone to join her in affirming a good and successful outcome of their plight, for she understands very well how a caring heart feels when one family member is lost or wounded. She says that her mother's heart wouldn't rest until the lost or injured fledgling would be recovered and well again and under her care, and that she now wishes the same for the mermen and their lost brother.

Loriolan extends his gratitude to Whalla and expresses his hope that all the effort from their side won't be in vain but will instead render Torilander's liberation successful, as everyone is hoping for. The calf clicks its voice in agreement, then retreats to the pod to play with its siblings and friends. Only the older generation of whales and dolphins exude an air of tension, for they have taken a friendly interest in the mermen and their fate, ready to do whatever it takes to help them in their misfortune.

After what seems like an eternity of nerve-wracking patience and waiting, the whales approach, for they received word from their brothers and sisters that the royal Carthaginian ship has been sighted near the shore of the King's city, and that many small boats have already begun to row back and forth between the main ship and the harbor, hauling loads of captured treasures onto land, with Torilander lying half-conscious in one of their bigger freight carriers, being heavily guarded by fierce-looking, armed men, and more than a dozen slaves rowing the freight carrier under whippings frantically towards the shore. The whales explain they decided to not interfere with this situation for two reasons: the slaves are chained to the boat, and if the whales would try to ram the boat to capsize it, the slaves would certainly drown and die, for they could not escape from their chains, thus rendering the whole freeing act a massacre. The whales assume the mermen would not want to risk so many lives for their brother's, even if they are human. But the fact that they are chained to the boat indicates they are prisoners and slaves as well, and it goes against the whales' ethics to kill many defenseless, innocent men. The second reason is that the boats are already way too close to the shore, with the water being relatively shallow and inaccessible for the whales, and therefore they would risk their own lives very dramatically, especially when considering that armed guards are lined up everywhere along the fortification bordering the shore.

Loriolan and Chekilian give off a sigh of disappointment. Nevertheless, they thank the whales for their good intent and say they agree with the whales' assessment of the situation on location, even if it means losing their brother for good into the hands of his human captors. They can just wish that the King will be merciful and kind to their brother, and that pursuing their journey to its final destination will help rescue their dear brother, rendering his captivity purposeful and meaningful in the end, and have him be reunited with his family again, with everyone who loves him so dearly that they cannot imagine a life without him. With tears streaming from their eyes, the two mermen ask Whalla whether they could just have one more wish, namely to ask the whales in front of Carthage whether they could possibly convey to Torilander that his brothers have not forgotten him, and that they will return to free him once they have conquered the elements, and will restore him to his former glory and beyond. Whalla thinks this message can be arranged, and indicates to one of her juveniles to deliver the message from a safe distance. Then she turns towards the mermen with a feeling of regret and apology for raising everyone's hopes in vain, and offers to overtake the transport of the mermen from here on out. She says that members of her pod can alternate in carrying them, and that the speed of their journey can thus be doubled and even tripled in comparison to how fast the dolphins were able to take them. She looks kindly at the dolphins, assuring them she doesn't mean to interfere with their business and come across as arrogant, but as whales they are used to the colder waters, and truth be told, they just are a breed much larger and stronger than the playful, sun-loving dolphins. She says they are migrating towards the North anyway, and as far as they know, they think the dolphins would probably prefer to stay in the warmer waters anyway. Before she can continue her apologies, however, the dolphin mother who has been leading the transport expedition shrieks with joyous excitement, thanking Whalla for her generous offer that seems to come just in time, for the dolphins have been feeling increasingly exhausted from the fast speed and energy loss due to the colder zones they have been entering. Whalla laughs and jokes that, as whales, they are meant to roam the deep and the cold, with their skin boasting a blubber buffer several times thicker than that of their dolphin siblings, allowing them therefore to endure greater pressures and temperature differences, which will come in handy if these two mermen are really serious in wanting to attempt the humanly life-endangering penetration of the frozen belt around the North Pole.

The dolphins begin to utter their many conflicting feelings about such High North adventure, admitting they wouldn't want to go that far North with the mermen, and therefore they feel thankful to the whales for butting in and taking over the responsibility for a continued safe journey their precious friends deserve. Loriolan and Chekilian look a bit surprised at the turn of events, but are happy to have found a ride of even greater leverage and speed than they have been enjoying so far. However, Loriolan needs to express some concerns he has when thinking about the travels ahead. How will they be able to hold on to the hump on the whales' backs, or the ridges between this hump and their tail flukes when going at a considerably faster speed and through waters of increasingly colder temperatures? Will the whales notice when they might lose one of them? Because the water friction will most certainly be quite overwhelming for them! And to lose another brother would be traumatic for either one of them at this point!

Whalla interrupts his worrisome thoughts, proposing the whales can transport them in the safety of their huge mouths, having the mermen hold on to their lower jaw teeth as if holding on to some sturdy and strong poles. And upon seeing the mermen's shocked faces, she assuages them, saying that she would only place them with members of her pod who possess the discipline to not swallow just anything they feel in their mouth, but instead are eager to lend their help in this selfless and wondrous way, knowing and taking pride in the fact that they would shelter their little friends from the bitter cold temperatures of the North, that ultimately have the power to kill humanoid beings who don't possess a blubber layer under their skin thick enough to withstand the roughest temperatures this Earth harbors, temperatures that exist far up North like an impenetrable ring of death, surrounding the North Pole with ice and high, freezing winds that keep every human and merman away, or else they might succumb to death, if their hearts and souls would not be strongly anchored in the highest source of life.

Loriolan and Chekilian look at each other aghast. What strange set of options have they left open to them? Loriolan's fervor in getting to the heavens via the Earth's core is triggering a string of rather undesirable challenges and questionable circumstances, and on top of all this strangeness, they feel they should be grateful for Whalla's offer, for there seems no other alternative available to them at this point that strikes them as more comfortable, smooth, and easy. And so they bow their heads in agreement, ready to enter Whalla's mouth, when word comes through the juvenile whale that Torilander received their message, and that he is thankful for their efforts, hoping and wishing they will be successful in their mission, and for them to return as soon as they can to free him from his bondage. He says he will hang in and get better and will not give up on life for as long as he knows they are pursuing the goal they set out to accomplish. He sends his love and peace, and his prayers are with them!

The mermen exclaim a shout of joy, for they know now that their brother is okay and knows they are pursuing their journey so they can come back and rescue him. With a whiff of fresh air, the mermen thank their dolphin friends for taking them the long distance, wish them all the best on their further journey into the sun, then bid them farewell, laughing relieved while watching the rescued baby dolphin do a buoyant somersault that has everyone cheering, and which then triggers other dolphins to follow his example, playfully and cheerfully jumping into the air, bouncing off the water, and happily vanishing towards the Western horizon, into the distance to their sun-drenched home habitat.

When they can't see them anymore, the mermen turn their heads around to look north, the direction they will be heading, and an ominous, gloomy feeling overcomes them, for the descriptions of Whalla in regard to the deadly ice ring around the North Pole don't sound very inviting but, if they are honest, rather distressing. They also feel quite trepidatious thinking they will have to crouch down in the crevice of a whale mouth for a relatively long time, as nice and kind an offer as it is. But with a word of gratitude to their new support team, the mermen swallow their fear and trepidation and enter the mouth of Whalla.

"At times we will dive to deeper and darker regions of the sea in order to avoid the lurking dangers of treacherous sea mountains and moving icebergs," she lets them know telepathically. "Plus, all of our herd will have to feed throughout the journey to stay strong for our purpose, and our food — mostly yummy squid — lies many hundreds of feet below the surface. My calves can't dive as deep as I do, for they need to breathe more frequently, but we will manage to maneuver through the waters as best we can given the extraordinary speed we normally don't travel at. I hope you will still enjoy the ride, for I will try to buffer you from the water pressures and cold temperatures as best as I can."

Loriolan kindly reminds the whale that, as mermen, they are able to transcend harsh dualistic appearances, and through raising their physical frequency, they are able to move through the waters without feeling its squashing properties in a too overwhelming fashion. But he thanks her, nevertheless, for offering her protection, for he thinks he and Chekilian might falter in their ability to vibrate on a higher level of existence throughout the overwhelming strain and stress of their long, arduous journey, and especially throughout the upcoming life-challenging penetration process of the icy North ring. A shudder overcomes them, and at the thought of it all, the mermen decide it is time to wax their skins and slip into their thick kelp sweaters. They rummage through their backpacks to find the items required, then help each other get prepared for the next stretch of their journey.

Whalla smilingly feels their efforts inside her mouth, then resumes telepathic communication with them. "Know that whoever of our herd carries you in its mouth will mostly stay close to the surface of the water, waiting for the others to return from their feeding excursions. And even though we have an enormous appetite and each of us needs a ton of food every day, we will put our priority on this journey, transporting you guys as speedily and safely as we can to the lands of the North, for a few of our kind have been able to penetrate the ring of death, and those few would surely have been able to lead you through the North Pole entrance vortex into the interior of the Earth. All we can promise, however, is that we will certainly try our best, and if we succeed, we will accompany you for a short distance into the bay of the river Hiddekel, a river our ancestors told us exists beyond the barrier. But then we must return to the salty waters of the Northern Sea of the outer world, for this is where we find our feeding grounds at this time of the year. Be aware that many fantastic adventures lie ahead of you. Take a peek at the lands and sights that will rush by us; soon you will see what humans call the island of Lernis (Ireland) showing up to your right, and later the volcanic land of Iceland, followed by the huge ice-sheet-covered landmass of Greenland, both to your left! Enjoy, and hold tight!" And with this said, the mother whale begins to lobtail to get to a deeper water level, then glides through the waters like an arrow with speed and purposeful direction, and the two mermen can't help but feel in awe of the humongous whales that have suddenly become their biggest allies and friends.

CHAPTER 5

Oh, how good it was to receive a message from Loriolan and Chekilian through the whales' communication lines! Torilander still can't believe his good fortune to have heard from the friend and the brother he was so forcefully separated from. How painful and humiliating it feels to be so harshly and rudely cut off from the journey he enlisted in for the sole purpose of being a strong and reliable support to his best friend on his life's quest and mission. Instead, he needs to contend with being the freak sensation for an endless amount of excessively curious humans, who either look at him as if he is from outside of this world, or insinuate amongst themselves that catching him will surely trigger more of Poseidon's wrath, and the captured merman is therefore a great threat and danger that should be gotten rid of in the most direct and fastest way possible.

Trying to ignore the countless staring eyes that all look down at him as if he is a magnet for controversial energy, Torilander lies motionless in a small boat, carried by four guards with leather straps slung around their big, strong shoulders. Occasionally, another guard pours a bucket of saltwater over his body, as instructed by his commander, to help the merman stay conscious and alive, lest he die away right before arriving at the palace and meeting with the king of the empire. All throughout the relatively short sea journey, the merman looked almost half dead already, with the ship's physician trying to exclusively attend to the wounds and fragile soul state of this most unusual catch, which the captain expects the King will most certainly congratulate him for. Hidden from the crew's view, Torilander thus spent the last few days in the stern of the ship, in a secluded area specifically arranged for him, with seawater being poured over him in regular intervals to keep his spirits alive and functioning. But all this intense attention on him could not prevent Torilander from overhearing occasional conversations of crewmembers in his vicinity, expressing their dismay and anguish at the thought of carrying a sea animal on their ship that, most likely, will provoke more of

Poseidon's wrath, which the crew anticipate could at any moment thunder down on them in the open sea, ready to swallow the ship, along with everyone on it. But Poseidon must have chosen to look the other way, because the ship obviously made it safely to the targeted shore, leaving Torilander stranded amongst the human race, and his hopes of rescue smashed as a result of it.

The human masses keep murmuring, whispering, and resounding in Torilander's ears with their negatively and sometimes positively charged utterances he seems to trigger in them, as the boat is carried through the streets of Carthage towards the palace. The young merman stares into the sky, wishing he could be with his friend and brother, swimming alongside the dolphins towards the North Pole. His mind keeps drifting in and out of realities, for the whole spectacle he seems to provide for these humans with his mere presence feels surreal to him, and has even an undertone of the most hideous danger he could ever imagine. Who knows what is to become of him, and whether the King will let him live in the end. As it turns out, this king is in the habit of turning people into slaves that are forced to do his bidding without so much as being able to express any of their many suppressed aches and pains, at least not without the fear of incurring punishment, torture, and merciless whipping. This thought alone provokes fear in Torilander, for his future is unsafe and much at stake.

After what seems like an eternity of physical and emotional discomfort for Torilander, the parade arrives at the palace, having to convince the guards to let them through. The captain describes the great fortune of having caught a rare specimen of the ocean waters, one that the King will most certainly want to see right away and without much delay. The guards take a look into the boat and, upon seeing Torilander, begin to laugh abruptly and heartily, then yield the gate to the arriving party to let them enter the palace courtyard under escort of a small division of the King's army.

Eventually, the group arrives at its destination, the royal center courtyard, garnished with a tall, gracefully ornamented, three-tiered fountain opulently pouring and spraying its flowing waters into a spacious marble basin, and reminding everyone of loftier realities than the ones they are most likely accustomed to. Torilander takes heed, for his senses respond to water, and to lively water especially. How his body and soul ache to be refreshed by taking a deep dive into his oceanic home world! This fountain just jumpstarted his memory and triggered the urge to throw himself into his native element. But in the same way as he felt imprisoned in this self-reduced, immovable position for the duration of his three-day-long captivity, he still cannot follow his natural impulses and instinctual desires and express life the way he is used to, but has to rather resign himself to his miserable fate, unsure whether he wants to recover and play into his predators' violating will of showcasing him to a world which — according to his experiences so far — couldn't care less about his wellbeing and life. Life sure has taken a frightful turn for the worse, a downward spiral of debilitating events that leave him tarrying in a state of inner and outer paralysis, rendering him unable and unwilling to come out of his inner shell for fear of directing even more unwanted attention to himself and, with that, more violation of his free will. And so he retreats to his innermost spaces again, hovering somewhere between life and death, anxiously awaiting to see what kind of character this king is and what he intends to do with him, now that a merman is in his hands.

The group waits for quite a long time, with the guards trying to keep onlookers at bay by forming a large protective ring around the boat Torilander lies in, making it impossible for the crowd to catch a glimpse of the novelty, news of whose arrival and presence one of the guards leaked to the palace crowd. Curiosity is building and escalating, even though everyone knows that the King has the first right to cast his eyes on such an unusual creature everyone has a hard time believing exists. But finally King Ahiram arrives. The Royal Family strutting behind him, he immediately wants to see the unbelievable fang his ministers just announced to him to have arrived. With his wife and grown children coming to a halt at a safe distance, the King dares to approach the boat, ready to react in any way necessary should the creature jump out at him.

But to his surprise, the merman lies in the boat peacefully with his arms crossed over his chest, his eyes closed as if already dead. Softness radiates from his countenance, a vulnerability even, which the King has a hard time placing in his mind for lack of relevant information about this merman's nature and natural habitat. He wants to know whether the merman is still alive, which someone from the trade ship crew affirms to him he is. The King's immediate concern is for this half-man's health and wellbeing, and so he inquires whether the merman has been medically adequately taken care of during his transport, and whether he was fed. After taking a deep, reverent bow, the captain addresses the King, informing him that medical attention was afforded exclusively for this merman's health but that he, so far, refused to take food of any kind that was offered to him, which, on top of him having been heavily wounded by the spears of his captors, seems to add to and now account for his present weak state. King Ahiram doesn't like the sound of it and orders for the royal physician to be at once asked to attend to the merman's needs and for his assistants to try to strengthen the injured sea creature by either making him accept food or trying to get him to swallow a strengthening medical potion. For how can he get to know such an elusive phenomenon if it would die at his feet?

Overhearing his communication and deciding it is safe to approach, the King's wife and children draw near to take a closer look.

"How peaceful he looks, and how resigned to his fate!" the Queen remarks, her motherly protective feelings triggered by his helpless, forlorn sight. "I hope he comes to and tells us all about himself!" She looks down at Torilander, smiling.

"I wouldn't hold my breath. He looks quite dead to me already!" the King's oldest son, Danel, injects with a haughty attitude. "But he sure would make a nice trophy, don't you think?" he asks his father, who nods distractedly, because his concern is still with the wellbeing and functionality of his new acquisition.

"Make sure nobody forces him to eat, though. Don't just shove the food down his throat!" the King orders the servant next to him, expecting him to relay the message to the doctor he sees hurrying to the site.

"Fine trophy this is!" Hanno, the second oldest son of the King, responds to his older brother. "This tailed thing here couldn't even clean your high and mighty sandals, let alone engage in any intelligent conversation, if it speaks at all." He grabs the spear of a nearby standing guard and begins to poke the merman's tail. "It's really good for nothing, if you ask me!"

A reflex causes Torilander's tail to twitch under the poking. But he doesn't want to give in to the provocation and open his eyes. He does not want to stare into the arrogant eyes of his supposed new owners, and of who knows how many thousands of curious eye contacts with the surrounding crowd. And so he continues to keep his eyes shut, hoping the martyrdom will soon be over.

"It lives!" Danel exclaims with an air of played interest. "I guess I stand corrected!"

"Just leave him alone!" Princess Elissa, the youngest of the children, shouts at her brothers, taking the spear from Hanno's hand to return it to the guard. "He looks so innocent and helpless! Quite adorable, to be honest!" She takes the Queen's hand to draw her closer to the boat, enlisting her help and lenient attitude in making sure the merman won't be bothered anymore.

"Innocent my ass!" Hanno continues to murmur rebelliously. If it were up to him, he would just throw this thing right back to where it came from or put it into the deepest dungeon to rot away. What's the use of it anyway? What's all this fuss about a humanoid fish? He has problems of his own, and this thing just managed to draw the attention away from his own needs, and very likely, it will continue to do so for the foreseeable future. Maybe it will even side with his boastful, incompetent older brother, his real nemesis. That thought really ignites the fire of resistance against that thing in him, and his mind is made up that it must be of an evil nature, because evil is what he experiences in himself, and evil is what he knows to project onto others around him.

"It's pretending to be asleep, or even dead," Hanno tries to discredit and to add fuel to the investigation, because the physician just entered the scene and, upon seeing the merman, reacts with considerable surprise that such a creature would in fact exist. After receiving his instructions once more from the King directly and hearing from the captain of the ship that brought this creature what medical attention was given to him so far, he and his team immediately proceed with a measured approach to stabilize the merman's condition.

"Daddy, I want him in my chambers!" the Princess exclaims, trying to beg and plead her way with her father. "I will take good care of him, I promise!"

"Elissa, this is not a toy!" the mother reminds her. "He probably has feelings, and certain needs I myself wouldn't even want to know about, let alone have my daughter be exposed to!" She looks at her child as if declining her a fancied, but improper fantasy.

The two Princes laugh out loud at this hilarious suggestion, ready to add to the ludicrous hint with their own concocted, demeaning jokes, when the King cuts through the baseless talk, announcing to everyone the merman will be placed inside the Royal Family's assembly hall, a place where the Royal Family will have the common chance to observe and witness the doings of the creature, should it survive. He turns to Yutpan, his most trusted minister, to have the carpenters start immediately on the construction of a spacious tank that is to become the merman's showcase cell, a place where the King and his family, as well as a team of specialists, will have the opportunity to study and understand the unusual creature's behavior and characteristics.

After receiving word from the doctor that the merman is out of any danger of dying, King Ahiram waves his hand, and the captain is handed a handsome reward for the excellent goods he was able to provide. Everyone is satisfied with the deal, and with a deeply reverent bow, the captain and his men retreat from the courtyard to return to their ship and their own further destinies. Who knows, maybe they can come up with even more of such elusive brood. Considering the generous amount of various jewels he just received, the captain feels pretty motivated to give it another good try, spotting the kind of fascinating creatures only the fables of old talk about.

The royal appearance has come to its end, and the crowds are allowed to come a few steps closer to take a look from still a reasonable distance, while the merman is lifted from the boat and temporarily placed into the fountain, until such time that his showcase is built and he is transported into the palace. A young servant boy is consigned the duty to keep a close watch on the merman at all times, and to report immediately should any disturbing signs come up or should the merman decide to open his eyes and maybe even talk. The King wants to stay informed of any such progress, but for now, urgent state business calls on his attention and thus he retreats back to the palace, followed by his whispering and giggling entourage, for seldom has the palace hosted such a delicious distraction and wildly entertaining phenomenon.

Relieved to feel the presence of staring eyes withdrawn to a safe distance, Torilander exhales deeply to release his tensions, then lifts his eyelids a tiny crack for just a moment, to try and make out who is still around and close to him. The guards lower him into the fountain basin, and the water immediately revives Torilander's senses and body. Nevertheless, he doesn't want to move yet, for he wants the crowd to not get excited and linger around needlessly long. He can't wait for the night to fall and for the crowd to go about their normal business. But it takes several hours for the last curious onlookers to finally leave the scene, greatly disappointed for not having been granted access to see the creature from up close, for the guards are stationed all around it, unwilling to let anyone through and defy the King's orders. And so the crowd is left hanging to speculate about the creature in their wild imaginings, wondering whether they will ever be granted the luxury to see such fabled being from up close and in real live action.

Many hours pass, and Torilander tarries in an unmoving position. The servant boy has his eyes on him, and Torilander is not keen on having him shout to everyone that the merman finally has opened his eyes and would therefore deserve another painstaking look at him. Instead, Torilander would like to wait with moving his body around — an overwhelming urge he actually feels in order to feel sane again — until the boy hopefully falls asleep sometime during the night. The guards have long lost interest in him, and most of them are now conversing and joking amongst themselves. Just the servant boy seems to be still a nuisance, because for some reason, he made it his honor and duty to stare at Torilander incessantly for fear of missing the slightest but, for everyone around him, infinitely significant changes and developments in Torilander's recovery process! A battle of wills seems to reign between onlooker and prey, and Torilander is getting weary of his pretentious charade, for he longs to loll and sprawl, and to swim a few rounds around the falling and cascading water, as cumbersome as such a swim might be in this rather shallow basin.

"You can open your eyes now," the boy conveys. "The guards are either drunk or asleep, and no one has looked in your direction for at least an hour! You are safe with me! You are probably afraid of us boastful humans, aren't you?"

Torilander is puzzled. This doesn't sound like a boastful human to him. Can this offer be trusted? After being shot at, hunted down like a crude animal, thrown around from one prison entrapment to another, and gazed upon by people who talk as if they own his soul, Torilander has a hard time trusting any nice words directed at him. But the boy continues to try opening up the merman's heart and trust in him, speaking to him from his heart that conveys deepest understanding and compassion with the plight of the merman.

Finally, after several minutes of heartfelt address, and after the boy has stopped talking for a long moment to let his words of compassion sink in, Torilander dares to open his eyes, gingerly meeting the boy's eyes as if to gauge whether he is still in danger or whether it is safe to trust this boy's intentions and allow himself to return to the living.

The boy holds Torilander's gaze without interrupting the long eye contact. Torilander sees that the boy truly has a good heart, and upon reaching this conclusion, he turns his gaze away from the boy and onto the scenery around him. He beholds the most remarkable, out-of-this-world kind of sights: a palace and courtyard in the open air, with trees lining certain paths, and grass and flowers accentuating the picture! It feels weird to behold such impressive sights outside the water kingdom he is used to, but nevertheless, here it is, existing in its own right, with him right in the middle of it! The guards have turned their backs on him, but he still huddles low in the water so as to not risk attracting their attention back on him.

The boy introduces himself as Philosir, and a wonderful friendship is struck up this night, one that is to hold for as long as their paths are meant to go and flow together. Mainly Philosir initiates Torilander that night into the ins and outs of court behavior, telling stories about the decadent and the more virtuous courtiers that either suck up to the King or try to change a few things here and there for the better. Torilander also hears stories about the three spoiled children of the King and Queen of Carthage, and how they like to fight amongst themselves every minute they can spare from their idle pursuits. Philosir expresses his regret and pity that Torilander will have to contend with being displayed in front of these rascals of young adults, and wishes for him to come out of the experience unscathed.

At some point, Torilander feels safe enough to share a few bits and pieces about his own upbringing, but still carefully avoids talking about anything of importance, like the journey he was on before being captured. Who knows, maybe the King ordered Philosir to befriend him and hear him out, only to have Philosir report to him in the morning. Torilander realizes that it will take him quite a long time to trust any of these human beings after the way he was treated. But it feels good to have someone to talk to, and so he enjoys most of the night with this stranger, who certainly could pass as a friend, if Torilander could just be able to forget about the many pains he experienced at the hands of this boy's fellow humans. But for now, the pain is still very fresh, and trust only flows where unconditional love and deeply reliable compassion can heal the inflicted wounds.

With puzzlement and some trembling in his voice, Torilander dares to describe his excruciating experience of how he was wounded by a spear while trying to rescue a dolphin baby and innumerable fish from the net of a fishing ship, how he was bargained away into the hands of a captain, a seasoned tradesperson who delivers goods into the hands of the King of Carthage, as it seems, how he involuntarily overheard many people talking and complaining about having a sea creature on board, and how Torilander felt the sweat and anguish of the many slaves under deck, who — chained with iron chains to the ship — had to perform the hardest of all labors, rowing the galley for hundreds of miles across the ocean. He says that feeling the pain and hopelessness in their combined hearts added greatly to his own sense of hopelessness, for he was able to deeply sympathize with their plight. He also couldn't understand how any of the officers could enjoy their lives knowing they were inflicting such horrors on their fellow humans. It would have been impossible for Torilander to pretend that all this anguish under deck didn't exist and to behave as if all this collective pain and suffering did not matter at all. In his opinion, it just demonstrates how cruel and indifferent a heart these so-called leaders of mankind possess, for they certainly step on their brothers to advance their own selfish and greedy interests. His conclusion, therefore, naturally is that he is glad to have been born under water, as a merman who is free to roam the endless seas, if he wishes, without having to witness such unbearably cruel behavior exercised towards any of their own kind.

This observation prompts Philosir to reveal some pretty hairy conditions about Carthage's social structures, especially about the ones that evidently exist outside the palace gates. He says that within the palace gates, the King has banned the use of chains on slaves, for he does not want his children growing up with this image on their minds, but as soon as one steps outside the gates, the image changes much to the worse, for it is common to see chained slaves walk through the streets, trying to fulfill their masters' many varied wishes and commands. The chains tell members of the small group of rich merchants that the bearer of the chains is some other merchant's property, a slave and therefore a condemned soul who is not allowed to seek or accept help by anyone other than his own master. To help a slave free himself of his chains or even escape is punishable with all kinds of torturous practices and happens therefore hardly at all. Some slaves might have earned their master's trust with many years of hard, loyal labor and often have their own children or relatives owned by their master as well; thus, these slaves feel bound to their master and are allowed to go about their chores without the choking chains. But from whatever angle one looks at Carthage's social life, it remains a very imbalanced and utterly unfair situation that has a few rich and wealthy people enjoying all that they can squeeze out of life and out of their fellow humans with their cold-hearted, selfish attitudes while the vast majority of Carthage's citizens live in daily misery and soul imprisonment. Philosir says he is happy he was born inside the palace gates, to parents and their ancestors who have served the King for many decades already.

Torilander sighs heavily, for he does not like to be enslaved to a king whose people live in such drastically unfair conditions, and who condones slavery and harsh punishments as part of his kingdom's social fabric. He hopes and wishes Loriolan will be successful with his mission and able to come rescue him, for he fears he cannot really effect any lasting changes in the human world anyway. Nevertheless, he conveys his condolences to Philosir, who seems to have found a friend in Torilander he feels he can trust with his innermost secrets and pains. Because at some point, the conversation between the two reaches an emotional revelation, as Philosir feels the urge to talk about the Princess. He tells Torilander that he grew up closely around her, as she loved to play with him and other servants' children in the meadows and forests surrounding the palace. She seemed to favor him especially, and often the two of them would get lost in the woods, trying to find reasons to not have to return back to a world that would separate them from each other and from the love they began, at some point, to feel for each other. But as of one year ago, the Princess gave in to the urgings of her parents and tutors, and has since then stopped noticing him in any way and fashion, much to his pain and dismay.

Once more, Torilander expresses his sympathy with Philosir's situation and just showers the sad young boy with his love and emotional support. But the boy's heart won't heal so easily, for he just saw the girl of his dreams, and she didn't even look at him once, torturing his lovelorn heart with her seeming indifference — that's how much she has changed and now seems to despise him. The love they felt for each other seems to have dissipated from her heart, and there is nothing he can do about it other than to give up and resign himself to a bottomless melancholy, for he still loves her the way they both used to love each other when looking into each other's eyes and seeing their whole worlds reflected back at each other. Torilander understands these feelings all too well, for not long ago, he had to relinquish his love for Hedna for the duties of friendship he and his beloved feel towards their royal masters and friends. But it does not feel satisfying or even healthy to dwell on these feelings, for until the mission is accomplished and he is able to see her again, he won't be able to convey his love for her and she won't be able to accept his love, allowing a happy ending to their delicate feelings for each other to manifest beyond the present constrictions.

Carefully, he begins to move around the basin to stretch his body, and before too long, the two tired young men slowly drift into a listless doze.

CHAPTER 6

"Good morning, my Lady!" Hedna greets her Mistress upon seeing her waking up with a yawn. Indirali opens her eyes, answers the greeting, then beholds the environment of their resting place by daylight, for it was late at night when the carriage finally arrived at Menelaus' home in Heraclea. Menelaus turned out to be a friendly man who delighted in the young women's company, even though they spent half the ride out of his sight, on top of a pile of trade-good packages within the covered wagon. At first, they sat next to the tradesman, enjoying a pleasant, light-hearted conversation, but further down the road, another business friend of Menelaus got on the carriage, causing the girls to retreat into the interior of the wagon to make space for him. Nikandros, Sophos' servant, had introduced the Princess and her maid as the daughters of a dear friend of the doctor, for it was deemed wise to keep the Princess's identity a secret and not invite mischief of any kind towards her royal origin. Because of the late arrival hour, Menelaus kindly extended the invitation to let the two girls stay in his barn, and find much-needed rest within the many haystacks stored in it. Surrounded by an array of farm animals, the two girls tiredly sank into the hay and were at once fast asleep. Hedna was woken by a goat licking her face, and soon after, two maids entered the barn to begin milking the goats. The many varied noises soon woke Indirali up, and still half in a daze, she now looks around to acquaint herself with their new surroundings.

"A good morning to you ladies!" one of the maids cheerily addresses the sleepyheads, for in their opinion, the morning has already progressed far into the day, with the maids being used to feeding and handling the animals way before dawn, and performing other such early morning activities. "The lady of the house extends her invitation for breakfast, if you would be so kind as to freshen up at the well outside the house."

The girls nod excitedly, for they have been noticing the sweet and aromatic flavors of freshly baked bread and pastries lingering in the air, and nothing sounds more enticing to them right now than to be invited to partake of and enjoy a meal consisting of some of these tempting smelling items. And so they gather their few belongings, and walk out to the well to pull up a bucket of water for their refreshment. After washing their faces and arms, they decide to approach the main residence, for a male servant is waiting by the entrance door indicating for them to step inside.

The family is gathered around the table, and Menelaus introduces the girls to his wife and children. He recalls fragments of their conversation from along the road to convey a feeling about their guests to his family. Eunike, Menelaus' wife, radiates warmth and hospitality, and tries to make sure the girls are well fed before leaving and getting on with their journey. She also wraps a whole loaf of bread, a cluster of grapes, and a big slice of cheese for them to take along, for she and Menelaus warn the girls about the rampant poverty that is sweeping the coastline towns, which didn't even stop at Heraclea's city gates but has, over time, turned it from a prosperous city into a place of filth and amoral values. Sadly, they recall their home city as a once proud and flourishing metropolis that used to sponsor the famous general assembly of the Italiot Greeks, an event of great spiritual and political importance that regularly attracted religious and political figures from all parts of Magna Graecia, and how this thriving city has since then declined and lost its luster.

But since Heraclea was founded by and was a colony of the neighboring city of Tarentum, a city that lent its fostering care and protection to Heraclea for many decades, the citizens of Heraclea felt it their duty to assist the Tarentines — who were fiercely led to war by the war king Pyrrhos they specifically hired from Greece for this matter — in their exhausting fights against the Romans, as well as against the neighboring Messapians, a tribe from the east coast who were after their fertile land and after new slaves and cheap laborers, trying to subdue and enslave as many Tarentine and Heraclean citizens as they could possibly get their hands on. However, with Tarentum's help, Heraclea managed to stay an independent city-state up until so far, but the resulting ravaging poverty is tempting many city elders into considering an annexation to the Roman empire, an act most Heraclean merchants detest and resist, for it is known that the Romans — like the Carthaginians — like to enslave people as well, steal their land, and either employ them as day laborers or exploit them by allowing them to rent the land that was once theirs and, on top of that, pay a hefty tax on their harvests, thus driving the majority of Heraclea's citizens into a never-ending spiral of loss, debts, compromises, and a fatal dependence they don't see a way out of.

From whatever angle one looks at the situation, it feels that Heraclea is slowly ceasing to exist, and its former grandeur and glory are vanishing off the face of the Earth. Eunike says that with each generation Heraclea is sinking deeper into depravity and people are losing hope right and left, finding themselves increasingly absorbed in a collective downward spiral that has already turned many once righteous people into criminals, who steal from others out of despair and who have developed a false sense of ethics based on their own pain and suffering, a distorted and self-serving sense of justice that allows them to justify their desperate, violating acts, and which poses an increasingly strong threat to the few remaining, truly ethical business people who are trying to produce and meet the many demands of the populace, providing much-needed products and services to disillusioned, emotionally hardened citizens who unfortunately seem to appreciate their efforts less and less. She recalls how people once pursued work of many kinds, thus contributing to a high collective income and gain, enabling the citizens to enjoy a more refined and affluent lifestyle and, with that, a strong sense of peace and harmony amongst each other, but the constant strife with greedy and aggressive neighboring city-states has weakened their city, and beholding all this greedy nonsense, the Ocean God Poseidon finally turned his back on many seafaring cultures — including Heraclea — cursing them to suffocate under their own ignorance and violence, and to encounter a similar fate on the ocean that they are creating for themselves and their neighbors on land, namely self-inflicted destruction. The ocean has long since become a place of highest risk of losing not only one's life but also one's fortunes. Poseidon's curse triggered a chain reaction of fateful events that left many once wealthy ship owners without the necessary means to continue their seafaring craft, thus crippling their enterprises and leaving a host of people without work and income. And with Heraclea's merchants losing their foothold, the Roman offer of annexation looks dreadfully near and real, driving many of Heraclea's citizens into a profound despair, for their beloved state of independence and freedom is shattering, and a cloud of darkness is forming at the horizon. They fear that neither the King of Lucania nor their friends from Tarentum will be able to protect them from Roman dominance, especially since Poseidon's curse has weakened all kingdoms that rely heavily on overseas trade.

Indirali listens with increasing agitation. Never has she heard such a desperate account of a city's fate and shattered aspirations. So far, she grew up under her parents' loving protection, kept out of the loop on all matters of politics and war. To all of a sudden hear someone speak the truth so bluntly to her face is rather shocking to her, but also triggers her infinite compassion and desire to help, if only she could find a way. Trying to keep her composure and her tears from flowing, she continues to listen attentively to what more anguish wants to release itself from the merchant's family's hearts and lips. And so she learns that once the majority of people couldn't afford to buy and trade their goods with other tradesmen anymore, a gripping poverty began to take over, leaving many once prosperous citizens destitute and despairing in its wake, along with an enormous amount of simple workers who felt the lack and poverty even sooner than the fast diminishing middle and upper classes. Because of this tendency, and because of the threatening takeover by the Romans, selfishness among members of the small upper class has been growing; trying to save their privileged and responsibility-laden status in society, many of them have ganged up in elite clubs to support their own kind from becoming extinct and getting run out of business.

Learning from the Roman example on how to subdue and enslave the masses, and trying to prevent having to rely on or be tempted by the hefty financial offers the Romans are throwing at the wealthy city elders in order to render them compliant with the Romans' will and strategy, a common fund has been established to financially help members of the elite to stay functional and ahead of the game should disaster ever knock on one of their doors and put them in the vulnerable position of having to lend the Roman offer some serious thought. This club is closely associated with the workings of the government, with its public as well as hidden agendas, and has become the pool from which the fiercely profit-driven landowners are emerging, greedily amassing as much of the land as they can get their hands on and mercilessly monopolizing the agricultural trade — the very area every individual depends heavily on for his own survival — thereby forcing many destitute people to compromise their lives, working for wages that barely cover the needs of their families, pushing them deeper into the abyss of endless debts and heart-wrenching dependencies on their landowners. Many day laborers or land tenants thus never feel the freedom to change their profession and/or move away, but feel forced to stay in one location and work for their cunning and selfish landowners for the rest of their lives, leaving their children to continue trying to pay off the pile of debt they inherited from their servant parents, only to never see the light of freedom themselves.

Indirali is startled at hearing the extent of Heraclea's problems and poverty, which prompts the family to recount incidents portraying the many threats hard-working merchant people like them are under these days, for envy and greed are rampant amongst the poor and desperate, and many good-willed merchants have lost heart, as poverty-induced problems either cause them to close off their hearts towards their fellow humans, becoming cruel and indifferent towards their suffering and misery, or cause their business to fail, rendering the once proud and successful incompetent and, ultimately, as impoverished as everyone else around them. And to have the productive middle class crumble like that is not a good thing at all in Menelaus' opinion, for it is the merchants who contribute the most to a healthy economy since they are able and used to carrying the burdens of responsibility for the large number of workers who depend on them, creating jobs and coming up with opportunities to trade and earn the money coins to keep the markets rolling and the economy thriving, thus providing everyone with an income and the material goods and human services that constitute a social life of relative abundance. For as long as the merchants have their source of wealth and resources open to them, they can in turn channel these benefits towards their workers, thus fueling the economy, but should this source be compromised or closed off altogether, the system begins to falter in the same way as the fields dry out when the well stops providing water throughout a drought. And unfortunately, after a series of exhausting wars in the recent past, the upper elite class is now increasingly working against the vast majority of people through manipulation, abuse of their work force, and through monopolizing and domineering their economic influence over the land. Poseidon's workings against humanity reflect man's evil ways and augment this destructive influence on the whole country, with the fishing and overseas trading business having dwindled to an all-time low, resulting in the dire situation at hand. Menelaus hopes the girls will stay out of harm's way while traveling the land, rather erring on the side of caution when running into raggedy-looking folks, for the likelihood of these desperate souls robbing an innocent traveler is, in today's world, far greater than the likelihood of them helping him in any noticeable way.

Eunike nods to show her agreement with what her husband just relayed, adding that many of the poor would even use violence for the sake of stealing a bit of food, especially when it is homemade, something more tasty compared to the foul little fish that occasionally get washed ashore, a food many poor and homeless people have come to depend on for their survival, as they scout and pick through the sand and rubble along the coastline for this rather unsatisfying poor man's dish. Eunike strongly suggests the girls stay off the trodden paths and eat in the solitude of a protective spot in nature.

So imploring and genuine are the family's concerns and advice for Indirali and Hedna to please circumvent the vastly reigning terrors of poverty and crime along their way, that the Princess can't help but feel compelled to learn more about the conditions that led Heraclea's population into the desperate state they are in right now. Gingerly, she asks why people gave up their land in the first place, why they sold off their land to people who paid them only a few tokens for their valuable land, and why did they allow themselves to be disempowered to the extent that they are not able to grow their own food anymore?

Menelaus thinks for a moment, then tries to answer as best he can. He explains that first of all, many later immigrants from Greece were not able to secure themselves any land, often ending up working for those who settled here before them as their simple workers and servants, living pretty much from hand to mouth. When the fishing business took off, however, many men — landowners or not — liked the idea of traveling the oceans and making a good income from that, leaving the hard labor of cultivating the land to their wives and children. Floods, droughts, and heavy storms have, over the years, also added to the desire to earn money elsewhere, for way too often natural disasters have easily destroyed the hard work and income of a family. And if one can imagine just a fraction of the distress a mother of several children goes through when her husband is absent from home for most of the year, and the day-to-day survival stress rests on her shoulders alone, then one can understand that the idea of congregating and moving closer to other such abandoned, torn families must have been pretty enticing, even if it meant leaving their land behind and moving into a small home in the fast growing harbor city that originally promised and offered a greater variety of cultural attractions, commercial wealth, and social interactions. And for many decades, Heraclea was able to not only satisfy its inhabitants' needs and desires for an abundant city life but also attract, as stated before, the prominent gatherings of the country's spiritual and political elite. But things didn't work out, and not owning land in today's volatile political and social climate, with foreign city-states vying for Heraclea's resources and land, seems to only catalyze and enhance the already devouring problems and poverty of the city, for people are disowned, jobless, and disempowered, and therefore a threat in and of themselves. Menelaus casts his eyes down, disillusioned with the worldly authorities who enslave rather than free, and punish rather than support and uplift, weary of seeing the world hurl into tighter control by a few and into a looming spiritual darkness that seems to choke the courage and life joy out of people's hearts and souls. Reminded of how hopeless the situation all around him has become, he longs for a hero to show up, the kind the legends of old talk about, one who fights the darkness and evil with the purity of his Divine Will-aligned personal will and with the courageous heart of a powerful lion. But where would such a man possibly come from? Menelaus' eyes fill with helplessness as he looks at their guests as if they would be able to provide an answer to his question.

"And to make matters worse," he continues, "the many homeless people living in the dirt of the streets and under harrowing conditions have now begun to suffer under malaria, a hideously infectious and deadly disease that is fast spreading around in the whole area, increasing the number of casualties with every year, and making our people wonder whether the Gods have forgotten about us."

"And the priests and priestesses of your temples can't and won't help the poor either?" Indirali wants to know incredulously, with her heart feeling increasingly disheartened.

Menelaus and Eunike shake their heads and confirm what Indirali already fears to be the case, namely that they are either too self-absorbed to care for the many problems around them — and as one business associate once told Menelaus in secret — even conspiring with the Roman temple elites to secure their future interests and dominance over the population, or they take a judgmental stance towards the many trespasses poor and desperate people exercise against those who possess power and wealth but don't care to share it with the needy, nor help out in any way to alleviate their problems. Menelaus' children speak up, recalling some hefty events in their neighborhood that demonstrate the temple's indifferent and aloof stance towards the suffering of its people, and say that for these reasons, their family has stopped attending the temple services, which, in turn, has drawn unwanted attention from some of the priests who had grown accustomed to the generous donations their parents had given them on a regular basis. There only seems to be one small temple left whose high priest is a more genuinely caring man, but since this temple is on the other side of town, the family only attends occasionally, and unfortunately, the old high priest's health has begun to dwindle, leaving the temple's fate hanging in the air. In his agony, the old high priest has called on more reinforcement, and the family can only hope that this reinforcement is comprised of good priests with a helpful character; otherwise, there won't be a Hellenistic temple left in this city worthy of any decent person's attendance and devotion.

Indirali and Hedna nod their heads, understanding how forlorn a population must feel when the spiritual elite of the city cannot be trusted, and is unable to tend to the many problems and wounds of its helpless and hopeless citizens. Again, the Princess thinks of her own idyllic upbringing, with the temple priesthood of Posidonia behaving around her as if she mattered, and as if the Olympian Gods mattered, all the while leading a double life, spanning many generations, that fooled the public as to their shady, behind-the-scenes orgies and political schemes and, on top of that, vastly fooled not only her father, the King of Lucania, but many of his forefathers as well as to their true financial ambitions and extensive betrayals. This realization prompts Indirali to turn her attention inward, and to silently exclaim a cry to her Goddess, wondering why those who claim to represent the highest connections to the Divine and who therefore should care about human suffering very deeply, why do these people behave like the biggest hypocrites of all and betray not only their fellow humans but the Divine Source of Life as well and, with that, their own higher-self interests and needs, whose violation will come back to them eventually to haunt them and to bring them the kind of justice they created for themselves. This ultimate justice, Indirali presumes, will help them to reawaken to the highest, most uncompromising truth, namely that what a person sows he will reap, and the selfishness and suffering he creates, he will have to deal with and suffer through as well. Knowing that the righteous people can ultimately trust in the Divine workings and all souls will have to eventually account for their actions and beliefs, Indirali settles into a feeling of equanimity, ready to thank the family for the ride and wonderful breakfast time they so generously extended to two strangers. Wishing them the blessings of the Olympian Gods and receiving the same blessings from their hosts, the two girls slip into their men's clothes and finally set out on their further journey, illumined as to the area's fate and conditions, and ready to find their way through it all in pursuit of their goal which, Indirali hopes, will give her the power to effect much-needed and prayerfully asked-for change in as many people's lives as possible.

CHAPTER 7

On their way out of town, Indirali has a hard time debating inside herself why it is prudent to keep their food safely bundled up rather than giving it away to the many beggars they encounter along the roads. Her heart wants to reach out and make a difference, but her mind keeps telling her that she won't be able to reach her goal if she won't have anything to eat and so be unable to enlist the Gods' help and wisdom as to how to effect lasting change for all these destitute people who yearn for a betterment of their life's situation. For a while, her intellect has the upper hand, especially when seeing the overwhelming amount of broken souls and their insatiable hunger, but finally, her heart begins to take over and, pushing her own interests aside, prompts her to take out the food from her backpack, unwrap it, and offer it to a group of starved, dirty-looking children. Tears well up as she looks into the melancholic eyes of one of the children, a little girl of about seven years of age with dark, big eyes that openly show her deepest amazement that a young, handsome man like Indirali would even stop, give his food away, and take the time to inquire about the girl's name and her parents' whereabouts. After giving all of her own share of food away and learning about the girl's sad story — her father lost at sea, her mother ill at home, and now it is up to her and her two elder siblings to provide for their family by begging in the streets — Indirali has a hard time tearing herself away from the children's sad fate, wondering whether she should return to Posidonia and her parents' palace, empty their treasure chests, and return with enough jewels and coins to be able to make a difference in these poor people's lives, whose miserable existence she has a hard time accepting as being unchangeable. But then her intellect begets the question: And then what? Will she be able to turn the tide of destiny for Heraclea, let alone for the whole kingdom, and prevent the gloomy fate of feudal and Roman land ownership and enslavement of those kinds of people who lack the cunning and ruthlessness their oppressors demonstrate so freely? What if she would give all of her parents' wealth away, bankrupt them, and paralyze them in regard to being able to run their kingdom's affairs, thus rendering them vulnerable to the very life-usurping, control-seizing, and violence-threatening elite groups whose destructive influences she is trying to eliminate from any poor person's life in the first place? Wouldn't she just hurt her charitable cause even more in the end? And to give her parents' wealth away isn't her right and privilege anyway since she is not the governing ruler of the kingdom, and therefore has no right to Lucania's state treasury. No, she decides, to think in this direction is just a futile undertaking, one that leaves her just as clueless with regard to the bottomless problems all around her as any person of no means would ever feel when faced with the overwhelming hardship caused by a handful of ill-intentioned and hideous, but powerful people. And so the disguised Princess turns her attention back to her path, to fervently pursue her own redemption from the evil of this world, so she may share her gained insights, wealth, and powers with those who can hear and come to her for their own redemption.

But the road that leads out of Heraclea is long and arduous, with more misery and poor, begging faces staring at them than the compassionate, delicate heart of the Princess can handle. If she had a cartload full of goods, she would give them all away to these hungering souls, relieved to be able to alleviate some of this enormous suffering and pain, but her hands are empty and tied, and her identity must remain hidden, lest she risk losing sight of her goal and faltering from the insanity all around her. If not for her own sake, she now must go on and achieve her goal so she can gain the necessary means and powers to become a big and crucial support to these poor and helpless people, whose sad fate she was oblivious of so far, but was now rudely made aware of on this most challenging, illuminating journey of hers.

Trying to not allow the suffering along both sides of the road to get to her anymore, Indirali nods at Hedna, and together they focus on the horizon in front of them, imagining seeing the light of the Olympian Gods and Goddesses guiding them and greeting them with every step. This thought begins to lighten their steps, and soon they find themselves almost floating by the last remaining city buildings, out and away into the promise of a better future for all the good and loving of heart.

But then a woman's crying rattles their souls, overthrowing what little newfound inner peace and determination for their own way the two girls had established, heartwrenchingly aiming at the deepest core of their compassionate souls, and thus forcing them to halt and take a better look.

In some distance to the right of the road, the girls behold a long, high, voluminous hedge, sheltering what looks like a small temple behind it, with the desperate woman standing by the entrance gate, crying her soul out and leaning against the gate as if she wants nothing more than for the gate to fling open and let her pass into the temple courtyard.

The girls look at each other, uncertain as to whether to abandon their focus and desire to get on with their journey or whether to try to get to the bottom of this woman's anguish. And again, the heart wins out, a no-brainer so to say, and the girls begin to approach the scene.

With friendliness showing on their faces, the girls stand right beside the woman, allowing her to notice them in her own time. The woman stops her sobbing, wondering about her sudden company. Indirali inquires about the cause of her distress, only to learn that the new priests of the temple have caught her two young sons while they were trying to steal a loaf of bread from a market stand, brought them here, and had them whipped by one of the temple servants. Now they are tied to a stake and left hanging in the hot midday sun, with blood oozing from their wounds and their souls broken. She explains that since her husband died several years ago during war, their family has been suffering greatly under the present depression, and not being able to find any work herself anywhere, her sons have begun to bring much-needed food to their dwelling place, a cave outside the city, and only now did she learn that they must have stolen it rather than earned it from a baker the way they portrayed it to her all this time. But they are still very young — she implores the girls as if asking for their understanding and forgiveness — and should therefore be treated accordingly and with kind mercy, especially by the priests who always claim to have their followers' best interests at heart, instead of being killed by them with a whipping too harsh and long for such tender bodies to endure, a whipping, in fact, so cruel and harsh that it left her sons lifeless after the ordeal, making the mother wonder whether she will ever see her sons anymore. Because, on top of that, the priests shooed her angrily away, scolding her for being a bad mother and informing her that the boys are now the possession of the temple and, as such, their fate is of no concern to her anymore. In fact, they threateningly demanded of her to leave at once, lest they would sell her as a slave to the next best bidder that comes along.

Indirali is enraged at hearing such evil nonsense. How can anyone claim another life and call it his own? Are these boys material goods that can belong to just anyone except the loving mother who nursed them into life? How many different nuances and facets can evil still assume? Indirali feels like faltering from all this pain she encounters, ready to sink into oblivion she hopes can make her forget and drown out all of this rampant, overwhelming negativity she has a hard time handling anymore. 'Aphrodite, my Goddess,' Indirali turns, inside herself, to her Matron for help, 'why have you forsaken these people? What have they done to deserve such cruel, inhuman treatment from amongst themselves, and why is there no way open for me to help these people in their need?' Tears are sitting close to running, all too often, and Indirali feels strangely incapacitated, incompetent, a new and harrowing feeling she is not used to and which seems to drive her towards the edge of sanity.

The woman continues saying that she never heard such hard words from a priest, but unfortunately, the former old high priest is no longer in charge, and the new ones just seem cold-hearted and indifferent to her, a frightful new change that just adds more agony to the plight of any poor person's life who has been begging nearby the temple for many years now. She says the new priests have already announced that beggars will be hauled away and discarded by the authorities, and that they will make sure of that.

Indirali feels jolted out of her agony, as it seems Goddess Aphrodite just spoke to her, for the woman's report just gave her the necessary idea that could possibly help her get her sons back. She has one piece of precious jewelry left from her initial belongings, a pin that bears the imprint of her royal origin. She cleverly had stowed it away in the sole of her shoe, for showing it to anyone would immediately reveal her identity to that person. To use it in a direct way for this matter does not seem wise or prudent, considering the corrupt mindset of the priests, but there is another way that this pin can help the mother and be applied for the maximum benefit of her situation. Putting her arms around the woman's shoulders, Indirali convinces her that help for her sons can definitely be provided if only she stays out of the priests' sight for now, because the boys need their mother to come back to and not lose her to some heartless slave master. With few words Indirali begins to describe her plan to the woman, who, halfway through the speech, stops her sobbing entirely, for the plan leaves her amazed and with rekindled hope.

Retreating into the shelter and protection of a nearby bush cluster, the woman is poised to wait it out until the two girls return from a half day's trip that is to bring reinforcement for their intended approach of the temple priests. With a trembling voice, Indirali asks Hedna to please leave some of her food with the woman, for she looks meager and exhausted from her ordeal. Hedna obeys her Mistress's command, for it was for her that the maidservant kept the food, trying to make sure her Mistress would stay healthy and strong on their journey. The woman gratefully accepts the offered meal, now more than ever convinced that a miracle just happened, for the Gods answered her pleading prayers and have sent two angels to the rescue. Choking down her tears, she decides to leave most of the food for her two darling sons and just have enough to feel alive again herself.

As they leave, Indirali gives Hedna a more in-depth explanation of her plan, while the two of them turn around from their intended path to walk back to the very same residence they had left earlier in the day. How odd, Indirali thinks, they end up returning back to their hosts again, which is the same thing they did in Grumentum. But if it is for a good cause, she is willing to accept a delay on her journey. The most important thing on her mind right now is to come to the aid of those two unfortunate boys and make sure they get reunited with their mother. And so the girls rush through the streets, reclaiming every step they thought they had already left behind, eager to see Menelaus and his family again, and hoping they will agree to help and will be able to do so in the end.

Tired from the running, the girls finally arrive at the farmhouse, and are warmly welcomed back. Puzzlement as to why they have come back shows in most everyone's faces at first, but when the girls explain their reason, the family understands very well. Having traveled a long distance himself the day before, Menelaus thankfully didn't go to the market today, and so he and his wife invite the girls into a private room to reveal the whole story of their problem.

After describing what they had run into along their way, and how deeply touching the pain of the mother felt to them, Indirali takes out her royal pin and holds it up for Menelaus' inspection.

"Sir, Madam, you have the honor to find yourself in the presence of the Princess of Lucania," Hedna informs them with an air of regality.

Both, husband and wife, take a step backwards, for they doubt what they just heard, but at the same time, they can't help but believe the unbelievable announcement, because the girls struck them as sincere and genuine throughout the whole time they have been spending time together. To think they would just play a joke on them doesn't seem to fit with their upright character. And so the couple share a look with one another, amazed, then back at the girls, and especially at Indirali, the supposed Princess. But all they see in the girls' eyes is steadfast sincerity, no flicker of a played prank or joke, and so Menelaus and Eunike begin to melt in the presence of true nobility, a purity and regality of character they have seldom come across. Going to their knees, they show their respect and honor to the simple-looking girl whose infinite compassion has begun to transform their own hearts. With awe in his eyes, Menelaus asks: "How can we be of service, my Princess?"

"This pin is yours if you will help us," the Princess offers. "It is worth more than you will earn in many years of your business. You can bring it to my father, King Eurylochos of Lucania, and he will shower you with riches beyond your imagination, for it was his plan to leave me with this pin, as one more way to help me along my path of self-discovery through a world he knows to be as cruel and merciless as it obviously is, but which also, thankfully, is filled with people of good heart, people like you and your family, souls of deep and compassionate character, who deserve to be enriched in exchange for the valuable help they might lend to me and my causes along the way. Know that we would have left your home unrecognized as to who we truly are, if it weren't for a desperate mother's unfortunate fate and deep worries about her mistreated and stolen sons."

The couple understands the situation and inquires how the Princess imagines the rescue mission to unfold that she is obviously planning. Indirali wonders out loud whether Menelaus and some of his strong men would consider going with her to the temple and convincing the high priest to let the boys go. It seems evident that the temple in question is the very same temple Menelaus mentioned earlier this morning, the same one the family visits only on occasion because it is so far away, the one, according to their report, that is run by an old high priest who still shows a decent amount of respect for his congregation. The fact, however, that two boys got kidnapped from the streets and whipped nearly to death points to the alarming and disturbing fact that the new reinforcement priests are of the same cold-hearted nature that most other temple priests have obviously assumed over the years. Menelaus is not sure he will be able to simply talk the priests into letting their catch go, for it is known in certain circles that priests like to have young teenage boys and girls around doing their various chores for no compensation at all, and being available for who knows what repressed urges the priesthood uses their victims for. He thinks he must make a financial or trade offer big and appealing enough that it gets their attention and convinces them to accept the bargain.

With a voice revealing some consternation but also the vulnerability of her soul, Indirali asks whether the merchant would be willing to do this if he knew that King Eurylochos would compensate him richly for this kind of sacrifice. The Princess offers to put everything in writing and to seal the papyrus roll with the impression from the very pin he is to take to her father. She says her father is a wise, just, and generous man, who will gladly reward Menelaus for his services to his daughter, knowing she was helped thus greatly along her way. Menelaus nods reflectively, then adds: "I will do more than that! I will enlist the help of a business friend of mine. He is a kind man, and will be more than happy to help. It will make the priests feel under a heightened sense of scrutiny to see two well-reputed men showing interest in their first mistreatment of the poor. Secondly," he smiles and looks at his wife, who seems to read her husband's mind right away, then answers him with a nod and a smile herself, "we will take the two boys and their mother in and offer them work and a place to live. I can always use a few more hands with my loading and unloading of goods …"

"And I can always use another maid in the kitchen," Eunike continues his thought, both satisfied with their side of the plan and with the fact that they are able to please the Princess of Lucania, who happened to stumble across their humble abode and lives in this unpredictable way.

Indirali and Hedna exclaim their exuberance. "You would really do this for these unfortunate people? How generous and loving of you!" The girls begin to dance around each other, hooking their arms into each other's, and continue to whirl and spin, laughing and exclaiming their joy and relief until they are dizzy from the action. As if a heavy stone was just lifted off their shoulders, they affectionately hug the friendly couple, thanking them from the bottom of their hearts and with a great sense of admiration for their kindness in their eyes.

Touched by this outburst of emotion, Menelaus clears his throat and suggests they all get going right away to do whatever they can to shorten the hardship of the boys and mother. The girls agree, and the plan is hatched to have the girls, accompanied by four strong servants and stable boys, return immediately to the temple to comfort the mother and let her know that help is on its way. Menelaus intends to pick his good friend up and follow as quickly as he can. And so the parties pursue their separate ways, to shortly reunite in front of the temple and handle the issue together according to plan.

This time the girls sit on top of a horse-pulled cart, unable to tarry and interact with any of the many poor people they see begging by the street, unable to share anything but a compassionate smile with them, wishing they would already be at their ultimate goal, able to flood the people with the goodness and abundance of a higher, better life experience. No matter how hard Indirali tries to not let the poverty get to her, she finds herself compelled and unable to pull her attention away from it completely. Part of her stares incredulously at the often shocking images as if it never could have imagined such dire destitution and misery. There are dead corpses lying by the wayside, rudely shoved out of the way by someone who didn't care enough to bury the dead in front of him; some unfortunate ones are sick and decrepit, limping along as if the Gods never cared and life is just this merciless, endless showdown of cruelties of all measures. Indirali thinks she can't take any more of these terrifying pictures, only to find that a super-worldly compassion opens her heart up and lets her gift a smile to however many casualties and victims try to vie for her attention in a world that has spit them out and left them to rot in the lonesome corners of an inhuman world.

Disillusioned with the privileged world she grew up in, Indirali tries to stay focused on what little difference she hopefully is able to effect in the present moment, and thus resolved, she finds herself with everyone else on the cart arriving at the temple site. As soon as the girls jump off the wagon, the mother lets out a cry of excitement and comes running out of her hiding place to meet the young men, who evidently kept their word to her. With pride and slight excitement in her voice, Indirali begins to describe the extent of fortune the little family is about to experience, as soon as Menelaus, a newfound friend of hers, will arrive with his friends to bail out her sons and offer them all shelter and work at his farmhouse.

The woman reacts with great surprise, unable to grasp the meaning of the young man's words. It takes her a moment to digest the turn of events, listening to more of the descriptions as if under a trance. Finally, it sinks in that her sons will be with her again and they are given a home and livelihood, something they have not known for many, many years, and the thought of which makes her cry and express her gratitude over and over again to the young men and their companions, who seem like a flock of angels to her distressed heart right now.

After just a short while, another carriage stops at the temple driveway, with Menelaus descending from it, two stately-looking business friends right behind him. With a friendly voice, Menelaus introduces himself to the woman as her new employer, then introduces his business friends to the Princess and her maid. He says he was in luck, for one other good friend of his happened to be at his first friend's home when he arrived, allowing him to request both of their support for this undertaking. Indirali smiles happily and stretches out her hand to both of the men for a greeting and thank-you handshake. The men laugh and say it is a welcome break from their dreary business activities, and they can't wait to see the bafflement in the priests' eyes, for they deserve to be put in their place right from the start, and a lesson ought to be taught to anyone who dares to mistreat even the most weak and poor among them.

Indirali and Hedna are glad to have them on their side, and with a sense of solidarity, the group enters the gate to stride along the meandering path towards the center courtyard. To the right, they behold the gruesome sight of the beaten boys, each hanging limply from a stake, with several priests sitting or wandering around the place, lost in conversation or contemplative thoughts. Upon seeing the group arrive, however, their attention shifts towards the intruders, and quickly, one from amongst them addresses the strangers to state their business, for it is against temple policy to disturb the inner sanctum of the priests outside public service hours.

Not being able to hold back any longer, the mother runs up to her boys to try bringing them back to consciousness, showing them that she is here for them and all will be well. However, upon seeing her approaching what the priests deem their property now, the commanding priest raises his voice and begins to shout profanities towards the woman, ordering the other priests to shut the old hag up and to restrain her at once.

Menelaus has never seen this priest before and assumes he must be new to the temple, for he certainly behaves out of line. Trying to get his message across throughout the priest's agitated shouting, Menelaus begins to raise his voice, demanding to speak to the high priest at once, for he has come to represent this woman's case, ready to back her up one hundred percent.

A shock runs through Indirali's and Hedna's veins, for they recognize the priest as one of the three who almost had raped them by the river, with the other two of them seizing the mother's arms in an effort to separate her from her sons. Startled, the girls look at each other, wondering what will become of this awkward situation, when the commanding priest catches their insecure glances and at once recognizes them for the pretentious bitches he still harbors a tremendous grudge against, since getting his pleasure with them failed so miserably at the time. Torn between the emotional charges of the recent past and the present moment, the priest finally explodes, accusing Menelaus of taking the wrong stand, for he has fallen into the trap of these two conniving bitches, who make it their business to screw men over with their hideous and seductive behavior.

Instead of gracing this outrage with any acknowledgement, Menelaus orders the priests to let the woman go, then invites Indirali and Hedna to follow him and, followed by his friends as well, begins to stride towards the high priest's quarters. Indirali and Hedna don't have to think about the invitation twice and immediately begin to walk after the men, even if it means to leave the boys unattended by any friends, for the girls sure don't care to fall into the priests' hands a second time. The mother stays behind, in enemy territory so to say, tending to her sons' many wounds. The offended priest keeps shouting after them, but Menelaus doesn't intend to let him get the better of the situation. He summons a temple servant he knows well to go ahead and show the group to the high priest's chambers. He is told that the high priest is resting and that he is not feeling well. Menelaus answers the servant that this is all the more reason for him to see the high priest and to please go ahead and announce his visitors to him. The servant does as he is told, then scurries along the long hallway of the atrium.

When the group arrives in front of the high priest's chambers, the servant is already holding the door open for them, bowing down in reverence and letting them step inside. The high priest sits at his desk, sunken in his position, meekly smiling at the group as if to welcome them. Menelaus apologizes for the intrusion, but two young lives are at stake, he says, and a mother's pain and suffering cannot go unheard.

The high priest indicates for everyone to sit down, then gives his attention to Menelaus, who takes it upon himself to describe the unfortunate situation his priests have just created for a mother of two desperate little sons, who now hang from the stakes, unconscious and bleeding from the whipping.

The high priest nods sadly and, with a feeble voice, begins to express his agony over the upcoming takeover by a bunch of priests influenced greatly by the Roman religions that steamroll over the Hellenistic Gods of old Greece, and who are turning his temple — dedicated to his beloved Goddess Hera — into the temple of the Roman surrogate Goddess Juno. He says for quite some time now this Roman influence has been bothering and breaking him with its offensive takeover tactics, but he is too old now, and his spirits are waning, and all that he can hope for is that his congregation will have someone to continue leading them towards their spiritual goals, like he tried to do during his lifelong mission and service to the temple.

Menelaus takes the opportunity to thank the old high priest for all he has done, and wishes him all the best for his health and the challenging times ahead, but then he addresses the issue everyone from the group has come here for, asking for the old priest's help in freeing the two boys and to name the price this would entail.

The high priest looks at the other visitors, acknowledging that this incident must have gone against Hera's will and desire to have conjured up such a group of advocates for the boys. But unfortunately, he says, his hands are tied, and the new priest who is to become his successor seems a very willful and boastful character, as far as he can tell from his short encounter this morning. He hasn't had time to get to know him yet because he and his two assistant priests only arrived late last night. But if there would be a good financial compensation, then he is sure he will be able to have the priests release the boys at once. The amount, however, would need to be high enough to impress and appease the new high priest's bruised ego, especially since he is trying to establish his new authority before all the other temple priests, as bad as he is coming across with that for now.

Menelaus confirms that it is his intention to pay whatever amount is needed to get the job done. His friends back him up on that, saying they will each contribute a share to this arrangement, for in their opinion, the new priest should look out to not estrange the patrons of the temple, lest he lose their support entirely. The high priest agrees, and after some back and forth negotiations on the proposed amounts, he sends for the new priest to include him in the final decision.

As soon as the priest enters the room, the atmosphere assumes an uncanny darkness of emotion; it's as if a dark spirit of the underworld has come to wreak havoc in one of the last bastions of liberal spiritual practice, the one important location, source, and means for the Greek colonists to identify with their own Hellenistic origin. With arrogance oozing from every pore of his vain skin, the priest stands provocatively in front of the desk, ignoring everyone else when addressing the high priest with a voice that allows no misreading of his contempt for the old, sick man.

"What is there to talk about?" he glares at him. "You should stand behind my decisions instead of listening to conspirators against your own temple, people who obviously question the reasoning of this temple's leadership and put a poor man's fate above the wellbeing of the temple and its congregation."

"These men have come to request a bargain that would allow the mother to take her sons with her," the high priest suggests, hoping to be heard. But the priest is not in the mood for mind games and underhanded conspiracy against his decisions. With a harsh tone of voice, he calls the boys and their mother part of the filth of the Earth and asserts that any good, hard-working citizen should see it as their duty to rid the world of this dirt and mess that clogs up the streets and causes malaria to spread all around, even infecting the most innocent amongst the members of the temple congregations, only because the lazy and poor people's unhygienic lifestyles create an environment conducive for these deadly diseases to flourish in. "No, …" he waves his hands about as if trying to ward off a pile of nonsense, "don't tell me to take pity on these parasites, for I sure as hell don't want to support the downfall of our generation and society by allowing these incompetents to suck the life force out of those who are decent enough to work for their living."

"That's enough!" Andronikos, one of Menelaus' friends interrupts with a resolute voice. "Shouldn't you help and uplift rather than condemn and punish? I'm more afraid of our future as a people when looking at your practices and hearing you speak thus, heartless and judgmental. The world is decaying not because of the poor people's incompetence, but because of selfish and cold-hearted people like you, who drain the life blood out of everyone they come in contact with."

"In every poor person there is a potential criminal!" the priest counters. "Give them any power and they will abuse it in the same way they are accusing their apparent oppressors of doing. They are just as hypocritical as anybody else. And because of that, they are in just the perfect circumstances for their growth right now, able to learn from the strong and victorious, and able to pay their dues according to their weaknesses and higher justice!" He looks at Andronikos with an air of superiority, unwilling to bow to anything he might have to say to that.

"This kind of self-serving reasoning is exactly the reason this world finds itself in the miserable state it is in," Andronikos retorts heatedly, "with men on one side possessing more wealth than they can possibly spend in several lifetimes, hording it, being greedy, unconscientiously violating, and becoming more and more sick and corrupt from it, and on the other side, you have those unfortunate souls who have to suffer under the lack and impotence of being manipulated and cheated out of what should rightfully belong to every citizen on this earth: a piece of land, and a good community of heart-centered individuals that lend their loving support to one another."

"Dream on, brother. I have yet to see that the Gods drop this kind of utopia in our laps without us having to take matters into our own hands!" The priest belittles his opponent with a sarcastic remark and another one of his superior grins.

"I guess only in this world can evil get away with it and still come across as looking virtuous!" Andronikos shows disgust in his face.

"Fine successor you found here for yourself," Gennadios, Menelaus' other friend, interjects while leaning forward towards the high priest.

"Gentlemen," Menelaus appeases, "we are here to make our offer to the temple. Let this priest here be the judge of our generosity." And with that, he begins to make an offer, which the priest immediately declines with a demeanor of played offense taken.

"You won't teach me a lesson on this one!" he assures, ready to disrespectfully leave the room. But then Menelaus utters the magic formula, namely for the priest to name his price. The priest stops in his tracks, turns around, and begins to think, for such an offer is worth his time all of a sudden.

After a few minutes of silence, he peevishly addresses the high priest again, telling him he would consider a deal between the parties if they would agree to enlist and pay a sculptor to create a larger-than-life statue of the Roman Goddess Juno, a Goddess he has been growing quite fond of, and which he would like to see replace the present statue of Hera above the altar as soon as possible, allowing Hera to take the place next to the entrance for worshippers to pay their — over time hopefully dwindling — respects to. He says that his superiors stand strongly behind him on this new trend and that it would be wise for the old man to yield to this new power and influence that is quickly and vastly spreading throughout the new empire.

The old high priest lets out a heavy sigh, for this is exactly what he was afraid might happen, that the Greek temples vanish and are absorbed by the Roman religion. Unable to find words for this betrayal of his heritage, he sinks his head into his hands as if trying to hide from the dreadful tendencies he seems hardly able to change anymore.

Perplexed, Menelaus looks at the Princess, wondering how to proceed. To be the fostering agency for Juno to take Hera's place seems a rather high price for a whole Greek congregation to pay in exchange for three lives. Sadness fills his eyes as he tries to read the Princess's mind. But her eyes are so insistently pleading for his help and mercy that he cannot deny her this wish. After all, who can weigh a person's life in gold anyway, be it a poor person or not?

But now Menelaus' friends speak up, enraged with the priest's self-assuming stance. If he behaves thus coldly, they argue, and cuts the Greeks off from their spiritual heritage, he will most likely lose everyone in his congregation. The men know for sure that the temple will lose their own support and attendance should such outrageous intent be considered. The temple is supposed to tend to the beliefs of its followers, and not the other way around.

The priest, fending for himself the way he does, doesn't allow the men to get the better of him. A loud argumentation ensues in which he portrays the dangers of resisting the Roman influence; how he has seen people of any status disappear if they didn't behave, and how this can happen anywhere and for any reason. The men don't like to be threatened, and a fistfight would most certainly have erupted would Indirali not have spoken up to remind everyone of their civilized nature and the true reason of their gathering. Thus brought back from the heat of their tempers, the men calm down and look at the situation from a more agreeable angle.

"Okay," Menelaus sighs, "let's say you can get away with this enormous betrayal and change of the Greek belief system. Do you really not care to lose what little congregation this temple has left anymore? What if our people decide to build another temple that would allow us to continue revering our Goddess Hera exclusively as our ancestors have done for many millennia?"

"It will be occupied by a Roman-friendly priesthood sooner rather than later," the priest counters without having to reflect on the answer. "Hello!" he laughs disrespectfully, "you still haven't caught on to the fact that you are on the wrong side, my brother. It's just a matter of time before the whole continent is under Roman rulership. Do you really want to go down with the vanquished?"

"Don't brother me," Menelaus rebuffs him with irritation in his voice. But then he overcomes his obvious aversion and proposes: "How about we get you this statue built for as long as we three family men here are able to be more actively involved in the temple decisions and changes from now on. It would help you to have us as a mediating agency that makes sure the congregation can be with you no matter what radical developments you throw their way!"

The old high priest looks aghast that Menelaus would even consider the new priest's infamous request, but the self-absorbed priest quickly injects: "Throw in a talent (about 30 kg) of silver coins for every year, and you have yourself a deal."

The three business friends look at each other to see whether they can accept this ludicrous offer. Then Andronikos negotiates for the new high priest to be easy on the poor and to not whip them anymore; if he can do that, then they all have themselves a deal as long as none of the men and their families are offended by the temple and its priesthood to the extent that they would want to leave the temple for good, in which case they would owe nothing to the temple anymore.

The priest nods and extends his hand for a handshake, glad to have found this kind of support on his first day of unofficial office, and glad he grabbed those little thieves at the market, for whipping them was the best thing he could have done for his own start at the temple as it turns out.

Reluctantly, the three businessmen seal the deal with their handshakes, unsure whether they will be able to stand by it with their full hearts over time, but certainly willing to give it their best efforts. Roman dominance is happening with or without their participation; at least they secured their own influence for a little while longer in one of the few remaining temples that still honor the Greek Gods the way the Greeks are used to, even if Hera is diminished to standing by the entrance rather than in the center of every worshipper's attention.

With anguish in their hearts, but smiling along with Indirali and Hedna about the positive outcome for the whipped boys, the men show their respect to the old high priest, wishing him much-needed strength and clarity for what lies ahead of him, then leave the chamber to walk back with the priest to the front courtyard of the temple.

The mother has been waiting for them, her eyes trying to read whether the outcome is what she wants to hear or not. Indirali's smile convinces her that the young man has kept his word once again and has performed a miracle for her and her boys. Tears start rolling down her cheeks as she hears the priest ordering the other priests to untie and take the boys off the stake and escort them out the gate.

Somewhat stunned at the sudden turn of events, the priests follow his command and set the now half-conscious boys free from their captivity. Two of Menelaus' men approach the priests to take the boys off their arms, then carry the rather still lifeless-feeling bodies to the cart outside. There, the boys and their mother are lifted onto the cart, while Indirali and Hedna keep standing by the road, ready to pursue their journey again, now that another calamity along their way has been successfully dealt with.

"How about you young gentlemen?" Menelaus inquires about the girls' fate. "Isn't it quite late already to be attempting this rather long walk to Tarentum?" And upon noticing the mother trying to feed the boys some food she must have obviously gotten from the girls, he adds, "How about celebrating this joyous occasion with a nice dinner, everyone invited! You can stay another night and leave tomorrow early in the morning. How about that?"

The Princess is overwhelmed with his generous offer, but even though it is nearly evening, finally getting on with their journey feels very urgent to her now. She is about to decline the friendly gesture, when Andronikos pipes up with a friendly offer of his own.

"Yes!" he smiles, "this sounds like a splendid idea for you guys! I myself have my own dinner to go home to, but if to Tarentum you want to go, I can offer you a ride with my son who will be leaving Heraclea early in the morning to deliver a load of pottery to one of our trading associates in Tarentum. I bet you would arrive at your destiny even sooner this way, and feel more rested as well."

This most welcome offer convinces Indirali right away that accepting another night's stay at Menelaus' home is the right thing to do, and so with a warm smile, she thanks the men for their extraordinary help in freeing the boys from their certain demise, gratefully accepts Andronikos' offer for a ride, and also thanks Menelaus for extending another invitation to her and Hedna, which, in her expressed opinion, only demonstrates his selfless heart and great sense of hospitableness. With a laugh of relief, she mounts the cart, followed by Hedna, and takes a seat in between the little freed family, able to take a better look at the two boys whose lives she just helped to change for the better.

Their backs full of lash wounds from the whip, and blood running from them, they lie in their mother's arms, the older one with his eyes open now, afraid to hold Indirali's warm-hearted gaze, for not too long ago life treated him miserably, and he is not sure whether he can trust it so soon again. And so the little company atop the cart begins to move, as the horses begin pulling the heavy load.

CHAPTER 8

Oh, how he hates his new environment! Torilander screams with inner pain and torture. Earlier in the morning he was brought into this tank, which is just big enough to allow him to pace about four yards back and forth in it, a showcase for the Royal Family, situated along the eastern wall of the Royal Family's assembly hall. He is to be their entertainment now, a rare specimen that the humans look at and study with all the intellect they possess, to figure out how such a creature could exist in their universe and what to do about it. Torilander winces with pain at the thought that this might be his new, and one and only, home for whatever indefinite time it takes Loriolan to master this earthly plane and be able to secure help from the divine planes, so he can come and rescue his friend from his imprisonment. Other than that, his life looks pretty bleak right now, completely at the mercy and will of these undeveloped beings that strike him with their unmannered, controlling, and self-absorbed ways as a species bereft of any higher, divine impulses and virtues. How vulnerable and exposed he feels towards their possessive nature, and how lonesome and non-understood in their ignorance- and obliviousness-imbued presence!

The fountain was already bad enough, shallow, small, and exposed to the public eye as it is, but this showcase serves one purpose, and one purpose only, namely to entertain and satisfy the Royal Family's insatiable taste for new sensations, unusual spectacles, funny distractions, and a creature they deem inferior and can, therefore, look down on. It was nice spending time in the presence of Philosir yesterday, for they both felt united in their pain of unreciprocated love for a woman. Philosir actually turned out to be a pretty decent human being, full of compassion and genuine interest in Torilander's life and goals. At some point, Torilander felt safe enough in Philosir's presence to disclose to him in vague terms that he was accompanying his best friend on his life journey towards the heavens, where his friend hopes to be able to unite with an Earth woman, when Torilander was seriously injured while trying to rescue a net full of fish from their fatal capture. At first, Philosir had a hard time understanding why Torilander would give his life for some fish, and why the heck he didn't even feed off the fish in the fountain which the King had made available for his consumption, but when he saw Torilander's pain in trying to justify his action, saying that for him and his friends even the smallest of fish deserve to live and that he doesn't want to be part of nor the reason behind any of their demises, Philosir softened his stance and began to reflect on his own attitudes towards the weak and meek and towards those who cannot fend for themselves, only to realize that even though he himself is a slave of the King, his heart has actually closed off quite a bit towards the pain and suffering of most other slaves, realizing that — like everyone else around him — he actually condones the killing and slaughter of animals to be able to feed off them. To question the righteousness of these actions and attitudes seems very unusual and uncomfortable, even dangerous and against the grain, if he thinks about it, for most everyone he knows depends on their regular meat dishes, and there does not seem to be a collective awareness for living any other way. In fact, he would feel quite unsafe if he were to question and go against the mass conscious tendencies, as the life of a slave is hard enough already, and very volatile, because a slave is not allowed to possess an opinion of his own; his thoughts and actions are expected to be completely aligned with those of his master and should not challenge him in any way whatsoever, lest the slave's life be terminated or sold off to some other brute. But deep inside, Philosir wishes he could afford to be compassionate with other slaves, and also with animals he grows accustomed to and even fond of during his yearlong care for them, because it feels good to feel unconditional love, and it feels good to allow even the lowest of life forms to live and thrive with their own momentum and drive for life.

When Philosir pointed out that ultimately everything belongs into a cycle of life, and that it seems the strong devour the weak, and that's just how it is, Torilander made him aware that there are innumerable different cycles in life, and many higher and lower worlds most humans cannot even perceive within their limited sensory range, and that any being can choose to what kind of life cycle it wants to belong, whether to be caught in the cycle of predator and prey, victimizer and victim, or whether to thrive in the cycle of a higher-oriented nature, to live and let live, to thrive and to uplift any life form around itself. Any soul, Torilander said, chooses his level and world of resonance, of whatever degree of spiritual darkness or light the soul feels naturally attracted to, based on his level of maturity and developed virtues. And it is because of this inner knowing that, as a merman, Torilander feels love and compassion for his co-inhabitants under the ocean surface so strongly and empathically that it is unnatural to him to consider anything but chlorophyll-rich sea plants as his food, for he loves playing with and admiring the various forms of ocean life far too much to want to hurt and obliterate any of them. And he is not the only one of his oceanic family who thinks and acts that way; in fact, most of his relatives and friends live by this code of ethics and therefore enjoy a relatively joyous and prosperous life as a result of this peace-loving attitude.

Upon hearing such relatively unfamiliar thoughts, Philosir became silent for a long time, reflecting on this unusual way of life and beginning to yearn for such an environment that allows all life forms to coexist in harmony and peace, an environment devoid of mass control by a few, devoid of punishment, devoid of any fears for the safety of one's life, a life so free, prosperous and enriching that it obliterates the need and urge to dominate, subdue, and imprison others, for the lack of life force does not exist anymore and the need to feed off the life force of others is therefore gone as well. In such a beautiful world, Philosir and his beloved Princess Elissa could very likely be together, with no king or other worldly authority being able to interfere with their true feelings for each other anymore, unable to prohibit their good fortune and happiness. What a heavenly, peaceful world this would be, where the lion lies down with the lamb, and the humans have become true brothers and sisters of the spirit. Philosir liked this thought and kept dreaming about such a world for most of the day, thus conversing with Torilander about better times and circumstances, and about higher-worldly experiences he never heard or knew of before. Torilander even went so far as to explain that he hopes to one day be able to live off the higher frequency energies more directly, thus eliminating his need to even feed off the algae plants of the oceans altogether, and allowing the plant life to stay intact and untouched by him and by other beings who strive for spiritual enlightenment. He said he knows of mer-beings who underwent such personal transformation processes and who now dwell in higher frequency worlds as a result of it, worlds of much higher light intensity, greater life joy, and more fulfillment in all areas of life, with personal powers that make living within the lower frequency worlds feel like wearing a suit that has been outgrown, a suit that has become way too small and too tight for them.

Only twice was their peaceful chatter interrupted yesterday; once when the Queen came to check on the merman's wellbeing, bringing with her the doctor to feed him a potent liquid for the purpose of boosting his immune system and health, and the other time when Princess Elissa showed up with two of her female companions, giggling and chattering about the oddity of the merman's looks, with the Princess boasting that he will be in her care very soon, announcing that she has all sorts of experiments planned for him already to see whether he possesses any intelligence whatsoever.

In both cases, Torilander pretended to still be mostly unconscious, leaving his eyes shut and his mind numb towards their self-assuming stances, but today, since transitioning into this dreadful tank, completely exposed to any visitor's stare, he feels tremendously violated and a victim to human will and intention, without Philosir to buffer and console him anymore, his heart afraid and faltering at the thought of what is to come, and how he will be able to handle and survive his imprisonment.

The tank is pretty empty except for a sandy bottom and some small stones strewn around it, with no plants, no bigger rock to hide behind, nothing. He is to lie on the bottom of the tank for everyone to behold, or to hang in suspension in the water; whatever he does, he will have spectators for every move and every glance he decides to throw around the weird-looking, big hall the humans call the Royal Family's assembly hall.

Not long after he was placed into the tank by a handful of servants, the oldest son of the King and Queen, Danel, enters the hall, accompanied by three other young men. Danel throws himself onto an upholstered big chair, puts his feet up high, and begins to pluck some grapes from a plate to then lustfully cram them down his throat, all the while looking extremely bored and disinterested in what else is going on around him. The behavior of his companions, on the other hand, is rambunctious and loud, with the three companions throwing a ball around, bouncing it fiercely off the floor and walls, oblivious to when they hit a piece of furniture or when they even happen to destroy a vase during their wild throw-and-catch game. So oblivious are they towards their environment that it takes them several minutes to notice the merman in the tank. But once he is noticed, the laughter and ridicule begin, and soon Torilander is the target of their bad jokes and superior, arrogant remarks and demeaning looks. Two of them begin to shout loudly at Torilander, trying to frighten and startle him and make him react to their nonsense, but Torilander keeps lying on the bottom of the tank, curled into a fetal position, without giving in to the urge to react and to wanting to smack them in the head for their disrespectful and nasty behavior.

A loud and agitated shouting discussion begins, with the young men hypothesizing about Torilander's seemingly primitive origin and outrageously awkward physical build. They have a fun time backbiting the sea creature that cowers on the ground as if dimwitted and out of it. All that Torilander can hope for is that they won't climb into the water and mistreat him physically; other than that, he tries to drown out their noise and human stink, for to give in and react to any of their offensive attacks would mean the beginning of a fight Torilander is sure he does not want to entertain and risk.

Then a female servant enters the hall, bringing with her a tray and several chalices of wine. She places the drinks onto the table, ready to withdraw to the door with a curtsy, when Danel grabs her butt, fondles her, and pulls her down onto his lap as if she is a thing ready to satisfy his sexual hunger anytime he feels like it. He begins to uncover her breasts, when she indicates her shame and embarrassment in front of the other men, and especially in front of the water creature. Following her reasoning with half of his brain, he finally has a moment where he agrees with her that doing it in front of the animal would indeed be creepy, and so he stands up, his pants bulged out, and informs his colleagues he will meet them in the arena for their lance throwing competition as soon as he is done with this. And they should expect to be vanquished by his prowess and valor, for there is only one of him around, and they better look out! The three men laugh out loud, then pour the drinks down and follow Danel out the door.

Only now does Torilander dare to relax and breathe freely again, slowly releasing the pent-up stress, anger, and fear these barbaric creatures caused him in their fervor to make him as unwelcome to their world as they possibly could. A deep sadness overcomes him at the thought of being stuck with these idiots, unable to remove himself from their presence and mockery. He continues to lie on the bottom for a while longer before he dares to float up and take a better look around the big, empty hall. Considerable havoc has been caused to the scene in front of him, with chairs tilted over, shards scattered over the thick, decoratively patterned burgundy carpet, some wine spilled over the table, and the curtain hanging loose on one corner of the large windows. Torilander shakes his head at beholding this mess, wondering how the Royal Family puts up with these men's rowdy behavior, and still has an assembly place to come back to and feel comfortable in.

The answer to his puzzlement and wonder comes in the form of a group of servants, who quickly slip through the door, equipped with cleaning devices of all kinds, and swiftly take care of the mess the spoiled brats caused with their inconsiderate and immature behavior. Occasionally one or more of them look at Torilander, who, for the first time since interacting with Philosir, doesn't hold back with his open gaze, and so their eyes meet, but the servants are too busy and preoccupied to dwell in front of the tank for too long as they are expected to clean the mess up in no time at all, for the next visit of one of the royals can occur at any moment and should not be held up by their presence and work. Torilander is amazed to see how unconditionally and demurely the servants do their dirty work, as if it's the most natural thing in the world to take care of someone else's droppings and waste in the same way as a mother changes a baby's diapers so it can go ahead and poop again according to the implicitness of its dependent, immature nature. But to compare the Prince's corruption to the innocence of an infant would be an insult to the entire human race, for the Prince ought to possess a full-grown brain, as underused as it appears to be, and as such, his disrespectful behavior comes across as violations and disturbances rather than as innocence and inability. Watching the cleaning process with open, amazed eyes, Torilander thus forgets about his urge to hide for a moment because this scene is just too ludicrous, maybe even funny. He knows from having grown up around Loriolan and going in and out of the underwater palace that servants do clean the palatial environment, but never has he seen such mess caused in such a short amount of time and then removed within minutes so the next upheaval can commence again. And hardly has he finished his thoughts when the servants also finish up, ready to leave the hall. One servant, however, quickly before disappearing through the door, opens a big bag he had brought along, takes a vase out, a precise replica of the one that got smashed by the rowdies, puts it on top of its predestined console, then hurries after his colleagues. They have barely set foot out the door when Hanno, the second son of the royal couple, barges in, chasing after a young woman who obviously tries to escape his smothering attempts to get the better of her. She shrieks with her unmelodious voice to startle him away from her, but he keeps coming after her from all angles until she gives in and lets herself be caught. But when he tries to impose himself on her, she becomes fierce with him, rejecting his advances aggressively as if to make it clear to him once and for all that she can never be his because she is promised to his brother in marriage. This reminder really ticks Hanno off, and with much agitation, he accuses her of being a gold digger who would marry his dim-witted, lazy, and decadent brother just for his inheritance and status as the future king of Carthage but certainly not for love, because this notion is unbeknownst to him. Then he reminds her that it was him, Hanno, she loved when they were children and that her father does not have her best interest at heart when he wants to marry her off to some male whore who won't ever be able to appreciate the sweetness and depth of a true love relationship, the kind Hanno and she are fortunate enough to experience.

"That might all be," she confirms, "but my father thinks that being queen of Carthage cannot be trumped by anything, not even love. He keeps telling me how much good I can do for our family lineage, and when we look at you, you just don't cut it. You will always live in the shadow of your brother. Do you really believe I will choose the moon, when I can have the sun that gives her light to the moon in the first place?"

Hanno is red with fury. "You dumb little thing, do you really think my brother will allow you to exercise any power over or under him? He doesn't even like you; I don't think he even likes himself. He is just after young girls and boys, anything he can put his tail into; that's where the seat of his intelligence is located anyway, because it's certainly not in his brain, no light in his brain at all! But if you feel comfortable around such a dimwit, then go ahead, destroy your life and the love we used to have." Hanno looks offended and angry.

"Oh, look at the creature!" the woman exclaims upon noticing Torilander, happy to be able to distract Hanno. "It has its eyes open. How curious he looks, and how knowingly he looks at us; it's almost uncanny, as if he is able to understand every word we are saying!" She takes a few steps closer to the tank. But Hanno doesn't like this kind of distraction; in fact, he doesn't like the creature whatsoever. One lame brother is enough to have around; to bother with another male competitor in the family is more than he wants to put up with, especially with things hanging in the balance between him and his woman, Corinna, the way they are. He grabs her gruffly by the arm, trying to yank her to the other side of the hall, but Corinna shrieks with pain from his hurtful touch, trying to resist his pull. That makes him even angrier, for he feels betrayed enough by her, and this merman creature just adds fuel to his already consuming jealousy.

In that moment, the doors fling open, and Princess Elissa, accompanied by two of her maids, enters the hall to remind everyone of her own important and cheerful presence. Her eyes immediately fall on Torilander, and upon realizing he has his eyes open, she exclaims her exuberance at such a wonderful development, for she has taken a personal interest in this captured pet that has her heart flowing with a nurturance she can hardly explain to herself. Steering herself and her maids past the angry Hanno and the confused seeming Corinna, daughter of one of the wealthiest merchants of Carthage, and one of Elissa's former playmates and confidantes, the Princess steps in front of the tank to take a better look at the merman as he floats lightly in the water, his eyes open with alarming astonishment.

"Aren't you a gorgeous looking creature!" she addresses him, showering him with her love and attention. "I bet this must all be foreign and frightening to you, am I right?"

Torilander gulps down the frightful tension he wasn't even aware of until she mentioned it, for watching the happenings around him has strangely drawn him into their world already, as repulsive and foreign as it all has come across to him so far. But he still isn't sure he wants to start interacting with these humans; he is afraid that if he does, they will focus on him even more and hone in on his weaknesses in ways that might be abusive and controlling. And so he just keeps staring at them, and a mutual evaluation of each other's features and looks ensues, with the Princess deciding that she likes very much what she sees and realizing that she is very happy to have this interesting-looking merman in her care. With a side look towards one of her maids, she indicates for the bell to be rung. When the servant enters, the Princess orders him to have the men she earlier sent to the seashore bring the natural elements she had them gather for the merman's comfort. The servant retreats with a bow of his head, ready to follow her command.

"We'll get you some useful items for your new little home here!" she informs Torilander. Then she begins to recapitulate for her maid friends what she understands Torilander's capture and journey to their palace to have been like, exaggerating the part of his being wounded terribly by some rough seamen, intending to draw her maids' consternation and compassion to the merman's plight. Hearing his sister defending and taking the side of this dreaded sea creature, and especially being pissed off at his love interest's silly interest in this increasingly bothersome and irritating half-animal, Hanno leaves the room with a hiss, demeaning the girls with his words as being a bunch of retards who let themselves easily be blinded by a dim-witted creature's pleading eyes and helpless air. But the Princess won't be swayed from her enthusiastic observations and comments, frequently looking back at Torilander as if to secure his goodwill and admiration for her selfless act, as she takes it upon herself to be his mouthpiece and advocate for the suffering she imagines he incurred along the way of finally coming to be with her. At some point she even mentions that the Gods must have delivered the merman to her doorstep because they must know she is the right person to take care of his needs, and who knows what beautiful future might be in store for them both, for when she looks deep into her heart, she feels tremendous care for this adorable creature, the likes of which she has hardly felt before.

For a while, Torilander almost began to hope that his fate might have taken a wonderful turn for the better when the Princess entered and began to see in him more than a despicable brute, showering him with her warm attention and caring words, but as she now continues to spout her irrational future hopes and mysteriously unfathomable feelings towards him, a different kind of fear begins to emerge and spread in him, one that seems to undoubtedly indicate that he is better off not to entertain her feelings for him in any way unless he is willing to forsake his deep feelings for Hedna, the woman who owns his heart, his one and only true love for as far and wide as he can see! And so he turns his gaze away from the Princess, which causes her to immediately go into a frenzy of disappointment, trying in all sorts of ways to win back his eye contact, for she likes to look into his deep blue eyes and behold his beautiful, mysterious soul, fantasizing about how he must surely feel the same way as she does, unable to let go of this wondrously beautiful feeling she imagines they must mutually share with one another. But Torilander is intent on looking the other way, hoping the intensity of her attention will fade away and he will once more be left alone and unto himself to ponder his hopeless seeming situation. The Princess, however, has made it her goal to please him in any way necessary to win back his attention on her, involving her maids in a cheerful game of hide and go seek that is to tickle his curiosity and urge to look back, with the Princess hovering and staying as close to the tank as possible. Corinna, who has taken a seat in the back, has a good laugh while watching Elissa's clumsy attempts, because the spectacle makes it very evident that the Princess is making a fool of herself, harboring strange and unbefitting feelings for an inferior being that are better left unexpressed and denied, but nevertheless, the scenario is paradoxical and comical enough to prompt Corinna to laugh heartily at the embarrassing scene, mocking the Princess's every move with her laughter, as if to convey to her the futility of such childish and abnormal urges and desires to try and bond with an animal. Elissa grows sour with Corinna's heartless laughter and begins to wish her out of the hall, for she is immersed in her dreamlike fantasy and doesn't wish to be disturbed or yanked out of it. Corinna has seen enough anyway, and so — with continued laughter and joking — she gets up and leaves the hall.

But as soon as Elissa deems herself in a safe and undisturbed space again, able to continue her dreamlike, romancing interlude with the elusive merman, the King and Queen enter the family assembly hall, both bringing with them an air of seriousness and businesslike authority.

"What is this business of fetching a big rock from the sea?" the King inquires of his daughter, who begins to gracefully taper off her efforts of winning Torilander's willingness to interact with her.

"Nothing!" she deflects with a sweet tone of voice, as if trying to break her father's somber attitude towards the matter with the lightness of her heart. "I just thought the merman would be happier with a few items from the ocean, his natural habitat, to keep him company in this bleak new environment we put him in, that's all."

"But a rock the size of a chair?!" the King frowns as if to express his doubt and concern in regard to her childish notion. "Really, Elissa, it will splash most of the water out of the tank if you try and have that rock lowered into it. Are you aware of that?"

"I just thought he might be happy to be able to sleep behind a rock instead of constantly having our eyes on every one of his moves, forcing him to contend with our curiosity at all times," she defends her thinking.

"I think her intention is in the right place," the Queen Mother comes to her aid, adding: "Why don't we try it out and see whether he likes the rock more than he would like to have more abundant water in the tank?"

"Well, I ultimately don't care, for as long as the carpet stays dry in here!" the King admits, waving one of the servants to have the treasures from the ocean brought inside. Then he steps towards the tank and takes a closer look at Torilander, who couldn't help but turn his attention back towards the hall, hoping the Princess will get away with her idea and he will be able to find shelter behind a rock whenever he feels like checking out and leaving the threatening world outside of his awareness. Torilander moves slightly backwards as the King stares at him with an intensity that tries to fathom the depths of the existence of this legendary creature from the sea. It strikes the King as odd to see such intelligence sparkling back at him through the eyes of the merman, and satisfied with what he sees, he begins to smile at Torilander.

"I'll give you a week to adjust," the King addresses him such, "but then I will introduce you to a select group of our country's intellectual elite, to researchers, doctors, and scientists who will get to know you better and teach you some of our customs and language. I bet there is a lot to be found out about you!" He grins contently at the thought.

Torilander does not feel to respond to this grin. If at all, the King's announcement just makes him more ticked off at the whole situation he is in. He doesn't need to learn their language; mer-beings can understand any human language intuitively, since their awareness is mainly located on a higher frequency reality which, by nature, contains many different realities of the lower frequency levels and thus enables the mer-being's awareness to simply tune in to the communication networks of different species. But he doesn't even want to be put into a situation where he is forced to explain any of the intricate workings of his brain. These narrow-minded human beings will probably never find out enough about him, and Torilander is afraid if he starts cooperating at all, he won't be left in peace anymore but might get handed around from one scientific community to the next.

The Princess, however, is overjoyed to hear her parents consent to her idea, for she truly, deeply feels for the merman's needs and woes. She would do even more for him if only he would talk to her and help her understand what he might still be missing. Because as wonderful as it is to have him here with her, she also feels for his solitude and anguish that must still reside in him as a result of his traumatic capture and transport.

At that moment the doors open, and several servants walk in with their heavy loads, with four strong men trying to balance a big rock between them, for they had to leave the cart it was brought on outside the palace. Under the King's instructions, buckets of water are removed until it is considered safe to try lowering the rock into the tank without spilling the water over the rim. Torilander retreats towards the left-hand corner of the tank, anxious to stay out of the way from all this action. Then the men begin to lift the rock into the tank and, held by leather straps, lower it towards the bottom right-hand side of it. Elissa and her parents are satisfied with the feat and begin to examine the maritime goods, then decide what goes where in the tank, making sure the merman will still have enough space to move around. And so Torilander's small environment begins to fill up with things garnered from the oceanic home world he already misses so much that it sickens him to his soul. The plants, little fish, even a turtle, sea stars, algae, corals, and sea shells just trigger his memory of better, more lighthearted times, and tears begin to form in his eyes as he observes his little world getting a little bit more akin to the vast oceanic world he was forced to leave behind.

When it is finally all done, Torilander doesn't know whether to gift the family with a smile or not. He still harbors resentment towards them for imprisoning him in this tank in the first place. The thought of being analyzed under the scientific scrutiny of the King's researchers just leaves Torilander feeling victimized again, reminded of just how impotent he is when it comes to determining his own fate. If they think for one moment that these added items will make a big difference in the way he feels around them, then they are simply wrong, for he hates every minute of being under their observation and good will or, in the case of the sons, under their ill will. But to let them know they were acting somewhat in the right direction, he moves behind the rock, looks at them as if to acknowledge this humane gesture of theirs, then crouches down to retreat from their attention, hoping to glimpse a more joyful future prospect inside of himself, by looking deep into his soul, and trying to connect with Loriolan, his best friend in this world, and Chekilian, his beloved brother, whom he misses more than he can admit to himself for fear of losing his mind. He also thinks about his parents, whom he misses so terribly much that it hurts his soul, and who don't even know he is caught by humans, unable to support Prince Loriolan on his life-risking mission, and reduced to just hoping the Prince will reach his goal now without him, because without the hope of Loriolan coming to his rescue, Torilander feels he has nothing much to look forward to anymore. With a heavy heart, he sinks into a half-conscious state, still hearing the family talk with each other, and occasionally referring to Torilander as if talking about a legendary creature they were fortunate enough to have come across and whose behaviors and habits they intend to study more deeply over the next while.

CHAPTER 9

How much Torilander would give to be with Loriolan and Chekilian right now! Not knowing about their fate seems unbearable to him, and so — in his mind — he drifts back down memory lane, back to those fortunate of times that had them all united as friends and brothers, ready to explore and conquer the world in their own playful, carefree ways, in environments that were conducive to their spirit of friendship and adventure. And as if by magic, Torilander feels pulled into a specific memory that has him laughing with his playmates in the gardens of Poseidon, as his family got invited by Loriolan's parents, the Underwater King and Queen of Azuris, to accompany them to an assembly, along with many other Underwater Rulers, called by the Water God Poseidon for the occasion of discussing and learning about the issue of upholding the God's curse on humanity. Many had expressed their doubts on the matter, and Poseidon saw it timely and fit to give his people enough insight into the conditions that led to this curse, as well as into the interactions between the mer-world and the human world that only hardened his stance toward the human world, to hopefully trigger them to wake up and perceive the wisdom behind what might otherwise come across as too drastic a measure.

Back then Torilander was still a young mer-boy, hardly interested in all this high-minded talk and argumentation; his two playmates' and his own interest was mostly geared towards climbing the highest underwater trees, hanging from the branches, and finding tons of reasons to laugh and have a super good time. At first the parents had the little mer-boys sitting with them among the congregation, hoping the boys would find Poseidon's speech and the audience's reactions attractive enough to hold their play-oriented minds for as long as possible by their parents side, but soon the boys escaped the seriousness of the meeting, finding their own kind of fun outside in Poseidon's gardens. Only later, when Torilander was already a seasoned teenager, his parents conveyed the gist of this auspicious meeting to him and his brother, making sure they were kept abreast of any important matters concerning their underwater kingdom. And thus he learned that that day Poseidon reinforced his curse against humanity, and after allowing many upset reactions from among his followers to be expressed and heard, he took it upon himself to demonstrate more directly how his curse is just the result of century-long violations of the laws of nature and of the human neglect to heal and remedy the toxic results and consequences they inflicted — and still inflict — on themselves and their environments. He said that his curse actually is helping the human race to balance out some of their most vicious deeds that otherwise would trigger even more severe calamities that would result in extinguishing human lives on a mass scale, like volcanic eruptions, droughts, floods, epidemics, and such. He conveyed that his curse is just one of several reactions from nature and planet Earth to rid itself of the inflicted diseases and stress charges the humans cause to their environment and people on a constant basis. He then went on to show his mer-being followers how dark and thick a ring around the planet the stress excretions of the human world have formed, and instead of working on diminishing and releasing the stress from the atmosphere, the human soul excretions just continue to increase day by day, threatening to choke the planet under this foul karmic stink that tries to squash out the light of higher realms, forcing the deva kingdoms — of which the mer-beings are a part of — to gradually leave this planet to retreat to higher frequency realities, and thus to increasingly disentangle their reality from the reality of the human world.

Poseidon invited his followers to meditate on his name, for this attunement to his essence would help them to elevate their conscious awareness to realms that allowed them to perceive the earthly energy aura more clearly, thus enabling them to notice the dark astral cloud belt around the Earth, and how the human race not only excretes their emotional and mental waste energies into the fine ether, but is also influenced by it in vicious cycles of self diminishing tendencies for lack of the understanding of their doings and of the ability to attune themselves to the Divine Source of Life. He said that many humans claim to serve and love the Gods, but their deeds speak otherwise, and their love often just reflects their lower-self-serving nature that justifies and allows them to manipulate, subdue, harm, persecute, and kill not only nature and everything in it but also and especially their own kind. This contempt for life and the constant transgressions against the sacredness of life have summoned the Gods and Goddesses to voice the decree of the law of karma upon the human world, to have them either suffocate under their own self-created debris or learn from it and thus outgrow it. Some higher-minded humans understand the fact that individual and collective karma can be reduced through the spiritual practice of meditation and mind-transcending, as well as through selfless service to life, but the majority of the human population rather rides on the mass conscious waves — which at the moment happen to lead towards the spiritual winter season on Earth — and thus continue to create more karma rather than dissolve it, and must therefore be forced by universal law to face and deal with their karmic loads, which is done through suffering and reintegration of alienated, repressed parts of one's self. Suffering can re-educate and wake people up to better their ways, and have them ultimately become strong in their stance to refrain from any further violations of life, including the killing of so-perceived inferior species, like animals and fish, as well as the plant kingdom, if ever the human race is able to purify their essence enough to be able to live off the life force of the ether and of the prana of the higher, more spiritual realms. Only when all the killing has stopped, in all its innumerable ways, shapes, and forms, will humanity, as a whole, be able to experience their world as the paradise it was intended to be. But for as long as there is still an urge left among the human race to live off another being's life force and energy, aggression and fear will keep running through the collective nervous system, infecting the individuals connected to it and rendering the world the place where evil can root itself to govern the world by means of organized threat and violence, able to draw the ignorant and gullible masses into further oblivion and disempowerment.

Poseidon then gave a short discourse on Divine Justice, saying that every thought, emotion, and physical action have their counterparts in the invisible realms, ready to manifest at the right time to teach the individual the lesson he creates for himself by way of his focus and resonance with whatever it is he tends to give his attention to over sustained periods of time. If someone puts his attention and actions on killing, he will be killed; if someone persecutes his fellow humans, he will be persecuted, and if the karmic feedback does not happen right away, then it happens some time later, and if not within this lifetime, then within another, but whatever the individual sows, he will reap, no matter when, and no matter how exactly. In any case, the intensity of his transgressions will return to him with the same charge, and the Gods and Goddesses can only hope that humans, individually and collectively, wake up from this game of illusion rather sooner than later, for unconditional love and absolute, unhindered freedom is the ultimate nature of the self, the state all hearts and souls originate from and return to, and it is up to every individual to realize this truth in his own time, after finishing with the path of suffering he holds so dear within his delusional soul and despairing heart.

And nothing teaches an incredulous crowd the deepest and highest wisdom of the Gods better and more vividly than their own experience of the truth, raising one's awareness and expanding one's perceptional range under the entraining resonance field of their beloved Water God Poseidon, to encompass a reality level normally avoided and left out from their attention span, to now include and shockingly behold the mentioned dark astral ring around the planet, how it rises like a monster from the surface level of the Earth to rear its ugly, fear-inducing thousand-headed face, spewing gout and cauterizing, etching fire into the ether, thus continuing to pollute the atmosphere around the planet, waltzing over life on Earth as if ready to devour it all into its endlessly vast and horrifying belly — the monster of all repressed and undigested karmic burdens and future ill intents, the collective subconscious material that keeps haunting and jeopardizing people with its irrational, weakening, and self-destructive influence, manipulating the weak in mind to go along with the masses and continue down the spiral of violation and victimization, as if nothing else matters anymore that could possess the power to instill hope and self-empowerment into the individual's heart and mind, no hope left, and no alignment with the Divine truth of their most ancient of ancestors, a lost generation that begets only more of its hopeless nature for the bleak future it creates.

Perceived from a higher, more cosmic viewpoint, this monster-like astral belt around the planet looks like a dark cloud and aura that overshadows the conscious awareness of planet Earth and its inhabitants to the point that they perceive themselves as separate from the all-encompassing unity of life. And like a non-functional nerve cell, Earth thus isolates itself from the totality of the cosmic nervous system, and overcome by Maya — the illusion of mortality and separation of life — life on Earth has become stale and uninspired by Divine values and thus ready to crumble under the life-diminishing influences of the progressing spiritual winter season. This tendency is expressed by the many wars people inflict on themselves, as well as an increase in sickness and natural disasters, and an increasing imbalance of the distribution of wealth on the planet. Considering all these humanly created calamities, Poseidon's curse is just one of many ways for Earth and nature to try to heal itself, to help discharge the negative charges of collective stress and present humanity with the karmic feedback of their negative creations so as to have humanity as a whole, and on the individual level, suffer through the karma and thus dissolve it.

So somber was Poseidon's speech on the self-created fate of humanity that the inhabitants of his Underwater Kingdom recoiled in disgust, ready to turn their attention back to the light-filled worlds of their peace-loving hearts and minds, hopefully aware that should any individual of the human race ever indicate his readiness and willingness to outgrow this collective purgatory hell they call their world, the mer-beings would hurry to his side to lend their help, guidance, and support to him who is able to hear and understand the workings of the higher, more light-filled realms from whence the nourishment for any soul flows in abundant streams of golden liquid life energy, which translates into heart-fulfilling bliss and freedom. Because, as Poseidon also pointed out to them, there certainly are many exceptions among the human race, individuals whose hearts are steadfastly anchored in highest, Divine truth and who therefore possess the strength, unconditional love, purity of character, and clarity of mind to outgrow the monster of accumulated collective karmic stress and debris, able to transcend the gripping limitations it maintains around the globe. And because of the purity and courage of these well-intentioned individuals and their nonattachment and non-resonance with the mass collective realities, these spiritual pioneers are therefore able to free themselves from their mortal chains, to unite with their brothers and sisters of the light — who live beyond this dualistic, transient reality level in a world of eternal peace, bliss, and fulfillment.

And since the goodness of the mer-beings' hearts wishes to help and nurture anyone in need and hardship, it felt good for Poseidon's congregation to hear that individual help and consideration are still possible and wanted by the Gods, to be given to deserving humans who impress the mer-beings with their unconditional love for all living beings, small or large, and with their fervor to strive for the highest possible truth in all matters, trivial or important, to help turn the fate of the world around so it might one day again be the peaceful, yet infinitely dynamic paradise from which all conscious life sprang, as a reminder that the mercy of the Gods is endless, and the game of life is but an infinitely pleasing, blissful ripple effect in the ocean of life and Divine awareness. It was also agreed by the congregation that if a ship got wrecked in one of Poseidon's storms, the mer-beings who wanted to help would only rescue humans who were unconscious, administering first aid if necessary, and placing them onto water floatation devices or bringing them ashore, if possible, so as to not reveal their mer-nature to the humans lest they attract unwanted attention to their race that could end up deadly for many mer-beings in the end because of the rampant control urge and ill will from many superior-feeling humans. Having lost memory of the beginnings of life on Earth and in the cosmos, today's humans tend to hunt down and capture a species they most likely consider inferior and an object of great curiosity rather than peacefully sharing life on this planet with it.

Thus masterfully did Poseidon turn his followers back to the light of his divinely suffused ordinances, making them see reason and truth and prepping them for their individual learning experiences when interacting with the human race, in whatever shape or form, that all mer-beings went away from the meeting deeply satisfied and enriched, knowledgeable about the humans' uncanny ability to transgress heavily against nature, but also compassionate towards the fate of any human individual who might ever find his way to the mer-kingdoms, who might impress them with his unconditionally loving attitude towards life, and who would be in need of the mer-beings' help and support in any way. They all agreed they would be most delighted if such an individual would ever show up and take them up on their willingness to help, for peace and true friendship among the species is something every mer-being aspires to, in the same way as the forest and meadow fairies and elves thrive on the energies of unconditional love and friendship that alone have the power to turn any world into the paradise every heart craves and longs for, because it knows deep within that this is the place it originates from in the first place.

This is the story Torilander was told by his parents when he was old enough to understand the significance of the meeting, because at the time, Torilander, Chekilian, and Loriolan were too busy being their carefree, frolicsome, and rompish little selves, examining the heavens in their own jolly ways and leaving the business of life to those who were able to conduct it and able to carry the burdens that come with it as well. But there was one incident during that meeting that Torilander had almost forgotten and that he now remembers fondly again, an incident he didn't make all the connections to until this very moment: Part of Poseidon's lush and exquisite gardens was a big spacious grotto, with the upper half of the garden being exposed to the air, and trees and bushes sticking out of the water. It was quite a fun challenge to climb way up the trees, and Loriolan and Torilander had a great time testing their prowess and agility that way, but Chekilian, little as he was at the time, didn't know how to wiggle his body up the tree nor did he possess the strength to do so. And so he remained underwater, screaming his lungs out for the boys to take pity on him and descend from their coveted lookouts in the top of the trees to come and lend a helping hand to him. Finally, Torilander decided to climb down and help his brother up, only to find that it was an almost impossible task, for the little fellow just didn't know how to move outside the water. Torilander shoved the heavier part of his tail up, but then he fell sideways, laughing and hoping Torilander would do it again, when all of a sudden, a tall and impressive looking merman came to Torilander's aid, set Chekilian on the palm of his hand, lifted him up, and had Chekilian continue to float upwards onto the top of the tree, much to everyone's amazement and delight. Chekilian screamed with joy, for he experienced a jolt of energy — as he later related — of a magnitude he never experienced before or after again, one that made it possible for him to reach the coveted treetop and had him joyous and laughing for the remainder of the day. The merman looked at Torilander with a smirk, winked his eye at him, and said: "Always remember that you are from the Light, and Light you will always be! With Light, all things are possible, and wondrously enough, the Light is always within you! So let it shine, little one, and let all effort subside like dewdrops in the morning sun! Be the Light, my son, just be the Light!" And then the merman put his hand on top of Torilander's head as if to nurture him with his love, saying: "And preserve your innocence always, little one, for it is the basis for happiness and your most efficient tool to help anyone around you who might ever need your help!" And then the merman disappeared, and for some reason, on that day, everything seemed to flow and happen effortlessly, with Torilander being able to almost float up the tree, even though the top was out of their native element, and the words of the merman always stayed like a treasure in his memory, one that Torilander often in the past came back to when things would not be as smooth and easy as he wanted them to be, and one he knows he can always draw encouragement and hope from whenever life happens to serve him a harsh lesson and he might lose hope in whatever critical situation he finds himself in, like right now!

He later learned that Poseidon has the ability to divide his essence up and appear in many different locations to take care of his followers, and the youngest and smallest from among his followers as well. Torilander's mother, Sudisheilia, an accomplished dancer and artist with a high sense of aesthetics, once sculpted a statue of Poseidon, and now that Torilander thinks about it, he saw a similar looking statue in Rhode's pleasure palace as well, and to his astonishment, he now makes the connection that the merman in the garden was indeed Poseidon, for he matched the statues pretty well. And it now hits Torilander that Poseidon indeed talked to him that day to give him this vital message he is in such dire need of right now, to remind him of his inner resources and light potential!

Torilander sits up straight. It just felt as if Poseidon just winked his eye at him again, encouraging him to master his destiny, and to turn the situation at hand around so it can begin to serve his highest purpose, however lofty it might be. A shudder of awe runs through his veins as Torilander contemplates the ramifications of this memory spark and his so far more subconscious, but deep connection with the God of the Underwater World. And it dawns on him that he is not alone and that he is not forgotten! His God has remembered him; from among all the many followers he has, he has pinpointed the boy he once helped in his garden and has put his awareness on him in his time of need! Tears run from his eyes as Torilander tries to bring back the lightness of that auspicious day in the garden, for if he can identify with that inner light, he might be able to make himself disappear from the sight of these humans and, who knows, maybe transport himself back into the sea, for nothing is impossible with the power of the Gods!

But then the talk of the humans reaches his ears again, as they are still discussing the possibilities of finding out more about the merman's home world and of maybe finding more of the mer-beings so their research and knowledge of this relatively mysterious and unknown species and world can become more thorough and complete and, with this, the mer-beings also more subdued by human control. And upon hearing their words, Torilander realizes that his meditation on the light is not as easy and simple as he thought it might be, for many different strands of emotions run through his body right now, tearing him in many different directions, some feeling good and many feeling bad. If he wants to master his situation and identify with the light of his true being, he will have to first conquer his fears and anger, of which there is a heavy charge coiled up in him right now. His father, Halikan, is the King's physician, a great and extraordinary healer who taught Torilander many ways of staying in his innermost center and to always try to draw from his own infinite healing powers and deep convictions that life is good and that the light is more powerful than the darkness will ever be in the end. How much Torilander misses his dad right now; how nice it would be to hear his wise words on the situation his son is in! Torilander sighs heavily, for the one-week deadline before a team of intellectuals will analyze the heck out of him sits like an indigestible rock in his stomach. The Royal Family still wonders about the merman they have sitting in their showcase, but Torilander does not want to engage in their thought processes; instead, he tries to ignore the talk of the humans and focus on Poseidon's name to attract his own essence nearer to the one of his all-powerful God.

Chapter 10

It is a hot late spring day, and the sun has been burning down on the little convoy of eastbound travelers; dust being whirled up by the front horseback riders envelopes the wagon and two rear riders in a big, dry cloud. Indirali wipes the dirt off her face, for she just dared to take a peek outside to try to gain an impression of the bumpy terrain they have been crossing for hours.

"Better keep your heads in for a while!" Hyacinthos, Andronikos' son, shouts at her and Hedna from above the charioteer seat. "This stretch is quite a tricky one in a lot of ways!" Then he continues to spur on the horses to give it their all in getting through what many consider treacherous territory.

Indirali tries to encourage Hedna with a smile, for her maidservant looks like she could throw up at any moment. But a smile won't suffice anymore; Hedna has been lying curled up in a fetal position for almost an hour already and now looks like she could just jump off the wagon and run into the bushes. So Indirali takes off her maidservant's sandals and begins to gently but firmly massage the soles of her feet. Hedna gives her a feeble smile, acknowledging her Mistress's generous and compassionate support. The gentle pressure immediately relieves some of Hedna's tension and nausea, and gently the both of them settle back into a more equanimous state.

No need to panic! Everything has been going very well so far, considering the Princess is traveling incognito and without her entourage and escort. Menelaus and Eunike have been real gems to have come across along their way. Instead of being eager to redeem the royal pin Indirali gifted them with for their extraordinary help and hospitality, Menelaus instead held the precious reward up into the air in the end, exclaiming he will hold on to it as a good omen until the Princess of Lucania returns to them to take it back from him and grace their humble abode once more with her noble presence and enlightening words. He, however, only exclaimed those words for the Princess to hear at her departure, and only once he was sure the Princess was far enough away to not be able to object to his decision anymore, and the carriage that picked the girls up in the very early morning hours was already at quite some distance, ready to take a turn around the corner and vanish from Menelaus' sight. It was his and his wife's intention to not leave any opportunity for the Princess to change their minds, but to leave knowing she found true allies and admirers in this Heraclean family of a simple businessman.

Indirali felt pretty touched by this unusually generous gesture and confidence in her victorious return and has, ever since the departure, reflected on every friendly word and action they shared with each other in the last two days. The mother and the two freed boys were shown to their simple but comfortable quarters, able to rest and adjust for a few days to their new environment before the mother resumes her work as a maid and the boys are extended the privilege of becoming apprentices to a handyman and a gardener. The mother was infinitely relieved to experience the incredible fortune to have been rescued and taken in by reputable and well-off landowners as Menelaus' family proved to be, and couldn't express her gratitude profusely enough for showing such kindness and care towards paupers as she and her sons have become over the last many years. Indirali had to calm her down, for at some point her anxiety began to release from her, and she started crying and sobbing, for she could hardly stop expressing her disbelief that such fortune could be real and of a lasting nature. The whole body of this poor woman trembled and shook, as one repressed layer of shock and trauma after another began to emerge and release, and only after Indirali took her into her arms would the poor woman finally give in to the safety of her newfound home and to the unconditional love of this welcoming new environment.

Yes, Indirali is sure that among all the hardship and misery she encountered along the roads, Menelaus' family stood out for her in many memorable ways, not the least of which is how spontaneously and agreeably they went along and supported Indirali's idea late last night — when everyone at the farmhouse felt happy and content after a delicious big meal and ensuing frolicking dance — to collect several big bags of food items and outworn pieces of clothing and cart them out into the night to where the paupers and homeless people spent their pitiful existence along the dirt roads, ready to make a small difference in their wretched lives and to gift them with a share of several business families' charitable contributions. And how good it felt for not only those of the paupers who couldn't sleep even after the midnight hour because of worries that kept them awake, to receive such an unexpected offering, but also for the businessmen and their families, who long bore a bad conscience and sense of incompetence in regard to the enormous differential of wealth and wellbeing that obviously gaps between the different classes of Heraclea's citizens. Many gifts were laid next to the sleeping paupers, as if angels had just come down from the heavens to encourage them with a spark of hope and remind them of the kindness that lives in every soul who has not lost the contact to its own higher self.

Everyone of the good Samaritans felt extremely happy with themselves when they finally fell into their beds at what turned out to be the early morning hours already, unregretful to have spent the majority of the night following the directions and urgings of the higher mind and of the Princess of Lucania, who got the ball rolling in the first place. Quite a trip she turned out to be, not taking 'No' for an answer when it came to helping those in need, and not resting until she did everything in her power to effect the maximum benefit for as many disadvantaged people as she could possibly reach. On the one hand, Menelaus and his friends were left feeling inspired by the Princess's good deeds and uncompromising attitude — with Eunike having found back her heart, as she announced she wants to organize a vaster charity network for the poor from now on — but on the other hand, they all look forward to a day or more of good rest from the late night ordeal, and from confronting through the new high priest of one of their last independent temples what many Heraclean citizens regard as a matter of controversy they would prefer to ignore and deny as having any importance whatsoever for their lives, namely the takeover by and intrusion of the Roman legions into the city's spiritual and political affairs and its wealth.

Indirali is torn out of her thoughts, however, when Hedna suddenly sits up to indicate her urge to throw up, which she does, leaning out from under the canvas of the wagon, to empty her stomach of what little she ate for breakfast, looking all pale and worn out from the late night activity, enormous heat of the day, and extreme bumpiness of the road. Indirali strokes and comforts her dear friend and servant so as to instill a good portion of strength and encouragement into her inner core, ready to absorb as much as she can from her companion's plight, for seeing her suffer like this makes her reel with compassion. After having relieved herself such, Hedna sinks back into her position between the hay-buffered ceramic pottery Hyacinthos is transporting for his father's business to the markets of Tarentum.

"Here!" Hyacinthos shouts above the galloping noise. "Take a sip! It'll help!" And with that he hands the girls a canteen of water, informing them they are just about ready to cross a narrow bridge leading over the Casuentus River, when all of a sudden, a horrifying shout yanks them all into alarm, as they realize that one of their front riders has just fallen off his horse, wounded by a spear that seemingly came out of nowhere. Indirali is on high alert, and so is Hyacinthos! Immediately he pulls back the reigns to stop the carriage so he can pick up the man and put him into the wagon, then continues to race towards the bridge, hoping to escape to safety, for he is afraid they might be forced into a fight with one of the many violent gangs that have sprung up in recent years, with the sole intent of robbing honest and hard-working businessmen of their well-earned goods and money. Hyacinthos was warned by his father and implored to take four more guards along than he ended up taking, for Andronikos' son felt certain he could master the challenges should any such detested rebels dare show their heads to him and to his four fierce warrior friends. His father could hardly afford these increasingly costly transports anymore, for the profits he makes on the markets have begun to fall short of the expenses it takes to get the goods there, mainly because of the escalating dangers along the road. But to encounter the possibility of a fight in real life is a matter entirely different from any thought of it — especially upon seeing a large gang of outlaws spilling out from behind the mountains, galloping their horses fiercely and fast within a big cloud of dust, and approaching rapidly from the front, thus blocking the way towards escape and safety — and feeling the burden of responsibility resting heavily on his shoulders, Hyacinthos authoritatively begins to shout his commands to his fellow travelers, ordering the girls to find refuge in the nearby rock formations while he and his men ward off the spears that keep coming at them at an impact and force nobody could have anticipated.

The girls run and hide themselves, while Hyacinthos and his guards get embroiled in a fierce fight for their lives. Quickly the outlaws surround them, demonstrating their superiority to the scanty little group that is greatly outnumbered by their attackers. One gruff old man jumps off his horse as his comrades aim their spears and bows at the few overcome men, commanding the men to lay down their weapons, go down on their knees, and surrender their valuables immediately to their leader. With anguish in their eyes, everyone of the captured men pulls out what little valuable possession he carries on himself, then hands it over for the old thug to take a look at, sack it into his big pocket, then poke his spear at them to provoke their reactions. He looks at several of his men, nods his head, and they begin to inspect the interior of the wagon. They report to him the men are transporting vases and pots and other such neat stuff, which prompts the old thug to exclaim a rough laugh, as he feels he has stumbled across some treasures his old nag of a wife will probably be happy about. Then he continues to provoke Hyacinthos and his men by shouting profanities at them, in which attempt he succeeds when Hyacinthos — all defiant and proud — spits at the old thug's feet, a sign of his contempt for this rude, thievish, and unwarranted behavior. This incites the thug even more, mocking Hyacinthos and putting him down for his ridiculously good looks, angrily announcing he and his men have served their purpose in life and it is time to return to their creator, for they will herewith be relieved of their debts to life and will be granted a swift and fast death by having their heads cut off.

Hearing this, Indirali jumps out of hiding to intervene on the men's behalf. Never has she experienced such lowlife self-importance, based on nothing but criminality, trying to call the shots and acting like he is God's mouthpiece. He won't get away with this nonsense, not for as long as she is around. Trembling with deep, gripping fear, she nevertheless confronts the old thug, telling him to not be so rash in his actions but to think about the future of his clan when he kills the very people he depends on for his future income. How can he continue to steal if everyone in his way gets disposed of rather than be able to continue to produce the goods he wants to continue to be able to steal?

Rather perplexed by this courageous little rat, the old thug commander is speechless for a moment, but then breaks out into a big laugh, joined by his men.

"There seems to be some logic in this, presumptuous as it seems!" He looks around to gather support and laughing confirmation from his ruffian gang members who are used to giving it to him in full measure. "But to be honest, young fella, I really don't care! — Now step out of the way, or maybe I'll make you one head shorter as well!"

"Why don't you do something different today, and impress your wife for a change by letting us live and go our ways!" Indirali injects, trying to step up her game. "In every woman's chest there lives the zest for life, and presenting her with our pottery here might cause her to show pity on us wretched people who make it our business to produce fancy stuff like this that you seem to enjoy."

The thug can't help but laugh even harder. "My Zoe is a hag, far from a saint, and yes, she'll enjoy the booties, but I doubt she cares about you guys any more than I do!" All the men laugh heartily; it seems some funny memory about their leader's wife just got triggered in their awareness.

"All the more reason to surprise her with your own better judgment," Indirali speaks up, trying to find a way to his higher senses, "because all we are are a bunch of simple people, men like you, trying to make a living any way we can."

"Don't you even dare to compare yourself to us!" he exclaims, enraged all of a sudden. "There is a hell of a difference between you ass-kissing system upholders and us freedom-loving folks, who have learned to take over the reins of our lives into our own hands, because all we were handed out by people like you before was just hogwash and bullshit, just barely enough to scrape by, but never enough to make us feel worth living! So you take your smart-aleck talk and shove it down your throat, for we are not the dimwits you try to make us out to be!"

His head seems to give off a cloud of smoky fire, that's how agitated he feels from all this nonsense arguing.

"I didn't mean to upset you, sir," Indirali subdues her tone of voice. "It's just that all of us here have family at home, like you do, and some of us have little kids to take care of as well," she looks at the four guards kneeling on the ground, with one of them hardly able to hold his composure, as he was severely wounded in his side from the spear, "… who would be fatherless and without provision," Indirali continues, "should you go through with your heartless intention. I implore you, sir, to please look into your heart and see that we are not your enemies; none of us wishes you harm. You can keep the carriage and everything in it …" Hyacinthos and one of his men exclaim a sigh of nonverbal protest upon hearing her bargain the prized possessions away, "… but please leave us our lives so we can continue to provide for our families, the way you and your people do for yours, allowing us to stay in business with our pottery making so people like you can profit from our skills and work."

An odd sensation befalls the old thug as he hears the young lad plead his case thus boldly, and still demurely as well. Could there be a shred of truth in his defiant speech, somehow aiming at his heart, no matter whether he likes it or not? Never has a city dweller and victim of his aggression argued with him thus convincingly, trying to point out the advantages of letting them live and assuring him of their good feelings towards him and his men, even in the face of death at the hands of him and his men. Instead, this lad talks to him as if he is his brother, trying to understand and sympathize with their situation and way of life as no man has done before; and not even from among his own men has anyone spoken thus collegially and touchingly to him on any occasion whatsoever. He stares in front of him, trying to battle a spark of conscience and higher impulse, confusedly scratching his head as if to come up with the right decision.

"Don't let this little fella make a fool out of you!" one of his men shouts, and others join in with their rough voices and comments.

The commanding thug, however, lifts his hand to quieten them down, then signals Indirali to take a few steps to the side with him.

"What did you say your name was?" he asks, bending towards her as if to shield their conversation from his gang members.

"Apollinaris!" Indirali reaches out her hand for a manly shake, which the increasingly confused old thug accepts with an air of puzzlement.

"Well, Apollinaris, where could such a simple-looking lad like you have gotten his educated mind from?" he wonders out loud, while appraising the lad from top to bottom, seeing only rags and worn-out sandals on this strange little fella.

"My father taught me a thing or two, but I guess I was born with a spirit of my own."

"Uhum …" the old thug thinks for a moment. "And where did you say you came from?" He bends towards her, and his foul breath makes Indirali want to step backwards, but she represses the urge and continues to play all interested. "Is it one of those stinking cities that spits out the poor as if they were some sort of poison to the rotten system?" he asks, accidentally spitting into her face. "Or did you come from somewhere completely else?"

"No," Indirali affirms, "I would never participate in such disdainful action towards anyone, least of all the poor who have ended up that way because they evidently can't help themselves anymore. In fact, only yesterday I inspired several business families to help distribute some of their possessions among the poor in the streets, and they gladly participated, eager to see a difference done in the lives of the less fortunate. No, sir, I assure you, my heart goes out to anyone who is left by the wayside because of whatever disheartening trends we see happening these days in our societies, and which probably are, to a great extent, an aftereffect caused by the many wars that keep ravaging our country. — I'm from the countryside, a simple farm boy from outside of Grumentum, on my way to Brundisium to catch a ship ride to Macedonia!" She lifts her hand to her temples to greet him with a sailor's salute.

The old robber commander acknowledges her salute with half of his mouth distorted to a grin, the other half questioning what's going on, then continues to question her, for something is different about this Apollinaris fella, and he can't quite put his finger on it. "So what did you say your business was in Macedonia? Are you some sort of haughty-naughty dissident who leaves his countrymen behind to find his luck elsewhere?"

"Not at all, sir," Indirali assures him, quickly thinking how to continue to appease him without losing his interest and good will. One faux pas, and they all risk losing their lives! She tries to tune in to some higher, inner guidance to say something that will win the old man over. She obviously can't tell him the truth about herself, but maybe something close enough to the truth that will make sense to him and pose no risk for her to be found out. "I'm actually trying to get to the Oracle of Delphi to find out about my brother. He served in the army, but at some point we lost track of him, and I'm afraid we might never see him again or that he was maybe taken prisoner by the Apulians. I just need to know for sure; that's why I need to consult the Oracle, to find out what truly happened to him, and where to find him. It's such a crazy time we live in!"

"Tell me about it!" the thug agrees, looking all of a sudden truly sorry for the young lad. Because he can relate all too well to this young man's story, for something very similar happened to his own son a long, long time ago. "So this brother of yours, you were pretty damn close to him?" he wants to know, his eyes sparking with interest.

Indirali nods silently, lowering her gaze.

"Tell you what!" the thug changes his tone of voice, sounding more cheery. "Why don't we tell each other our life stories over a drink of wine. — Hey ya!" he yells at his men, "Let's have these gentlemen comfortable around a fire! Yeah, a damn fire, I say! Don't just stand there like idiots!" he roars upon noticing his men's confusion over this turn of events. He puts his arm around Indirali's shoulder and begins to walk towards the spot he envisions for their camp, somewhere off the beaten path, and behind a hill; and again, he can't help but feel that something is strangely different about this young lad, as if he is almost as sensitive and agreeable as a woman, not the kind of either arrogant twit or boastful ruffian he is used to and has dealt with throughout his long, eventful life. Something about the lad reminds him uncannily of his own dead son, and that fact alone makes it worth probing deeper into this young man's story.

And so the captives are led to the new spot, along with the wagon and the horses. Two of Hyacinthos' guards help the wounded guard to walk between them, all the while spurred on by the old thug's men to walk either faster or slower, depending on the prevailing game-playing mood of the captors. Hedna steps out from behind the rock, fortunately outside the perceptional range of the men, looking all pale and weak from her sickness; her spirit wants to do the honorable thing and be at her Mistress's side no matter what her condition, but Indirali wards her off with a wave, mutely ordering her to stay put since it isn't certain at all at this point that they are yet out of danger. And so she prefers her maid to stay hidden rather than to risk her life unnecessarily and make the gangsters aware that there is another young lad belonging to this group of victims, one whose life they could also tamper with.

Soon after, they reach a suitable spot, somewhere out of sight from the road, protected by a cave on one side and small hills on the other sides. The thug signals his approval, and everyone begins to prepare for a fire, and for a lot of wine to flow. They find some jugs of wine in the carriage, which the gang welcomes wildly and joyously, because the few canteens of wine they brought along would not have taken care of their insatiable thirst, not if they would have to share it with their captives. Because as it looks, their leader is inviting them to some sort of peace drink offering, an act completely new and suspicious to many of them, as this is completely out-of-the-norm behavior.

Soon they all sit around the fire, and upon Indirali's persisting request, the thug advises one of his men to attend to the injured guard's wound, disinfecting it with a few drops of his own highly concentrated and therefore highly prized liquor, have a sword heated up in the fire, and have it pressed onto the wound to stop the bleeding. Without this relatively instant help, the guard would not have survived for long, and Indirali expresses this fact to the leader, along with her gratitude for showing mercy towards his victim. The gang leader introduces himself as Anatolios, and after passing the wine around several times for each to get their fill, a semi-drunk Anatolios leans over towards Indirali-Apollinaris to extract from him more detailed descriptions about his brother's fate and whereabouts. Slyly dumping the alcoholic beverage behind the rock she is sitting on to avoid getting drunk like everyone else, Indirali begins to draw on her feelings for the fate of her true brother, Athos, as well as from her longing feelings for Loriolan, and begins to spin and weave a story — fired up by Anatolios' deep interest and comments — that would have bent an iron pole out of shape with compassion. She conveys how she and her parents have been waiting for many years now for her brother to return, and when a soldier came back from the battlefield who had fought side by side with her brother, they had to find out that he was wounded during battle and was eventually captured from the infirmary by Apulian soldiers, who — according to word of mouth — sold him and other survivors off as slaves to a Macedonian slave trader. But since all this is just hearsay from many instances in-between, Indirali as Apollinaris took it upon herself to wanting to consult the famous Oracle of Delphi to find out the real truth of her brother's fate, and come to his rescue any way she/he can.

Indirali's account leaves Anatolios moved and touched, for something in the lad's voice, along with his obvious innocence and juvenile idealism for life, reminds the old man so damn much of his own young son he lost way too early in his life, and to see Apollinaris' determination and courage in wanting to get to the bottom of his brother's disappearance almost brings tears to the old ruffian's eyes, prompting him to caution this impetuous little fella, for the soldiers have only heard harsh reports of the unrest and battles going on in Macedonia, with the Celt tribes overrunning the Illyrian and Macedonian countryside, intent on seizing land that isn't theirs and crushing any man that stands in their way. He says he hopes Apollinaris knows what he is doing, and actually admires his sense of loyalty towards his brother. It also reminds him very much of his own painful memories about his son's premature demise that actually led to the way Anatolios and his men decided to live from that moment on, as outcasts in the mountain ranges outside of Metapontium. Supported by the alcohol he pours down in generous quantities, Anatolios begins to disclose with a shaky voice his own sad story that changed his life forever. He says that he and his men had been soldiers in

Pyrrhus' army for many years, bravely battling the Roman forces anywhere it was necessary, staring death into the eye on many occasions for the sake of regaining Italiot Greek independence in the south of Italy, when finally, over the course of several semi-victories and standoffs with the Roman army — which caused both sides to contend with heavy losses — Pyrrhus advanced directly on Rome to try to smoke the brutes out of their stronghold. But instead of getting anywhere near his target, and instead of regaining any hoped-for support and alliance with any of the tribes along the way, their army got trapped in the swamps outside of Rome, being constantly pursued and hunted down by the Roman consul, with the Roman Senate spitting in Pyrrhus' face when they rejected his request for a peace treaty. Anatolios remembers how tired and exhausted Pyrrhus' infantry and cavalry soldiers were when all their highest aspirations for a final victory over Rome got shattered, and the army had to instead scramble and flee the enclosing ambush of the two Roman consuls. Pyrrhus was Tarentum's big hope for winning the war over the imperialists but, in the end, turned out to be a letdown. When leaders of the Greek colonists of Sicily called on Pyrrhus' help against the Carthaginian siege of their island, he left Tarentum in a shambles and, against the city's will, went to Sicily and began fighting the Carthaginians to free the rather affluent Greek cities from their occupation and siege. But again, instead of bringing the whole fight to its victorious end, he gave in to the Greek leaders' complacency and failed to advance south to ultimately battle and try to vanquish the Carthaginians on their own ground, only to see — because of his negligence and incompetence — Sicily fall back into the hands of this second-biggest imperialist force on the planet. Anatolios thinks that someday soon, the final showdown between these two superforces will start, and the world will see who wins dominance over it, but he and his men have no intention to be in the middle of that. In fact, they are so tired of fighting the so-perceived noble cause that leaves good and decent men dead in its wake that they decided to fight their own fight from now on, since there seems no gain and purpose in fighting the war for others.

Anatolios stops for a moment to take a deep breath, then begins to reveal what lies at the bottom of his heavy heart. He describes that when he came back to Tarentum after many long years, his wife and two small daughters — like many other abandoned families — had left the city because of destitution and grave mistreatment by fellow citizens. When Pyrrhus first arrived from Greece, he forced the Tarentines to hand over the citadel, put a military general into power for when he was absent, and had constant recruiting and demanding military training exercises going on that all but exhausted and bewildered the Tarentine citizens over time. But how shocked was Anatolios when he found out that his son was sent to the dungeon because he didn't cut the requirements for physical strength and endurance and because of his intellectual non-alignment with Pyrrhus' dogmas and demands. When Anatolios finally succeeded in freeing his son based on his yearlong merits in battle under Pyrrhus, he found him in such a decayed state that it took just another month or so for Kyros to succumb to the ailments he incurred in the hostile dungeon environment. With slight tears in his eyes, Anatolios looks Indirali into her eyes to convey his pain to her from that horrible moment when his son died in his arms, not knowing whether his mother and sisters had survived their ordeal, and sorry for having let his father down by refusing to go to war. Anatolios needs a moment to let the pain flow out of him before he continues his recount. His men are all ears, and none of them dares to disturb their leader's confession to a complete stranger, for they weren't aware of the full extent of the pain their gang leader evidently bears deep within his heart.

He later found his wife and two daughters living with other destitute women and their children in the caves of the mountain range outside of Tarentum, and even though their reunion was sweet and a big relief, it was also and foremost overshadowed by the unwarranted death of their son, who wanted nothing more from life than to live it peacefully, and to retain the right of deciding his own fate and destiny in a world that is dominated and oppressed by arrogant, imperialist minds, and torn up by the futile wars they instigate on each other's subjects.

Anatolios is quiet for a moment, and Indirali lays her hand on his shoulder to impart her compassion and solidarity to him. Drunk and sad as he is, Anatolios begins to weep, irregardless of the image he needs to uphold in front of his ruffian gang members. But astonishingly, none of them dares to raise their voice in any disrespectful way; the only thing they wonder about is the fact that their otherwise aloof and superior leader, who hardly ever shows his deeper emotions to anyone, is all of a sudden pouring his heart out to a young man, who, for some reason or another, must be reminding Anatolios of his unfortunate son. Why else would this drama unfold in front of their eyes?

Trying to choke down his tears, Anatolios continues to fill his listeners in on all the many reasons why he became an outcast, and a ferocious leader of them as well, reminding everyone how Pyrrhus, their once highly regarded military leader and anticipated savior from Roman dominion, who wanted to expand the Greek empire to the west and unite the Greek colonies under one benevolent rule, ended up being as power hungry and preferential towards his own men as any Roman consul and senator when it came to dividing up land. He ended up abandoning the Tarentines before the war was won to sail back to Macedonia and attend to his own causes. Many Tarentine citizens, and especially the soldiers who fought for Pyrrhus with everything they had, believing this great war hero and acclaimed strategist would ultimately fulfill his promise to the city of Tarentum, were greatly disappointed in this wasted effort that saw many great citizens of Tarentum die in the futility of it all, including even — like his beloved son Kyros — many peace-loving folks who tried to stay out of the chaos and spoke out against the war in the first place.

Anatolios shakes his head when thinking about it. All these many years he tried to forget about this horrendous pain of loss and disappointment, but for some reason, it managed to surface under mysterious circumstances all of a sudden, as if an angel had come to lure the truth out of him. A few of his men begin to speak up as well, with similarly heartbreaking stories to tell about their own lives and families, all feeling in their own individual ways triggered to contribute their share of painful memories and console each other in their wallowing group pain. And lo and behold, under Indirali's compassionate words and healing presence, even Hyacinthos and his four guards find stories to share that all but talk about the same sense of betrayal and suffering that the outcasts had so far regarded as their own sad privilege. Instead, the outcasts now realize that the very same men they had a few moments ago announced to be killed in order to teach them a lesson — in case they were supporters of the overtaking Roman forces, or just ignorantly sympathizing with Pyrrhus, the pretentious promise-maker of the Macedonian empire — seem to actually suffer from the same disappointments and problems in life as they do, brothers in arms, and brothers in pain so to say, and a deep shame and regret overcomes most of them as they sit around the fire under God Bacchus' magic spell and influence, letting the long overdue release of their pain take its healing process, helping them lift their burdened hearts and broken spirits above the human misery, and once again learn to soar in the heavens of united friendship and lightness.

Following Anatolios' example, the ruffian gang begins to assume a more unguarded and lighthearted stance towards life, with Anatolios addressing his long-lost son as if he is with them right now in spirit, apologizing to his peace-loving kid for all the violent and murderous acts he committed in the name of freedom and peace, when ultimately he knows he degenerated under the way he chose to live his life — taking his wife and daughters down with him — to become just a shadow of his once idealistic self that wanted to stand up and fight for every individual's right of freedom and share of wealth, and for the dignity of life itself.

At some point the almost shamanistic healing session finds its natural conclusion, with Anatolios and his men apologizing to their captives for their inconsiderate attack on their lives, but — they say — they cannot quite be so nice as to leave them their possessions, for their families depend on the men bringing back booties valuable enough to feed everyone's starved bellies. He says that now that the Romans are moving in on Tarentum, and also having their eyes set on Metapontium and Heraclea, it has become even harder to stay under the radar of violence-exercising authorities, who make it their sport to head-count every citizen, register their every asset and head in the family, and then begin to tax and drain the life force out of everyone who is dumb enough to become part of their so-called civilized state. He says that heavy taxation and slavery have become the norm, and all this in the name of unification of the city-states into one big monopolistically controlled country that has senators spell out the rules everyone has to live by and is punished by, and pays for with his life so the elite group can enjoy a lifestyle of grandeur and luxury based on the little man's sweat and hard labor. He says under Roman rule it is a privilege to own a horse, which they assign to a person who earned it through their alignment and service to the senators of Rome; they call this class the equestrians, a step up from the plebeians. But Anatolios does not care to fall under any such fixed category; he knows that he and his men would be executed and made an example of should they fall into Roman hands, and so they prefer to stay unto themselves, riding their own horses, and determining their own self-value, taking from others what they think is the least the wealthy citizens of the three southern coastal cities owe their impoverished and forgotten soldiers for defending them all these many years, fighting many harrowing wars against the Romans, and giving their lives for what little independence is still left to the cities now.

Instead of arguing with him, Indirali takes it upon herself to represent the captives' group consensus in letting the gang get away with the robbery of their wagon and goods, for trying to hold on to those possessions might end up tipping the delicate scale and have the situation blow up in their faces after all. Upon noticing Indirali's determined facial expression, and having witnessed the magic she wove throughout this wondrous get-together with their captors, Hyacinthos quietly signals his guards to let this one go and be content with just staying alive. One important issue, however, Indirali can't just turn a blind eye to, and so she brings it up with an air of humility and determination. She makes Anatolios aware that Hyacinthos' father's business — as does the business of many other such families — depends upon trading with other cities' markets, and if the traders have to be afraid of traveling, then their livelihood is greatly at stake. "Is there not a bargain that can be struck between the parties," she wonders out loud, "that would allow trading to go on and so not choke the economy of the coastal cities to death to ultimately everyone's fatal detriment?" Anatolios nods his head reflectively, then concedes that out of ten passages, he and his men will let six go and keep the booties of four.

"Make it so you keep one out of ten," Indirali counters, "then we have ourselves a deal!"

Anatolios' face distorts under the unfair seeming offer, but when Indirali points her finger into the sky and mentions his son's name, the old thug reluctantly comes around, shouting: "Seven for you and three for us! And that's that!"

"Okay," she agrees, "two for you and eight for us it is, and for all the hard-working folks that depend on the safety of the trading routes!"

Anatolios waves his hand dismissively as if to give up, for in his heart he knows that this equation is what he and his comrades have been sticking to anyway all this time, but he won't openly confess to it or admit that he and his gang actually have a conscience that prohibits them from indiscriminately ravaging innocent people's lives. A faint smile shows on his lips when Indirali and Hyacinthos begin praising his generosity and good will, which, in the end, prompts the old thug to give his agreement and to seal the deal with a handshake between him and the boy.

And so the groups are finally ready to part, with Hyacinthos feeling the need to give it one more last try to secure some of his father's possessions from the wagon. With respect but determination in his voice, he turns to Anatolios to convey his plea to at least let them have one item per person to help pay for their expenses along the way to their final destinations, lest they all be stranded, unable to even provide for the medical care their wounded friend might still be in need of. Anatolios lifts one brow, as if to think about this bold request, but the goodness of his heart has long won out, and so he grants an exception, for the company he enjoyed touched upon long-lost feelings of hope and sanity, feelings he had almost given up on ever feeling again; and if he is honest with himself, his heart feels actually quite relieved to have been offered a way to show his wish for reconciliation. With an air of aloof generosity, he signals one of his men to lift the canvas and let each one of Hyacinthos' group members choose one article from among the pottery in the carriage. Then — out of the blue — he informs them that he never meant to kill them anyway, and that it has become a sport of theirs to frighten people into submission but to ultimately let them live and get away, hoping this fright and scare will deter people from ever returning — with or without reinforcement — and roaming this mountain region to search for him and his clan. This way, only the most business-minded folks dare to travel these routes, their urge for income from other cities' markets forcing them to accept the risks involved with traveling along these unsafe paths, which makes for good business for Anatolios and his chums since these are the folks that own precious things, and from whom stealing is — in the majority of cases — a worthwhile undertaking. This is the way the outcasts reclaim justice and payment for themselves, Anatolios explains, for the army just discarded his worn-out soldiers in the end without any retirement provisions. And in these economically and politically unstable times, this means starvation and hardship of all kinds.

The five released captives stand there with their mouths gaping as Anatolios tips his finger to his forehead as a farewell, then whistles his command, which prompts the gang to go into wild gear, swing onto their horses, and gallop speedily towards the mountains, a big cloud of dust whirling up wherever their horses set foot, until the last of them has disappeared into the mountain ranges that have become their home and refuge.

Indirali begins to run towards the rock she knows Hedna is hiding behind, only to find her maidservant fast asleep, trying to recover from the sickness and exhaustion from the previous night. Gently she strokes Hedna's cheek, hoping she will wake up with a good feeling, when her maid begins to yawn and rub her eyes, wondering where she is and whether she missed anything of importance. Indirali tells her she will fill her in, then helps her up so they can all begin their walk towards Metapontium, the city closest to them, to recuperate from their loss and aggravation and to find a doctor who can help their friend recover from his injury. Hedna's eyes open wide with shock upon seeing and hearing about the stolen wagon and Andronikos' stolen goods, but then her attention shifts to the wounded guard, who has a hard time walking between his two buddies who do their best to prop him up and have his arms lying securely around their shoulders. It falls on Hyacinthos and the fourth guard, however, to carry two large pieces of the pottery they garnered from Andronikos' possessions, with Hedna offering to carry one piece, and Indirali carrying a beautiful vase as well, all trying to be careful with the breakable wares as much as is possible on this bumpy dirt road. It's going to be a long walk through the dry, dusty landscape even though it's only about four miles to Metapontium, but because of the relatively vast intake of wine in the last hours, Hyacinthos and the guards are having a bit of a problem walking a straight line, and Hedna still doesn't feel her old self again. Indirali sighs, but then puts her mind on arriving at Metapontium, a city she thought she would have been able to skip on her way to Macedonia. Let's see what lessons and pearls of wisdom this city will have in store for her. Trusting in the infinite wisdom and foresight of the Divine Powers that seem to guide her ways very strongly, she begins to lead the way, followed by Hedna, Hyacinthos, and the guards.

CHAPTER 11

"And then she makes me do all these ridiculous exercises on how to walk upright and straight, sit upright and straight, talk charmingly and courteously while sitting straight, and anything and everything for me to do in a straight manner, in the hopes of turning me into a real lady," Princess Elissa explains, "all the while looking proper and uptight herself when exemplifying her points and teachings, as if she swallowed a board, and now it's stuck in her!" She pauses to take another look at Torilander, who leans over the rock as if he seems interested in her stories she has been confiding to him for the last several hours. "She doesn't even get that I make faces to Matina behind her back. Domentzia is just such a dense and rigid woman. It's almost hilarious! She's an infinite well of jokes that's fun for me and my maid to draw from; sometimes we reel with laughter when we try to imitate her!" Elissa laughs at the thought of her etiquette tutor, a woman of stern constitution and awkwardly tall build, who somehow always manages to elicit a strong reaction from her pupil, albeit most of these reactions find their expression behind the tutor's back. Princess Elissa admits to her new friend that Domentzia has a way of triggering a gut reaction from her that either makes the Princess laugh hard and loud about her tutor's awkwardness or prompts her to project her resentment towards the tutor, who has been given the assignment to tame the once wild and free-spirited Princess into a sophisticated young lady able to dazzle any noble young prince into submission with her alluring charms and well-behaved manners. Elissa, however, hates these charm school sessions as if they choke the life spirit out of her young heart and mind, and if she could, she would just always run outside and play with the servants' children the way she used to. But life is changing, she sighs, and she is not sure whether it's for the better, because she sure does not feel any better from all these weird, stringent practices she is subjected to lately.

Elissa looks into Torilander's good-natured looking, deep, blue eyes, and it strikes her that he must understand her better than even her own mother does at the moment; that's how lovingly and compassionately his gaze rests on her. With a shudder of awe, she tries to shake the strange feeling she has been experiencing since she set eyes on him for the first time, a feeling she cannot place, and therefore a feeling that confuses her greatly. Only one thing is for sure: she feels strangely attracted to this lovely creature, and if he were a human, she would have wanted to marry him on the spot. But he is not, and so she confides in him as if he is her bosom friend, a good and easygoing listener who never talks back but understands all too well. For over the last two years, the Princess feels her life has been dwindling in joy and a strange seriousness has set in, overshadowing her once cheerful attitude towards life and forcing her to contend with circumstances beyond her control that she just can't make herself to feel good about. She says her father, the King of Carthage, seems always in a rush, looking predominantly somber and gloomy all the time, and when he speaks, he talks about trying to secure Phoenician occupation of and trade with Sicily, for revolts have challenged the wealthy but lethargic citizens of Carthage into responding to a growing instability in locations their commerce greatly depends on. He says he wants to avoid war with the strong Roman Empire, but he is not sure how long war can actually be avoided, and if it would break out, he is afraid that it might hit the complacent citizens of Carthage pretty damn hard.

Elissa stops for a moment, reflecting on her family's dynamics. Melancholically she begins to describe to her newly trusted friend how her mother has pulled away from being the nourishing, warm-hearted center of the family, for her intuition and wisdom seem to have fallen short of being able to suggest the right strategies for her husband's many challenging decisions, and war is just not a topic she wants to entertain in her mind nor spend her time and energies on. A great tension has thus been developing between the King and Queen that seems to divide the household into two parties, namely the men with their more aggressive natures on one side and the women with their still loving, but as weak regarded constitutions on the other side. And much to Princess Elissa's dismay, this gap seems to be growing by the day, and unhappiness and disregard for each other seem to grow as well by the leaps and bounds.

At that moment the doors fling open, and Prince Danel with his three rambunctious friends enter the hall, disrespectfully throwing themselves all over the place, laughing loudly and shouting noisily at each other as if Princess Elissa is not in the room at all, and Torilander, the merman, even less. They brag about their sports achievements and tease each other for doing worse than the one who just expresses the tease, poking each other in the side or hitting each other's heads with napkins and other utensils they find lying around the hall. Eventually two of them end up in a wrestling match, with the other two spurring them on and shouting slang words at them for either measuring up to their expectations or letting them down. The match is fought with fervor and fever, and soon the other two join in to roll and tumble around the room as if it were their playground.

"Why don't you guys go to the barn and work it out there?!" Elissa shouts at them, trying to be heard over the noise. "We all would have more fun that way!"

Two of the wrestlers look up from their heated activity and, upon beholding the Princess, begin to tease her as well, calling her the beautiful, ice cold young lady that makes their blood freeze with her cold attitude and at the same time brings it to a boil with her hot body. One wrestler manages to disentangle himself from the match and feverishly grabs Elissa's butt, his face expressing a victorious grin, as if holding a precious fruit.

Elissa exclaims a disgruntled shout, angrily pushing the obtruder away, which finally gets her brother's attention, who immediately whistles to his buddy to lay off his sister if he does not want to be beaten up thoroughly by the royal champion wrestler himself. With a heavy sigh of disappointment, the obtruder complains about having a delicious fruit like the Princess right under his nose and not being allowed to bite into it. But Prince Danel is not in the mood for entertaining this kind of pleasure when it comes to his sister, and with a stern and somber look in his eyes, he orders the trespasser to lay off and zip up his pants if he does not want to be thrown into jail. This finally gets the young man's attention, and with a sigh of surrender, he moves away from Elissa to throw himself back into the rumbustious fight. Danel, however, lost his fire and passion, and with a look of preponderance, he demands to know from his sister why she is not with the other ladies doing their weaving business.

Elissa does not know how to answer this question, for normally she would have been in the weaving chamber at this hour, but to speak with Torilander seemed far more entertaining and charming than this boring weaving business could ever be anyway. Upon seeing her hesitation, Danel begins to notice the merman, how he leans over the rock as if observing the whole scenario with an air of aloofness and silent pleasure. "Oh, now I get it!" he exclaims. "You've developed a crush on this creature, haven't you? — How pathetic!"

"Have not!" Elissa proclaims sulkily, for to be found out in such a rude manner and in front of these mocking perverts is not something she looks forward to confessing. "He is a real living thing, you know, with feelings and needs just like any other living being, and for you to call him a creature is just rude and insensitive at this point!" She looks at her brother as if she is ready to fight him on this one. But he dismisses her notion: "Whatever makes you happy!" he says, whistling his team together to announce they should indeed continue their match in the stables until the gladiators begin their practices and they will be able to learn a thing or two from them.

And so the rowdy gang leaves the assembly hall, leaving a mess behind that is reminiscent of the one they left behind before, prompting the cleaning crew to show up right away and clean it all up, as if Prince Danel and his rowdies never graced the hall at all on that day. Any broken or rumpled item gets replaced, the furniture shoved back into place, and the last finishing touches get put on the hall, a flower replaced here, a picture straightened out there, as if the hall's beauty was never tarnished and thrown off balance in the first place.

Elissa gives a sigh of relief once the last servant has left the hall. "Some knuckleheads of brothers I have! One more self-absorbed than the other! I feel quite estranged from them for most of the time." She moves closer to the tank so she is able to interact better with her newfound confidante. "My mother told me she named me after the Queen of Tyre who founded Carthage many, many centuries ago. Her story, however, is a sad one, for she left the Phoenician capital under much agony and tragedy. She was married to a high priest with whom she reigned over Tyre until her still underage brother was supposed to assume the throne when he would be old enough. But instead, her vicious brother ganged up with a mob against her and her husband and murdered her husband so he could rule over Tyre sooner rather than later. Then he demanded all of Queen Elissa's wealth, whereupon she escaped with most of the aristocracy of Tyre, leaving the city to the lesser ranks of society. She and her escort sailed towards the West, and finally arrived at the site on which today's Carthage stands. Under her rule, the colony quickly prospered and developed into a remarkable center for commerce and trade, the likes of which the world had hardly seen before.

Elissa says she is quite proud to bear the original Carthaginian Queen's name, and often can't help but see similarities between herself and the Queen when it comes to their relationships with their doomed brothers, who, all in all, seem to pursue different goals than their sisters do and express themselves more aggressively while doing so. She confesses that she is tired of watching her brothers squander away what little self-respect they have left, and to either laze around the palace or fight amongst themselves rather than find a worthwhile purpose to pursue that could effect a difference in the lives of many deserving and needy subjects.

Torilander is quite taken with what the Princess says, for even though she is the youngest of the siblings, her words and deeds have impressed him the most so far. He feels a pressing urge to respond to her, to try to comfort her torn and hurting soul, but his fear of being found out as a thinking and speaking merman and therefore very likely being studied on the spot by all sorts of professors still binds him to a mute state. His eyes, however, speak more than words could ever speak, and an infinite compassion pours from them to show the girl in front of him that he understands and that he cares. For even though it was her father who ultimately brought him here into this small tank that is now his imprisonment, he can't help but relate to and sympathize with her situation, for he feels as lonesome and left to his own fate as she expresses for herself right now.

"It's quite challenging to think about getting married," the Princess continues to pour her heart out, "and to trust that there is a man who will honor me, respect me, and stay loyal to me for the rest of my life. I don't know whether such a man exists when I look at my brothers; how they compete with each other, and how they beat each other up over the least of things. — But my parents want me to get married soon. That's why I'm made to attend etiquette classes — to get prepared for the big event! As if it's so grandiose to leave your familiar environment behind and trust that whoever happens to marry you will provide you with a loving and comfortable home! I can't decide whether to look forward to leaving or to be afraid of it." She pauses and lowers her gaze.

"Not all men are like your brothers, you know!" Torilander opens his mouth to let the words of comfort flow out of him. "My best friend is on his way right now to overcome the challenges of hell in order to meet and unite with his beloved woman in the heavens of the Gods. He would do anything in his power to just be with her and see her happy. These kinds of honorable and loving men do exist; you just have to look in the right direction to find them."

"This might well be," Elissa answers, lost in her thoughts, "but what direction might that be? — Wait a minute!" she begins to shout. "You talk? You actually, really just talked to me?" She touches her head, stands up on her feet, and twirls around. "The merman can talk!" she exclaims over and over again, as if having to convince herself of it even further. "I have to tell father!" she shouts, and is about to run to the door, when Torilander calls her back decisively, asking her to please not betray him quite yet, for he does not feel ready for the onslaught of intellectuals who might want to pierce his very nature and, on top of that, rob the Princess of her opportunity to converse with him. This sentence makes the Princess stop in her tracks, and with wonder in her face, she turns around, halfway embarrassed by the fact that she confided her deepest secrets to a creature and stranger who actually understood every word of hers. Even though she saw his understanding reflected in his eyes before, it still hits her and makes her feel quite uncomfortable to all of a sudden know as a matter of fact that he has heard all her little secrets, and there is no hiding from it. With a sigh, she returns to the tank, wondering out loud why it took him so long to talk to her. She also wonders how on earth she is able to understand him so clearly when, obviously, he is under water and behind a thick glass pane. Most human voices would only sound blurry under these circumstances, but his sounds miraculously clear and loud enough to understand. Torilander wonders about this phenomenon as well, but then remembers that his race functions from a slightly higher level of existence than that of the human race, and therefore his expressions and perceptions often come from a frequency outside the range humans are used to. There seems to be a wide enough frequency range that allows the reality zone of his race to overlap with the one of the human race so they can perceive and interact with each other, but what comes across as a miracle to Elissa right now is but a natural phenomenon to Torilander when he functions from that higher level. He just wishes he could shift most of his essence to that higher level in order to be able to dematerialize himself from this tank and imprisonment right back into the freedom spaces of the ocean. But for now he takes it upon himself to explain to the Princess that his voice, in fact, has an easy time passing through the glass simply because his essence is anchored on a slightly higher frequency level of existence than that of most humans, and therefore his voice is able to penetrate dense materials and can still be heard clearly.

Elissa stands there for a moment, dumbfounded. Then she repeats her question from before, why he didn't communicate with her sooner when he understood her all along. Because she feels quite laid bare before him and needs to assure herself of his discretion! Torilander shrugs his shoulders, introduces himself by his name, then explains he has hardly overcome his shock of being here, wondering whom he can trust, when her words began to open him up to her, and now he can just hope she will honor his trust in her the same way he would do for her if the situation were reversed. Elissa understands his line of reasoning, and her sense of betrayal immediately yields to a curiosity about Torilander's friend, who — according to his words — seems an extraordinary example of a man.

And thus Torilander describes to her in a few words the incredible, out-of-this-world romantic love between his merman friend Loriolan and his beloved Earth Princess, Indirali, what a long, arduous journey their hearts seem to demand of each other, and what the two lovers are willing to overcome in order to be able to unite in the most ultimate way. — The account leaves the Princess stunned and in awe, for this story sounds like a heroic tale of old, and she would have loved to meet these two heroic characters, who right now, it appears, are far apart from each other, battling different issues and forces, to finally fall into each other's arms in the very happy end, so she hopes. The Princess sighs heavily, as if she just read a beautiful romance novel that made her hopeful for love again, and desiring of a similar heroic lover to come and sweep her off her feet.

"If only someone would do all this for me too!" she yearns. "Demonstrate his undying love for me, and deeply convince me of his lifelong commitment. I think then I would be able to give marriage a shot!"

"I know of someone who certainly would do that for you, because he loves you more than he loves his own life!" Torilander reveals.

"You feel that way about me?" She wonders out loud, quick with her assumption. "Already?"

"No, I'm talking about the boy you grew up with, and with whom you seemingly once shared a love so pure and innocent that the both of you would often hide from the adult world to be able to stay in your sacred, blissful world of love for as long as you were able to. — I'm talking about Philosir, the young man whose kind heart allowed me to let go of my fears and relax in this new environment I found myself thrust into against my will. He spent the first day and night with me at the fountain, making sure I felt comfortable and safe enough to close my eyes and actually fall asleep in what I assumed to be a hostile environment. He helped me greatly to stay open to what is to come, and not give in to my fear and hatred of the situation. You would be well advised to keep him as a lover, for he has a heart of gold, and if I were you, I would not ignore his pure feelings for you but respond back in like way, for you can rest assured with him that he will always just have your highest and best interest at heart in all matters that pertain to you."

"But he is a servant's son!" the Princess exclaims indignantly. "And as such, his rank is way too low for me! My father would kill me if I as much as even just looked at him again. — No!" she shakes her head vigorously. "My parents drove that point home to me very clearly. Over and over I was told by them and my tutors, and was even made fun of by my brothers, to drop this boy and focus on becoming a sophisticated and poised young lady who will win the heart of any suitor who happens to have the stamp of approval from my father, because this man is either of royal blood or wealthy beyond measure. According to protocol, these are the only acceptable criteria for a possible match for me. If I don't want to incur the wrath of my parents, or have Philosir killed by my brothers like it happened to Queen Elissa's husband, to the founding queen of Carthage, then I better leave this topic untouched, lest I have no hope of ever being happy and married in my life."

Torilander laughs out loud, but immediately apologizes for doing so. He says he does not mean any disrespect for her feelings, but in his opinion, she has it all backwards. "Maybe it's the norm to be miserable as a member of the human race," he reflects, "but in our world, we try to adjust our outer circumstances to our higher feelings more than the other way around. For ultimately, a world governed by the power of love is worth living in a million times more than living in a world governed by oppression and hate. I have a hard time understanding the degree to which the members of the human race are willing to compromise their innate desire for happiness and health when they decide so easily to give up on their ideals and on true love, as if it seems to come so easy and natural to them."

"Well, that's easy for you to say!" Elissa pipes up, feeling a bit peeved at being second-guessed in regard to her feelings. "You are not a woman, and you don't have powerful parents as I have, parents who have a crown to wear for the public and who demand the very highest standards from their daughter …" Her voice begins to tremble as she tries hard to find a reason why Torilander's viewpoint would be wrong and non-applicable to her life, but deep down, her soul knows he is right, and she has a hard time pretending otherwise.

"I can imagine how difficult it is to fulfill expectations that are based on public opinion and on the need of a ruler to appease and control conflicting parties, many of which live by a code of ethics far inferior than that which rulers and aristocrats of long ago lived by. I by no means mean to make light of your situation, but the anguish of your soul and the longing of your heart for your true soulmate encouraged me to speak thus boldly to you, especially after listening to Philosir's love confessions for you throughout the whole long night, last night." He looks at her in a friendly way.

"He talked about me the whole night?" Elissa wants to assure herself, looking at Torilander with an incredulous look on her face. "About his love for me?"

"He sure did!" Torilander affirms. "So much so that my heart went out to him in his suffering, for he is convinced that you have forgotten about him and your heart is with him no longer."

"What a dummy he is!" Her jubilant, child-like heart cries out. "How can I forget the boy whose pranks and jokes made me laugh as nothing else ever has! And whose hair I could run my fingers through endlessly, trying to comb his wild mane into something adorable and pleasing to the eye. He always was a wild one, my Philosir — that's what made him so special to me, that's why I always loved him so much! No, he needn't feel sad, for when I hear that, I myself become sad at the thought!" She looks as if she needs to hold back her tears.

"Too bad," Torilander conveys, "there are two beautiful lovers who are not able to be with each other because etiquette demands it so."

"I just don't know what to do!" the Princess admits, her tears starting to run down her cheeks. "If I resist my parents on this matter, they will expel me from the palace, never to be invited back in, and never to see my family again. My family would regard my act as unforgivable, and would send me to my exile, no matter how much I might cry and ask for their acceptance of my lover. — What would you recommend I do?"

"First of all," Torilander asks, "does your heart still belong to him? Are you still as much in love with him as you were two years ago?"

The Princess takes a moment to respond. This question is one she tried to suppress in her own mind for the longest time, and the answer to it is something she would not have wanted to admit to herself under any circumstances whatsoever. But now that this gentle mer-creature implores her to tell the truth, she is unable to keep it hidden any longer, and like a strong geyser shooting from the ground, her repressed love for Philosir finds its valve to escape and come to the surface. "I love him more than the moon loves the sun, my heart belongs to him and always will! — I just can't act on it, lest I lose the life I know!" She looks down, as if beaten by her own admission.

"You don't need to be afraid to admit your feelings in front of me," Torilander wants her to know. "I'm used to seeing people around me who are truly in love with each other, and have no hard time living and expressing it freely towards each other. But I understand that your family and state think differently." He pauses for a moment to ponder the issue. "Have you ever heard of the power of thought when expressed on a very subtle level of conscious awareness?" he wonders out loud.

Princess Elissa looks at him as if a flicker of hope just crossed her face. "What do you mean?"

"If you can manage to settle your mind into a deeper state of awareness, you can imagine any outcome to your desires as you wish, for as long as it is in alignment with the Divine Will, and doesn't interfere with other people's free will. It is best to affirm the Divine choice of whatever it is you want, because when you do that, you will only invite the best solution to your problems, the one that has no bad consequences, and ends up being a win-win for all parties involved in your manifestation process. And if you can hold the thought on this more subtle level long enough, and ideally nurture it with positive energy and emotion, it tends to manifest in your outer circumstances. Things might start to happen that somehow, out of the blue, begin to support the outcome you want."

"That sounds like magic," she finds. "Is this some kind of magic spell you are talking about?"

"Not really, but the result sure feels like magic when it does come true. The way to go about it, however, is very logical and practical, and easy to do once you understand the mechanics of it. Do you want to try it out with me right now, for I have a wish of my own that I would like to practice until it comes true for me as well."

"What's that?"

"Oh, I just want to be back in my native element, the ocean water, able to reconnect with my family and destiny."

"But then I lose you as my best friend!" she whines. "I don't know whether I want that. I just got to know you, and I must say, I like you a lot already."

"I like you, too, Elissa. But if you really like me, you will let me go, little Princess, for I'm not happy in this environment, and I don't look forward to being analyzed by your physicians and researchers. In fact, I have a girl as well that I'm in love with, and whom I intend to find again, and ask her whether she wants to spend the rest of her life together with me. Because with every mile that separates us from each other, my longing and love for her just keep growing, and I can't bear it any longer. I want to pursue my love the same way my best friend and hero pursues his."

Elissa's heart feels perked up. "You want to ask her to marry you? How romantic!"

"How about it? You manifest Philosir into your life, and I manifest my Hedna into my life?"

Elissa's eyes glow. "You are sure it will work?"

"Pretty sure. But it does require great motivational force, much practice, patience, and endurance, all qualities that are the hardest to be practiced. That's why it would be nice to do it together, to support each other in our efforts and weaknesses. Do you really want this, and are you in?" He holds his hand against the glass.

"Yes," she agrees wholeheartedly, "I'm in!" And with a big smile, she puts her hand against his from the other side of the glass, glad to have found a true friend in Torilander.

Chapter 12

An hour later, Prince Hanno storms into the room, cussing and spitting fire, for he was just overrun by his brother and his gang in the hallway, shoved to the side, and made fun of as being inferior in his fighting skills to those which his brother boasts. Everything in his way is pushed over and kicked around by his angry feet and hands, when he finally grabs the hearth iron poker and thrusts it into a pillow as if piercing his archenemy through his bloody, boastful heart. "Here, you jerk, take this, and this, and this!" he pants heatedly, ramming the poker deeper and deeper into the pillow, which begins to disintegrate under the cutting impact.

Torilander is shocked by the intensity of Prince Hanno's emotions and immediately tries to hide behind the rock. But his startled reaction whirls up a handful of small stones from the bottom of the tank that make a clicking sound upon hitting against the glass. This gets Hanno's attention right away, and he spins around, angrily looking at the tank to continue venting his immense, pent-up anger on whatever and whoever will take it from him.

"Hey, you little rat! Try to hide from me?" He storms towards the tank to hit the iron poker against the glass. Torilander is horrified to see him do this, for the tank could break and the water could gush out. "Do you think that rock can keep you from me, you hideous creature." He bangs the poker against the glass once more, his face distorted with pain and anger. "You don't have me fooled with your fishtail and lame, puppy-like facial expression that has my sister all over you and under your spell! You are nothing but a bad joke, a misshaped creature from the bottom of the ocean where you should return to if it were up to me!" He bangs the poker against the glass again with all the anger he's got, and a small crack appears on the glass.

"Please stop it!" Torilander rears up from behind the rock, trying to put some sense back into this raving, ravaging maniac. "I'm not against you, in fact

I'm all on your side!" Torilander looks at him with bewilderment. Princess Elissa was called out earlier by one of her governesses and is therefore not available to buffer him from this dangerous onslaught.

The Prince is startled for a moment to hear the creature speak. "What did you just say?" he wonders out loud. "You can actually talk? —That's ludicrous! You are even more ludicrous than I thought you were!" He gets ready to strike again, when Torilander commands him with a firm voice to put down the poker and hear him out. Puzzled, Hanno holds the poker in suspension, for deep within, he doesn't care to break the water container and have his father be all over him about it. But his anger often gets the better of him, and once he is under its spell, it takes a strong, authoritative voice to put him in his place and have him listen, which Torilander actually succeeded in doing. With a puzzled look on his face, he gives Torilander a moment to explain himself, before he decides what to lower the poker down onto.

"Maybe we can talk, you and I," Torilander suggests, "and maybe I can help you with whatever problem you might have."

"Nobody is ever on my side, and nobody can help me either," Hanno shouts angrily, smashing the poker onto the ground and stomping on it. "Everyone just keeps telling me how stupid I am, how pale in comparison to my lame-ass brother, and how I won't ever amount to anything."

"That's hard to believe!" Torilander gives in. "You seem to have the strength of several oxen; you certainly don't look like a weakling to me!"

Hanno blows off his inner steam as he allows the compliment to sink to the bottom of his churned-up, restless heart.

"The only area I can see you might need some guidance in is how to channel your incredibly vast energy to benefit not only yourself but also the people around you."

"That's just it!" he cries out loud. "There is no one I can think of whom I want to be associated with any longer, because they just all make fun of me or don't give a damn about my desires, ambitions, and goals. I'm just to keep my mouth shut and let Danel reap the laurels of success and acknowledgement.

I'm just the stupid second-born, somewhere between my heir-to-the-throne ass-brother and the cute, little, innocent princess sister who has everyone twisted around her little finger with her cuteness and charm." He kicks into a chair, over and over again. "I'm at the point where I want to do the same as my famous namesake, Hanno, the great King of Carthage who lived a little over two centuries ago. He traveled our vast African continent, went to Arabia, and Egypt. He played with gorillas, established colonies, and saw wonders no one even knows about. Sometimes I think there is nothing here for me, and I should just go and throw myself into an adventure like that."

"Why don't you?" Torilander looks at him with wide-open eyes, curious as to where this conversation might take them both.

"I really, really think about it!' he exclaims fiercely, as if ready to storm out right now, never to be seen or heard from again.

"Is anything still holding you back?" Torilander wants to know upon noticing the Prince's hesitation.

"Well, it's just …" Hanno scratches his head. And aware that Torilander is watching him, he finally blurts out: "I don't know if I ever can come back if I leave like this. — I think my father would not forgive me if I left without his consent."

"I see! And do you think your father would give you his consent if you asked him nicely?"

"No!" Hanno is sure, "I think he would kick my ass for not standing behind my brother in all these volatile and restless times, with the Romans threatening our butts every minute of the day. But I'm so tired of playing second fiddle in everything, sitting on the waiting bench until maybe my first-priority brother has a lapse that might require me to step in for a moment until he's recovered enough to take over again. What a stupid destiny to contend with, wouldn't you say?"

Torilander nods, reflectively. "Yes, I can see where you are coming from."

Deeply satisfied to finally have found someone to agree with him on things, Hanno sinks into the chair with a big, heavy sigh. "I told you, my situation feels hopeless and predetermined in a tight, strict, and awful way. My radius of freedom resembles that of a miniature clock, with me spinning aimlessly round and round in ways that only make me feel ever more limited and controlled. I really don't know where to take my life joy from anymore. I used to have a lot of it when I was a little boy. Back then it wasn't too obvious that my brother came first in everything, because I played outside with the stable boys, the only real friends I ever knew. But I had to give up playing with them; everyone just has to grow up and become a boring, lame adult who has to make it their priority to be unhappy and unfulfilled, trying to kick each other's asses, if not in your own palace and country, then overseas, with whatever superpower seems to have their heels up high at the moment." He shakes his head. "Stupid, stupid world!"

"I'm truly sorry you feel so imprisoned by your situation. I can relate!" Torilander points at the tank to make Hanno see his point.

And for the first time, Hanno laughs out loud for a second, for he sees how similar their situations really are, and that the creature he was a bit unnerved by in the beginning actually turns out to be a companion of sorts, someone who can understand the suffering and plight Hanno has been under for the longest time now, and in which he has felt extremely alone and misunderstood for as long a time as well. And so he takes a deeper look at Torilander, his eyes still vulnerable from the anger and confessions he just shared with the sea creature. But all he sees are warm and good-hearted eyes staring back at him, with no hidden agenda lurking in them that could betray an underhanded nature, a hideous agenda that possibly could have been able to strike out at him at any moment, putting him down and calling him names the way he is used to by his alienated brother and his decadent entourage.

"Do you really want to travel around the world, or is this just a way for you to escape the undesirable circumstances of your present situation?" the merman asks of the Prince.

Startled at the uncanniness of the merman's seemingly deep insight into his own nature, the Prince lowers his head. He actually never thought about this point. He just assumed running away and throwing himself into whatever adventure wants to absorb him fully would have gone right along with what he wants from life. But now that the sea creature asks this question so probingly, doubts surface in his heart, a fact he is actually quite surprised by. "I think it would be cool to do that," he states half-heartedly and with a low tone of voice. "I think I could prove myself out there probably more than I can here in this prison camp of mine!" He looks at Torilander, wanting to hold his gaze with strength in his eyes. But they falter, much to his amazement and embarrassment. "Well, I don't really know what I want, I guess. Nobody ever asks me that anyway. It's just assumed that I stick around as the replacement boy so to say. But I want to be more than that!" He rears up with a sense of dignity and desired self-worth: "I want to be the center of my life for a change, make a difference of some kind, you know, like the heroes of old, kind of!"

"I think that is everyone's good right!" Torilander agrees.

"That's what I think!" Hanno echoes back, for he cannot stress and hear this point often enough. How good it feels to finally have someone agree with him on something so important to his heart. The creature becomes more likable with every moment, he finds.

"Did you ever ask yourself what it is that you truly, deeply want in life? Vocationally, and personally?" Torilander ignites the conversation. "Have you ever given it any thought?"

"Not really!" Hanno has to admit, feeling pretty stupid all of a sudden. "My life has been so planned out for so long now, that I didn't even try to figure out what it is that I actually want."

"What activities make you tick, and what kind of goals would fascinate you if you dared to ever dream about achieving them?" The merman continues to probe into the Prince's soul and inner makings.

The Prince has to think for a moment, becoming real quiet and concentrating. Then, after several minutes of deep inner searching, he declares: "I think I would like to reign over my own city-state, kind of like my brother has the fortune of being able to do one day, lucky as he is, to be taking over the crown of one of the wealthiest and most prosperous cities in the world, our Carthage; but maybe it needs to be another city that I would rule over, and still try to build it up to one day equal or even outshine the splendor of Carthage. Yeah, I think I would like to compete with my brother in who runs the greater and better city-state, only that he has a natural advantage over me already through his birth, but I think I can beat him anyway because of who I am."

"Sounds interesting and highly motivated!" Torilander applauds him. "It sounds like your competitive spirit with your brother can serve you well when it comes to trying to excel in something that big and wonderful. It can fuel your motivation to go beyond any limitations and obstacles in your way if only you learn to harness this raw power and innate drive to be better and greater than anyone else, especially your brother. And I bet that if you do outshine your brother one day, you probably will feel only compassion and gratitude towards him for giving you such a precious gift as this powerful motivational force, this smoldering, intense fire within you, will most likely turn out for you to be."

Prince Hanno lowers his gaze. How odd to feel the way he does right now. What mysterious influence has this merman over him that he begins to feel his hatred towards his archenemy, his brother, diminishing? "But ruling over my own city-state will probably always stay an unreachable dream for me, for as long as I breathe!" he cries out his pain and doubt at feeling the glimmer of hope triggered by their conversation. "Why would I subject myself to such irrational thinking and wishing when, by the end of the day, I end up being the odd man out again that everyone laughs at and subdues to their wishes?"

"This doesn't need to be the necessary outcome!" Torilander explains. "If only you believe that there is another option, then together we will make it happen."

"How?" Hanno's eyes almost roll out of their sockets.

"By asking your brother directly, for if Carthage truly has colonies around the Mare Internum and Tyrrhenian Sea, then there could be an ideal and appropriate city-state for you somewhere out there, one that could benefit greatly from your leadership and from what you are able to offer to the development of the state. And if you also keep your loving, persistent focus on your desire and goal, then you might very likely have your dream come true rather sooner than later!" Torilander affirms, holding his knuckles against the glass wall to invite

Hanno's consent and cooperation.

Hanno stares at the friendly gesture as if to decide whether to give the whole conversation any credit at all. But then his innermost longings not only for a life of dignity, independence, and higher purpose but also for true friendship and love come to the surface, and with slight shame in his eyes, he puts his knuckled-up hand onto Torilander's to signal his final surrender to the merman's friendliness, wisdom, and incredible foresight.

"Sorry for earlier, man!" he apologizes. "I just didn't know how cool you truly are!"

"It's alright!" Torilander forgives him. "I didn't know what a great character you truly are either!'

Both grin at each other, and with that, Prince Hanno leaves to attend to matters of duty and training, for which he seems strangely and wondrously prepared and ready all of a sudden.

CHAPTER 13

Somewhat ill at ease, Torilander sits behind his rock, trying to think things through so as to not ultimately make a fool of himself, promising anyone he comes in contact with to help make them happy and fulfilled, and enable them to live their higher destiny. But when confronted with all these human miseries, he can t help but feel triggered in his own mature, higher nature and frankly express the truth and higher solutions he sees so readily written all over their faces. He actually feels astonished that these royal kids cannot see and tap into their own desires for happiness, and are even less able to pursue them. How odd that he needs to point things out to them and end up becoming their mentor on how to realize their own higher vocations and true love interests. Torilander shakes his head at the situation he is in, but an inner voice tells him to be patient and allow the process to unfold. Maybe he has been brought to this location for a higher purpose; maybe he is to teach these kids a lesson or two in how to develop a peaceful, creative attitude towards life that ultimately has the power to turn bad tidings around, individually and collectively as well, especially when the person he is to teach a lesson to is the future king of Carthage. For that reason, and for the reason of keeping his promise to Prince Hanno, Torilander hopes to soon have a private tête-à-tête with Prince Danel himself, and hopefully pretty soon, because the desire to leave this tank cell behind and experience the vastness and freedom of the oceanic world again and realize his true, and everlasting love, is burning in his soul, and becoming more consuming with every moment.

And divine providence seems to support his selfless will as promptly as possible when in the evening hours a girl comes rushing in, followed and chased by Prince Danel himself. Both exclaim noises of sexual foreplay, sighing and moaning as if the libido just wants to do its pleasurable thing, no matter what the reasoning mind might prescribe for the moment.

"Danel, I shouldn't!" she exclaims. "Tullia will kill me if I don't get those pastries done for tonight's dinner!" she complains half-heartedly, for being chased by her beloved prince is a treat way more delicious than those average-tasting baked goods she has to deliver by the trayful every day.

"Those silly little pastries need to wait!" Danel breathes into her ear, having caught up with her finally. Feverishly he tries to push himself into her, kissing her exposed skin wherever he can find it on her firm, alluring body.

"You are right," she answers playfully and seductively. "You are always so damn right!" And with that, she surrenders completely, allowing the sexual intercourse to increase in its dynamics, trying to find its fevered-for climax, with Prince Danel wanting to do his utmost to satisfy not only himself but also the damsel he has secretly cast his eyes upon, for her beauty stands out to him, and she manages to catch his attention any time she walks past him.

But for some reason, the climax is nowhere near in sight, for Danel's manhood seems to all of a sudden be strangely out of commission at this very moment.

"What is it, my dear?" the girl asks upon noticing Danel's struggle and dissatisfied face. "Am I not attractive to you today? Tell me, my Prince, is there anything wrong with my attire?"

"No, nothing wrong with you," the Prince admits. "I think I'm just not in the mood for it after all."

"What?" the girl has a hard time believing his words, for in the last weeks they had more fun doing it than she ever had before in her life, and Danel was able to perform every single time. "Are you sure you are not tired of me, my love?" she begs to know the uncomfortable truth.

But instead of answering the rhetorical question, he throws himself on the couch to get a breather from his obvious failure, exclaiming: "I think it has to do with what happened in this room earlier when one of my buddies tried to have a go at my sister."

The girl takes a seat next to him, then keeps staring at him as if to figure out whether he really means what he is saying or whether her steamy affair with the future king of Carthage has just found its inglorious, premature demise.

But the Prince keeps thinking about his sister, and more repressed feelings seem to want to emerge from his chest, an intimate get-together the kitchen-help girl has not yet had the privilege of sharing with him. But her demure heart knows to be supportive when a man wants to get things off his chest, and so she engages in a heartfelt conversation with him that allows the Prince to reveal things to her he would not, under any circumstances, have revealed to anyone else. Both know that their relationship is secretive, and what transpires between them, therefore, will stay secret as well.

Danel grabs his forehead as if trying to hold the weight of his combined responsibilities in his hand. "Sometimes I don't even like to spend time with these idiots who seem to have no manners at all," he confesses. "But they have been my buddies in armed war training and other combative sports for so long that it would feel strange to all of a sudden retreat from them and turn my attention elsewhere." He sinks his head deeper into his hand, as if feeling quite despondent at the thought of it all. "And where in the world would I turn my attention to anyway?!" He sighs heavily, letting his frustration flow out of him.

Livia, his girl, touches him gently to express her sympathy and comfort.

"My father wants me to become a warrior king," Danel continues with another heavy sigh, "to fight the Romans and extinguish their predominance on the world market once and for all. I think he feels pretty threatened by their natural inclination for supremacy, and wonders throughout his long nights about how exactly to get the better of this obstinate danger to Carthage's wealth and prosperous citizens. Because as much as Carthage's wealthy merchants love the commercial and trading possibilities my father keeps securing for our future, not many of them have shown interest so far in helping to defend our great city from this ongoing threat, which draws nearer from the north and has already progressed quite a distance towards the south of the Italian peninsula. The majority of our army consists of mercenaries, men who are hired to do our citizens' job in defending our glorious city-state, and it makes me wonder sometimes how safe we are putting our delicate security issues into the hands of non-Carthaginian warriors, into mostly Libyan hands. What do these warriors come back to after the war is over? Hopefully not to revolt, that would be just another nightmare!"

"It grieves me to see you thus worried, my Prince!" Livia utters with a voice expressing compassion. "For what it's worth, I truly believe in Carthage's good fortune, and I pray for its continued prosperity and global importance." She looks at him with her crystal-clear eyes, as if to uplift his spirits, which for some reason seem to be pretty down this very moment.

Danel smiles feebly at her, then continues his reflections. "Thank God this Pyrrhus, King of Greece, turned out to be incapable of turning the Sicilian Greek colonies against us; he is out of the way, but the Romans have been pretty persistent in expanding their borders to all sides, demonstrating to everyone that they are an imperialist force to be reckoned with. Pyrrhus, however, has been almost succeeding in the recent years to overturn Carthaginian occupation in Sicily, thus endangering one of Carthage's most important commercial and financial income sources. And he came damn close to battling us on our own ground!" Prince Danel groans loudly as he almost pulls away from his mistress's touch to be able to feel the whole damn impact of the dead-end situation he feels thrown into by his father and his seeming destiny. "Considering what I'm being prepared for, the crown feels more like a burden and curse than something to be worn lightly and with joy. — I don't even know what real joy feels like anymore. You are the closest thing to joy that I can think of!" he admits to her, gently taking her hand into his. "I just really don't know whether to look forward to becoming the king of Carthage one day or to dread this moment, for it will mean the end of any carefree and unworried times I can still spend with my reckless friends, as demeaning as their behavior is oftentimes." He buries his head in her lap, as if hoping to find refuge there from the cold realities of his life.

"You will carry the crown with dignity and will do it more than justice, my Prince!" the kitchen-help girl assures him, "and all the world will look upon you as the greatest king that ever lived!"

"If only you are right!" he wishes with a whisper, feeling quite sleepy all of a sudden, ready to fall asleep on her lap. "I really don't like to throw my life away in futile wars, you know," he mumbles. "I want to have fun in life as well! Why should our merchants have a more privileged life than their king himself? It doesn't make any sense, and still my father tries to raise me to be a war strategist to save the kingdom from its potential demise and to defend the lazy lifestyles of the Carthaginian elite, who already own thousands of slaves to do their every bidding anyway. I don't want to become just another slave to them, not me!" And with that the Prince dozes off, being gently stroked by his mistress, the girl who ever came the closest to meaning something to his confused and deeply worried heart.

Minutes turn into tens of minutes, and after about half an hour the girl's conscience in regard to her work duties sets in, prompting her to ever so gently pull herself out from underneath the sleeping Prince's body, leaving him in his curled-up position to continue sleeping the stress out of his nervous system while she rushes back to her work, lest she be scolded and punished for her negligence and tardiness. The Prince gives a sigh of relief as he is being moved gently off her body but then resumes his much-needed sleep, for he partied late into the night last night, trying — like he does so often — to forget about the nagging feelings at the bottom of his soul.

And so another half hour passes, with Torilander hearing Danel's rhythmic breaths coming from the couch; the hall has darkened, and he can hardly distinguish the Prince's body from the couch anymore. Looking upwards, Torilander prays to God Poseidon to help arrange a meeting with the future king of Carthage so he may be able to keep the promise he made to Prince Hanno. In that moment, a comet shoots across the sky, and a clashing noise outside the window, caused by swords striking each other, startles the Prince out of his sleep. He sits up, wondering out loud where his girl Livia might have escaped to.

Seeing his chance, Torilander answers the Prince from out of the dark that she had to leave to probably return to her kitchen duties, which has the Prince react even more startled, for he completely forgot about the merman and, even less so, expected him to be able to speak and understand every word he uttered in secrecy to his girl. Ashamed and slightly enraged, Prince Danel walks up to the tank to take a closer look at the merman. "So, you finally open your mouth, huh?" he asks provokingly. "Quite a scheming little fish you are to keep us all wondering about your intellectual capabilities. And here you are listening in on other people's secrets and problems."

"I don't really have much of a choice in the matter of where to be, so forgive me for listening in on your problems," Torilander apologizes with an openhearted look on his face.

For a moment, the Prince is indecisive as to whether to be angry with the merman or to just turn around and leave. But then he decides to make sure the creature won't disclose to anyone the delicate facts he must have overheard. And to his astonishment, Torilander assures him right away that these confessions will not reach the ears of anyone else, and that the Prince can trust his word and know his secrets are safe with him.

When Danel turns around with a thank-you on his lips, wanting to get out the door and get on with his evening, Torilander asks him to please stay for a moment, for he has something on his heart he would like to ask of the Prince. Puzzled to hear this request coming from the sea creature, the Prince stands still to hear him out.

For a moment, Torilander feels awkward and nervous thinking about the pleas he mulled over in his mind, and to which he hopes to receive not only a positive reaction from Prince Danel but also his much-needed help and attention on the issues he garnered from the Prince's siblings. And so he spontaneously decides to bring his own requests up first, for they seem trivial and easy to handle compared to Prince Hanno's and Princess Elissa's issues.

"I haven't received proper nourishment since my capture. This is probably due to the fact that everyone expects me to devour the little fish they put into my tank. However, I do not eat anything that has a face and is animated by some form of spirit but am rather used to eating sea plants and algae. Would it be too much asked to have your servants bring me a variety of sea algae from the ocean so I can get stronger again?"

Danel is a bit confused why the creature would address him with this demand, but then he acknowledges that he must just be starved and also needed to verbally convey his need to someone who won't blurt out to the King and his researchers right away the secret of his ability to speak. And so he nods his head, promising to take care of it right away. But when he turns around to leave, the creature calls him back again.

"What now?" he asks a bit irritably, stopping in his tracks to face the creature once more.

"The glass has a crack, and I fear it might give out at any given moment, emptying the water all over your valuable carpet. Do you think your glazier could take a look and see whether he can fix it?"

"How did that happen?" Danel reacts, surprised, looking all puzzled while approaching the glass window for a probing look.

Torilander shrugs his shoulders, for introducing Hanno's plea by betraying his impetuous behavior towards him earlier doesn't feel like the best strategy to accomplish what he intends.

"Maybe the glazier can go over it with a flame. It looks mostly just on the outer surface of the thick glass," Danel mutters while evaluating the crack carefully.

"The girl you were with …" Torilander begins his intended conversation.

Danel looks up at him and, upon noticing Torilander's pause, graciously fills him in: "You mean Livia, my sweet little kitchen-help mistress? What about her?"

"She seems like a very nice girl who seems to have your wellbeing much at heart."

Prince Danel laughs abruptly. "Well, let's say we both serve each other in ways that please us both very much. Very observant of you, though!" he has to admit.

"I thought to almost have felt some genuine love for you coming from her, don't you agree?"

"That might be," he agrees, "for I have only treated her well. And we do have fun together. But what is it your concern anyway?"

"None!" Torilander appeases. "I just feel happy when I see two people in love who seem to fit together as nicely as you both obviously do."

"You think so?" Danel takes a moment to reflect on what he just heard.

But then a cloud seems to overshadow him. "But it can't ever be!"

"Why?" Torilander bursts out with a hint of dismay in his voice.

"Because everything is predetermined in my life! That's why! My life does not belong to me; it belongs to the state, and as such, I have no say in the matter. I am to marry the daughter of one of Carthage's wealthiest merchants and financial supporters to the Crown, and that's that." He pauses for a moment, then adds almost derogatorily: "Besides, who would take a king seriously who chose to marry a servant girl? That's so ridiculous that I can't even go there!" He is ready to dismiss this whole conversation and get the heck out of the hall, when Torilander pulls him back in through the longings of his heart.

"What if there was a way to have her as your wife? What if the longings of your heart are the true measure of how righteous and in accordance with the laws of the universe you live, instead of you having to compromise your deepest, strongest desires for the sake of becoming everyone's whore anyway?"

Prince Danel stops in his tracks, again, almost shocked to hear the truth blurted out thus bluntly, but also becoming more intrigued and mystified with every minute he spends in this creature's presence.

"What if the love between you and Livia is the most real, the most genuine, the most worthwhile, the most eternally lasting, and the most infinite well of your happiness and wellbeing you will ever come across in your life, no matter where you will go and what you will be doing? Do you want to come near death before you wake up to this truth, only to find out that you have wasted your time on matters that don't really matter and which actually destroyed your fervor and love for life? How can the king of the state end up to be an idol of falseness; how will he teach the innocent children of his state what to look up to when he himself failed to live by his truth, failed to make himself happy and fulfilled in the lasting manner that alone counts when you evaluate the fleeting moment in time and compare it to the glory and bliss of eternity, in which the soul lives according to its true splendor and magnificence?"

Danel isn't sure whether he was able to follow the merman's reasoning, for his words sound elevating beyond measure, but what has it to do with his situation, even if he wanted it to apply? His face expresses utter astonishment, and he finds himself unable to reach for the right words. With a sense of defeat, he tumbles backwards to feel a chair and sink down onto it.

"I for my part would not want to marry a woman who feels for another man, be it in her past, her present, or her future." Torilander keeps going.

Danel frowns. Now what is he talking about?

"In fact, I would make it my priority to release her to the man she truly loves, if her greed for power and riches does not overshadow her true love feelings."

"What are you talking about, man?" Danel gets impatient. "Not about my Livia, I hope?"

"Not at all," Torilander assures him, "I'm talking about the woman you are to marry and who used to love your brother at one point in time, before parents on both sides began to put state business before true feelings and prime their youngsters for a life of unfulfilled love."

"My parents want the best for me, and I don't know whether I really care that much about my love life anyway when I'm out there on the battlefield, because that's what I'm supposed to do: sacrifice my life for the sake of securing peace and stability for my people, like any other good king would do!" He looks sulky and almost offended.

"I don't doubt that your parents love you and want the best for you. But if fighting to preserve peace is the kind of life they want you to adopt, then I doubt that they are the absolute instance on wisdom or the indisputable power that can keep the long-lasting peace and prosperity alive that our great ancestors knew and experienced throughout the Golden Age."

"You don't know what you are talking about!" Prince Danel reacts disgruntledly. "You have no idea what my father had to go through just to keep Carthage from falling into enemy hands already! Not only are the Romans an increasingly annoying threat to our empire, but so is Greece, with King Pyrrhus coming awfully close to marching into our city, trying to storm our Byrsa, our citadel, like the Greek-Syracusan king Agathocles several decades before him succeeded in doing, occupying it and thus startling our citizens into total shock at the prospect of losing our independence and identity as one of the richest and most successful commercial states of our times. Our Gods, thankfully, helped us to get rid of Agathocles, for soon after the occupation, he had to return to Sicily and quash his own revolts, but a scar remained in our collective awareness nevertheless. Plus, it looks like the Romans, with whom Carthage had several peace treaties over the last centuries, don't give a damn any longer about abiding by them but rather engage in taking the opposite side when it comes to interests in Sicily. According to all of the treaties, they are to stay out of Sicily altogether and not interfere with our trading business, but they have irritatingly shown increased interest in this fertile little island, and it feels like they are going to fight us on this one since their appetite for annexing any land they can conquer is becoming insatiable and uncanny." He sits sunken in the chair, reflecting on the topic that has him feeling increasingly restless, as adulthood and his destiny seem to start taking over his life and, with it, his innocence and his once fresh outlook on life. He lets out a moan, then retrieves his speech: "They probably felt peeved at us — the Romans that is — for trying to come to the aid of the Greek-Italian town of Tarentum a while ago. We sent a fleet of ships to just scare those aggressors a bit. We didn't really end up fighting them on it but just wanted to show them they cannot seize just any town against its will as they so please. They know we are the superior sea force, and they must have taken it as a personal offense, for since then our relations have considerably cooled down to the point where it might come to a long, arduous war between us superpowers, because none of us wants to relinquish interests in Sicily, the island that still separates our lands." He sighs again heavily, and Torilander can't help but feel compassion towards his heart that somehow seems to be very heavy from the royal responsibility he is born into, and from being deeply embroiled in his city-state's military affairs.

"You are right," Torilander responds kindly. "I really don't understand the full scope of your and your city's problems, nor do I want to pretend to understand. All I can suggest from the simplicity and humility of my heart is that, in the face of having to carry such heavy burdens on your shoulders, it would be even more important, in my opinion, to have a loving wife waiting at home for you to come back to, to tend to your wounds, physical and emotional, and to give you the strength and motivation to do what you must do in order to guarantee the safety of your people." He pauses for a moment, and Danel lifts his head to listen intently. "Imagine your wife doesn't really care to comfort you or show you her interest and compassion. Imagine always having to wonder whether her heart is with you at all or whether it is with someone else."

"Enough!" Danel exclaims with a shout. "I think I get your point. I don't like the idea either of having a lifelong love affair with my kitchen-help mistress, confiding my pains to her and then seeing her run off to handle the pastries my wife and I are going to partake of."

"Yeah, that wouldn't be very considerate to either one of them," Torilander makes him aware. Danel nods, as he is used to receiving support and solidarity on all his issues from his friends most of the time, but then he realizes Torilander actually had the women's interests at heart more than anything else, and so he feels forced to identify with his higher, more ethical self who wants to treat women right, not as sex slaves or prestige objects, but as the beautiful souls that they are who deserve nothing but his respect, loyalty, and kindness. With that thought, his face begins to assume an expression as if something just pierced him, and a layer of intense emotions surface, making him feel as if under some enormous soul pain that just got triggered. "I just don't know how to get my father to agree to my liaison with Livia!" He wipes his forehead.

"I might know how you can accomplish this!" Torilander reveals. "Where I come from, the power of thoughts and words is deeply understood and applied for everyone's wellbeing. If you can focus and hold a certain thought for long enough, it tends to manifest into the physical world. And when the desire you want to manifest is according to Divine Will, then you have only positive repercussions, a win-win solution for all parties involved. If you, however, focus and materialize something disadvantageous and of ill intent for another person or group of people, then the repercussions will come to haunt you and defeat you with the same impact and intensity of your sent-out negative charge. The reason

I'm telling you this is that I want to make sure you understand to only ask for the Divine solution to come to pass, because then all circumstances and interests are considered for the maximum benefit, which seems so important for your destiny as the future king of Carthage, but you should also know that it will be the solution that makes you the happiest and most fulfilled person around."

"I don't know, man, my situation is deeply linked with Carthage's fate. To think that thoughts and words can make much of a difference sounds a bit unlikely to me," Danel expresses his doubts. "How effective can this kind of mental work really be when it comes to overcoming major obstacles in your way?"

"Oh, it can be absolutely effective," Torilander convinces him wholeheartedly. "Our mer-kingdom lives in peace with other mer-kingdoms, and most of our inhabitants live a life of higher values, prosperity, and great fulfillment. Our race knows how to apply the power of the mind to our challenging situations, and brings the transcendental values to everything we do. Because of that, I think that our race lives more according to the blissful and fulfilling times that your race only knew throughout the Golden and Silver Ages, allowing our water race to resonate with higher dimensions and worlds which — to be honest — many of us are considering ascending towards in light of the darkness we see spreading at an alarming rate on this planet, turning our once beloved friends, the humans, against us and all of life. So, yes, the power of thoughts is real and very efficient when it comes to creating the kind of life that you truly want and that the Divine wants you to have, because it is the most fulfilling one that life has in store for you."

"Sounds like magic!" the Prince concedes, "But if it works, why not give it a try. It just needs to stay between the both of us; no one else is to know about it, promise?" He stands up to approach the tank with a questioning face.

"Funny you should say that!" Torilander responds, "For your sister and your brother have spoken to me on similar matters, and with both of them I now share a similar oath of secrecy, the same one I will share with you."

"My brother and sister talked to you? And Hanno didn't eat you up alive, that little cockroach?" he wonders out loud.

"On the contrary, he opened up quite nicely to his higher-self interests. It was an honor to witness his transformation, and I can just express my hope that you will give him the chance to express his deepest longings and desires for his own life to you, since he will one day need your approval and support, as you very likely will need and value his wholehearted support in everything you are doing as well, I'm sure."

Prince Danel doesn't know for a moment whether to laugh or take the merman seriously when it comes to his loser brother. But something in this whole conversation makes it difficult for the Prince to mock his brother as harshly and arrogantly as he usually does, for the merman is unlike his consenting buddies, and his words keep rather hitting into a subconscious pocket of his that seems to be loaded with emotions of an undetected and repressed kind, and of which he doesn't care to see the majority part releasing completely for fear of collapsing to the ground and crying his gut-wrenching pain out over the many things he finds so deeply unwelcoming at the threshold of his — by everyone else foolishly hailed — adulthood.

"All your little brother really wants is to be acknowledged by you, for I think he secretly admires you and wants to become like you," Torilander enlightens the Prince.

"You mean he would like the crown and all the privileges that come with that. I think that's probably closer to the truth, don't you think?"

"There might be something of that as well," Torilander agrees, "but only because he is deeply identified with you and your destiny at the moment. If you were to give him something to do, something he could feel responsible about and able to prove his abilities and self-worth, I think you would start to see another side of him, one you would actually grow to like and maybe even admire."

"Admire? That sounds a little farfetched at the moment. Maybe tolerate would be closer to the truth!" Danel counters, feeling too indignant and puffed up to be even considering giving his bugger of a brother a chance in life.

"I think it would be wise and advantageous for you to have as many friends as possible in these trying, war-stricken times, and being your blood brother, I doubt that Hanno would ever turn against you in any situation, no matter how challenging, but would probably always opt to support you and Carthage's cause at any given time. Think about it!"

Danel actually does need to think about it, for the thought of being surrounded by enemies and not having his brother to fall back on sounds scarier than he would have ever admitted to himself. His face lightens up, and any resistance towards the thought of acknowledging his brother as a decent human being has dissipated.

"Yeah, maybe you're right!" he exclaims with some embarrassment in his voice. "But why do you care for any of us, the way you do, after all we did to you, capture you and all?" Danel truly has a hard time believing this merman is for real.

"My kind thrives on harmony and bliss," Torilander illumines him, "and to see you and your siblings get along feels good to me, for I value friendship and goodwill over anything, and I'm sure everyone around you will benefit from your camaraderie and mutual support of each other as well. It will ignite the atmosphere with the light of higher, warmer, and more uplifting feelings that will bring everyone closer to the Divine Source of Life."

"What exactly did Hanno and Elissa confide to you?" Danel tries to extract.

"Why don't you speak to them directly, all the while aware that you all are not that much different from each other when it comes to matters of the heart and soul, and to the desire to be happy and fulfilled in life. If you can meet them with a sense of goodwill and openheartedness, I'm sure they will respond in like manner and will confide to you what deeply matters to them."

"I don't know, the rift between Hanno and me goes back many years," Danel interjects. "We just haven't been very interested in each other's lives for quite a long time, and to all of a sudden show interest in him feels almost unreal and pretentious. I wouldn't know where to begin to bridge that humongous gap between us ..." His voice falters, and he looks forlornly towards and out the big window, realizing how dark it has become over the past hour.

"As a leader, you will have to initiate peace offerings on many occasions, so why not begin with your alienated brother, who — as a matter of fact — wishes nothing more than to be reconciled with you. If you let your heart speak to him, and I mean the deepest levels of your heart, the ones that feel only love for all of life, then you cannot fail, but will come out victorious, winning the love and support, heck, even the admiration of your brother, a feeling so deeply fulfilling and wonderful that I would give anything to have it back in my life right now, for I also have a younger brother who sometimes bothered me with his immaturities and insecurities but who, all in all, has grown up to be one of the finest young mermen I happen to know from amongst all the kingdoms of the Tyrrhenian Sea." And now it is Torilander whose eyes become melancholic and his heart heavy from the weight of not knowing his brother's and best friend's whereabouts and circumstances. For all he knows, they could be in trouble right now, needing his help, or they could be very close to their goal already. Not knowing feels like a gnawing abyss of uncertainty in his soul, in the face of which his captivity feels unbearably hindering and challenging to any attempt at being patient with his situation. If he could, he would jump out of the tank right now, but then there are all these long, narrow streets to be traversed on the way to the ocean, with thousands of human beings barring the way with their weapons and ill-intentioned curiosity. No, Torilander knows, the solution must come from within, for if the King himself does not change his mind on Torilander's captivity, he won't stand a chance of getting out of here along the same path on which he came to this place.

"You have a brother as well? One you had to leave behind when they captured you and brought you here?" Danel can't help but feel for the merman, because all of a sudden it dawns on him what it could feel like to lose your brother for good, and it sure does not feel good at all, not at all! "Sorry, man, that sucks!" he exclaims upon noticing Torilander's inward attitude. And not knowing how to deal with it, he deflects with another issue that has been plaguing him for quite a while now: "Do you think this thought power can help resolve military threats as well, or even turn the tide in regard to political tendencies?" He takes a moment to make sure Torilander is listening, then continues: "Those Romans seem so greedy, trying to secure world commercial markets for themselves wherever they can conquer them. I wouldn't be at all surprised if they want more than just Sicily one day. Who knows, maybe they want to heist the island of Sardo to the west, and Illyria on the Greek peninsula to the east. Maybe they want to come after us in the south, and maybe after the Gauls to the north as well, all so they can expand their empire in all directions. How can this voracious power be stopped or averted? Can I simply think them away?" He rolls his eyes to underscore his dismay with the Romans.

Torilander can't help but smile at hearing it all brought to this simple formula, and he is happy to go into it for Danel: "It's easier to change your own personal life than it is to change the lives of many others around you, especially if you try to stem the tide of time, the negative trends of the Iron Age, or spiritual winter, that keep gaining momentum against the sacredness and intactness of life. My father used to tell me that during this present age it is easier for the collective awareness of this planet to plunge into darkness and lower-self absorption than it is to stay oriented and moving towards the light-filled realms of higher existence. And because it is that way, life is being oppressed, violated, and killed, and empires that don't shun these wicked tactics come out on top, imperialistically trying to overrun individualistic- and tribal-like settlements under the promising illusion of uniting them into larger segments of a monopolistically controlled system."

Danel's eyes almost pop out of his head as he hears the merman talk thus bluntly. "By the way," he introduces himself, "I'm Danel!"

Torn out from his thought process, Torilander takes a moment to respond to Danel's introduction. "Torilander, nice to meet you!"

"Torilander? Cool name! Torilander, where did you learn all this? Or better yet, where does your father, and your race for that matter, know all this from? Higher thinking, politics, all the works of it! You didn't strike me as that learned at first at all!" he has to admit. "Maybe my father is right and we can certainly still learn a lot from you!"

"Many of our race feel very connected to our Higher-Self nature," Torilander explains, "and through that to beings of higher frequency levels of existence, from where we receive much of our collective and individual guidance and inspiration. We feel fortunate that we are mostly able to resist the negative tendencies of the

Iron Age and are able to stay attuned to the realms of blissful existence, which in fact prevailed throughout the Golden Age on Earth. I never put much attention on these facts, nor did I listen too carefully when my parents talked about these matters, but now that I hear about all the wars and various threats the humans inflict upon each other, I wish I had been more attentive when the wise from among my race spoke about these elevating and liberating truths."

"You are lucky to even have these wise ones among your race, who still seem to have a connection to the Divine, for our priests — the people you would think should know best about these higher truths and levels of existence — are themselves very conflicted and ignorant on these essential matters, as far as I'm concerned." Danel gets agitated. "Did you know that whenever there is an enormous threat to our people and city, like there was during the infamous few years of the Syracusan King Agathocles' occupation of our Carthage and several of our surrounding African towns, our priests, who are supposed to be our connection to God Baal Hammon, audaciously suggest and enforce the sacrifice of hundreds of firstborn children. And if this kind of misery ever befalls our city, they even insist on sacrificing the firstborn of our wealthiest citizens! I myself am fortunate to have survived such an outrageously evil raid, but only by a hair's breadth, because in the end everyone agreed it to be wiser to have a future king to count on to defend and protect the city, and to keep securing our commercial interests throughout all our surrounding colonies." He pauses for a moment, trying to digest the heavy emotional charge this memory still has for him.

Torilander looks at him aghast. "You sacrifice your children to your God, and think that's pleasing to him?"

Danel nods his head, disgust written all over his face as well. "Believe it man, it's totally bizarre, I know!"

"No wonder your city feels under such threat and siege coming from all kinds of directions right now," Torilander begins to understand, "be it from the Romans, Greeks, or whatever other political power has their eye on your territory and wealth. Your own people are creating this sad fate for themselves when I hear you describing how they kill their infants and oppress and subdue their lower caste citizens into slavery. If the majority of the population suffers the agony of oppression and threat to their lives every day of their lives, this emotional charge tends to draw more of its kind to eventually create an overwhelming collective reality that corresponds with the oppressing nature of their lives, only that the oppressors now face becoming the oppressed as well, as the sacrificial killers and slaveholders attract foreign invaders into their own territory."

Danel is somewhat shocked to hear this truth, and with a reflective mind, he stares at Torilander as if he has all the answers this Carthaginian prince seems to be in great need of. "Quite a way to look at it," he admits reluctantly, for the expression of this truth sounds a bit scary and ominous to him. Where would it leave him, the future ruler of Carthage, were he to accept this kind of self-responsible thinking? "Our merchants and priests are all pretty set in their ways! They actually support and condition each other in a weird, corruptive way!" he reasons. "I wouldn't know where to start to try to change things around in our society. Who gives up their slaves voluntarily, owned possessions that are forced to give their lives in order to enable the decadent but comfortable lifestyles of the rich elite? Who ever wants to give up slaves whose tedious hard work enable the rich to continue enriching themselves, and why would the priests give up murdering and sacrificing the firstborns in a time of hardship if the majority of the population condones these practices and believes they accomplish the desired outcome, namely to appease God Baal Hammon so he will consider our human plight and come to our help?"

"I agree, it doesn't sound like an easy task!" Torilander looks as if he were pondering the mysteries of life and death, when suddenly he has an idea: "Why don't you create a new temple altogether, heck, even equipped with a new priesthood who listen to what you have to say, and who are ready to abandon their superstitious and self-destructive ways to adopt a new belief system that actually supports the good of the people, and helps to create a more benevolent reality for Carthage altogether?!"

Danel looks perplexed. Did Torilander just inspire him to revolutionize the temple and priesthood of Carthage? Not in his wildest dreams did he ever imagine he could take on the spiritual elite of Carthage and force them to either change their ways or be left outside the royal goodwill. He gulps down his astonishment at hearing such a bold suggestion, but then a strange feeling seems to emerge from the depths of his soul, prompting him to give this idea the credit and attention it deserves. Because if he is truly honest with himself, he often thought of himself as more of a peacemaker than a war strategist, only that he never dared to oppose his father's will and plan for his life, afraid of disappointing the one man he looks up to the most, and also afraid of what consequences it might have on him and his family's lives should he decline the crown. With a frown on his face, Prince Danel tries to ponder his destiny, not knowing how to realize the deepest promptings of his heart without endangering his future. But Torilander is used to thinking outside the human box, and with fervor in his voice, he keeps cheering Danel on to go for his true and highest vocation, for ultimately, love, peace, happiness, and fulfillment will be the only feelings remaining in the end that all souls will live by, the only feelings that are closest to the ultimate truth and that have any higher meaning at all. He tells him that good is stronger and more powerful than evil, and that unless a soul craves suffering and pain, there is no reason to dwell in the place of anguish a moment longer than is necessary, but that the wise man pursues his highest fortune and bliss as soon as he realizes he is separated from it.

"What about the very real threat of the Romans, who have the actual manpower to not only conquer and subdue us but also to wipe us out, should we not be able to conquer them first!" Danel interjects with a feeling of desperation.

"Of course you can decide to continue engaging in the battle of duality and world domination throughout the darkening Iron Age!" Torilander concedes. "Life force and spiritual energies are diminishing on this planet throughout this spiritual winter time; resources of all kinds seem to become more sparse — or hoarded by a few humans that try to control the markets — and humans in general become more desperate and aggressive in regard to what lengths they will go to squeeze a bit of life juice out of whatever they can lay their hands on. Like a parasite-infested body, this world starts to turn against itself, and instead of upholding life, it razes it, competing over territories and over what little resources its inhabitants see left, killing and subduing life in their way until it serves but one controlling, super-powerful master, who intends to feed his perpetually starved, bottomless belly with any life he now has under his control. But if you want to experience a different reality than that of a conquering or conquered people, and if you want to be a model unto those who ache to see a different, more peaceful and loving reality created for themselves, then you step up your game and become the hero you are meant to be, a bold, courageous man who consciously opens himself up to new ways, and who dares to go against the mass tendencies of his time, able to lead the way for those who want a life beyond the sad and limiting realities of the status quo."

Danel has to find his seat again. What adventure into his soul has this evening turned into! He huffs and puffs as quietly as he can, for Torilander's words feel like arrows targeting his heart, arrows of truth that one by one take down the self-imposed walls around his heart and soul, only to have them laid bare in front of a stranger, and a merman on top of that. "Give me a break," he whines, getting almost pale in his face. He buries his face in his hands, trying to figure out what his own inner truth is on the matter.

Torilander sits down beside his rock, mulling over what he just said and wondering how it will affect the Prince in the long run. Does this womanizing, brother-hating man truly have what it takes to become a spiritual leader unto the part of his society that truly wants to create a better future for itself, a future that is not based on hatred and killing, but on peace and harmony within the individual, and without in the environment it lives in?

"How can anyone change the times he lives in?" Danel wonders out loud. "How does anyone escape the negative downward tendencies of the Iron Age? Isn't that beyond the capacity of just one single man?"

"Yes, I think it probably is!" Torilander has to agree. "But you can change your own reality, and the reality of those who find in you a decent and strong leader, one who can help them turn the negative mass tendencies around most everyone on planet Earth suffers under in various shapes and forms, enabling them to live by their own higher truth, and ultimately helping them to reunite with their brothers and sisters of the light, here on Earth, and also in the so-called heavenly realms, or higher frequency realms of greater bliss and harmony."

"I don't know," Danel expresses his trepidations; "I really wouldn't want to leave my father and family, and the whole of Carthage to the woes caused by an imperialistic foray advancing on us. I think I couldn't live with my conscience if I had to see them all lose their freedom or even lives, only because I didn't live up to standard."

Torilander can see how much Danel wrestles with his issues, and how much his royal inheritance seems to burden him. "Even if Carthage would win the supremacy over the world market," he implores the young Prince and heir to the throne, "how would your soul be able to live with itself knowing it was a major motivational force in killing thousands of soldiers, be they on the adversarial side or on Carthage's side? What possible explanation or excuse could your soul have in front of its Creator and God? — Don't you think it's way more gratifying, in an ultimate kind of way, to be the source of inspiration for higher values that support and uplift life, and honor the Divine in every living being? And who knows, if the Divine is strong in you, you could even end up transforming many lives beyond your own city borders, and thus contribute more to the peace of this world than even the best rulers and senators would ever dream of accomplishing. This approach can even be more powerful than war itself, for it prevents calamities and creates more of what makes the human race as a whole happy and fulfilled, whereas war is the negative reaction of a mindset that has deteriorated over time under the wrong kind of assumptions about life, as such mind believes in scarcity of resources and excuses war as a response to the worst it sees and expects from the human race and nature," Torilander reflects. "Many of our sea water races try to primarily live by the motto that "one light-filled soul who ignites the light in another soul is worth more than a soul who tries to analyze or even fight the darkness, for the latter clearly demonstrates his ignorance of the universal law that says that like is drawn unto itself, and he who sends out goodness and love for life receives more of it, whereas he who perpetuates and dwells on problems and sends out any of the many forms of darkness and evil will also receive back what he forced upon others."

Danel is all ears. Never has he heard anyone speak like this before — certainly not his unaware buddies with whom he is used to having comparatively brain-dead interactions. It actually starts to dawn on him why the future prospect of becoming a vital instrument for mass killings has brought him to a state of indifference towards moral values, hurling him into a life of relative decadence and declining feelings of self-worth. It all of a sudden is clear to him that he has already given up on life before it has actually truly begun for him, all because he has seen no way out of his looming predicament and felt rather caught in what everyone considers his predetermined and inescapable destiny. Danel has to wonder about Torilander's role in his awakening, for hardly ever has he felt the Divine presence coming through anyone else as much as he feels it streaming through this underwater being. It's as if just interacting with Torilander opens up higher faculties in Danel's brain, allowing him to see and connect with his inner truths he didn't even know existed. He actually feels so enlivened and good from this talk that he seriously wants to continue probing his true higher destiny, lest he decide to go down the road of war and death. Torilander's words sure sound intriguing to him, and maybe he should allow himself to find out why the thought of turning his attention towards the spiritual renewal of the temple feels so enticing and empowering to him. He smiles at Torilander, for the merman certainly not only knows how to trigger the right kind of questions from his mind but also seems to be wise beyond his years, and gives him answers he didn't even know he was searching for, because — as he can now see — he has been trying hard to distract himself from his inner pains, with superficial pleasures and a false sense of obligation towards his father! And because he wasn't aware of his true inclinations, he had plunged himself into self-destructive behaviors that were all meant to help distract and appease his aching heart.

"Believe it or not," Torilander reacts to the smile, "but there might be some Divine providence here at work. I think some aspect of you has attracted me into your life to have this kind of soulful conversation that might enable you to change your life around for the better, towards peace and true prosperity for those who can grasp it and resonate with it permanently. And then, I think, it is safe to say that you have found your first brother in spirit in me, as odd and strange as it might sound to you."

Danel looks at the merman more intently, the being he at first identified as an odd creature from the bottom of the sea, someone as far from understanding his highest yearnings and inner workings as a lighthouse is able to lead the way for a galley, which — tossed around on the high seas in a storm — is unable to find its way back to the shore. That's how he feels, tossed around by the pressures and threats of life, not knowing how to find home, and how to get to the bottom of his own soul's destiny, until he met this sea merman, his lighthouse in the sea, to point him in the right direction and bring hope and purpose back to his drifting, lax will to live.

"Well, brother," Danel walks up to him, "I have to sleep on it all, and sort through my confusion to see what my ultimate destiny is really supposed to be. I must admit, the idea of running a temple actually thrills me to the core; however, it would have to be a temple that supports and celebrates the miracle of love between a man and a woman, between me and my Livia." He pauses to reflect on this idea, "Maybe this is the way to be with my kitchen-help girl for all times?!" He smiles contently, then asks Torilander whether he needs anything besides sea algae for the night.

"If you could kindly not reveal to anyone except to your siblings yet that I am an intelligent being who actually does speak and communicate well, I would appreciate that!"

"You got it!" Danel lifts his hand to regally wave Torilander good-bye. "I will have a gentle talk with my brother and sister!" His eyes sparkle with newfound joy. "And the glazier will take a look at the crack first thing in the morning."

Torilander lifts his hand as well to bid his new friend good-bye, then sinks back onto his rock to bask in the beautiful feeling of friendship. It's been a long day, but an important and memorable one, for he was able to crumble the wall of hostility around him, and connect with the Divine in the souls of his captor's children.

CHAPTER 14

It is late at night, pitch dark, and everyone is extremely tired. For hours the group has been wandering and straying around the city, trying to sell one or two of their pottery pieces in order to gain the cash needed to pay for a meal and for a one night stay at a cheap inn. The wounded guard is unconscious, with his upper body hanging limply in a bent-over shape, the two carrying guards huffing and puffing to keep up with Hyacinthos, who has been leading the group since they arrived at the city. The market was already over for the day when they finally arrived at the market square, and to find some buyer for the pottery has since been a total fiasco, with people wanting to cheat Hyacinthos by offering prices way below the market price, mostly just a tiny fraction of its value. One person they came across seemed quite interested in the vase Hyacinthos was carrying around, going higher with his offers than anyone else did before him, but Hyacinthos was just not interested in selling this particular piece for any price. This made the rest of the group even more frustrated than they already were, except for Indirali, who imagined that Andronikos' son must have his good reasons for this behavior. But everyone from the group seems extremely tired and exhausted, with the girls not having slept the night before; it feels like everyone has reached their limits of what they can take from this most fatal of days.

Finally Indirali touches Hyacinthos' shoulder, trying to make him aware someone has been following them for a while, and maybe it is time to find out who he is. Hyacinthos slows down his pace, trying to calm down his agitated, frustrated mind as well, while he consciously takes a look at the young man who has been staying about twenty steps behind them while following them for almost an hour now, as Indirali quietly relates to him in a whispering tone of voice.

"Hey, you!" Hyacinthos shouts at the man, trying to connect with him. The man looks around as if seeing whether Hyacinthos possibly could mean another person, but upon seeing no one else besides himself in the area Hyacinthos points his head at, the young man points at himself and looks at Hyacinthos with a questioning face. Hyacinthos nods, yes, he means him, who else! The man starts to walk and come closer. He looks a bit timid as he looks over every person of the group, but then seems to fasten his curious gaze onto Hyacinthos' vase for a moment. Hyacinthos begins to question him as to why he was following the group for about an hour, and who he is anyway, to which the young man responds by pointing at his mouth, indicating silently that he is not able to speak. He begins to, however, gesticulate that he understands the group is hungry and tired and that they should begin to follow him because, as it seems, he knows a place where they can find both, food and a place to rest for the night. Several times, Hyacinthos tries to assure himself he understands the man's gesticulations right, for he certainly does not want to continue leading his exhausted men further astray than he already has. But the young man seems to be very adamant about understanding the need of the situation and about having just the right solution for it, if only the group can trust his guidance. Indirali finally speaks up, encouraging Hyacinthos to give it a try, for they don't exactly know where they are going anyway, and according to her feeling of the man, after having looked him over carefully, he is a good and gentle soul, humbly but finely dressed, and with good-natured eyes that are able to extract her trust in him. This gives the overworked and undernourished Hyacinthos the last kick in the butt, so to say, and with a wave of his hand, his men begin to walk again, only now everyone is following the young man, who has so miraculously shown up out of the dark to take over the reigns of hope, ready to lead them to a place of compassion and nourishment, at least that is what the tired travelers wish for.

The young man is by far more awake, strong, and vital than the group members, who also have to carry the unconscious guard in their midst, and several times Hyacinthos has to call out to him to please slow down and wait for everyone. The young man indeed slows down right away and, with compassion in his face, looks at the wounded guard, who looks like he is having a hard time surviving this late-night ordeal. The walk turns from a half hour into almost an hour, with everyone groping in the dark, hardly able to distinguish the young man's figure in front of them. The group feels at their utmost limit of how far they can still go; several times the young man indicates that it's going to be just a little bit more time and distance until they reach whatever destination he has in mind, but this little bit of time seems to last forever, especially when the group members are as exhausted as they are. Doubts set in, and one guard expresses them to Hyacinthos, wondering whether they are just on a wild goose chase and might end up in a slaughterhouse of some sort. Hyacinthos has a hard time keeping it all together, and more and more often he begins to complain to their mute leader about the endless seeming walk that stretches everyone to their utter limits. The young man keeps smiling at them, gesticulating that they are almost there now and that it would be a pity if they gave up so close to the goal. Hyacinthos moans, then indicates to his men to continue trusting the guide, for he himself has run out of options, and as it looks, they have followed the man to the outskirts of the city and are now far away from any other inn anyway. And so everyone resigns themselves to the situation and trots demurely after their determined guide, too tired to think of any other solution and just hoping they will be rewarded handsomely for their patience, persistence, and enormous effort of the day. In fact, as Hedna and one guard start picturing things and start talking about their food cravings, juicy dishes begin to dance in front of everyone's tired eyes like a hallucinatory water oasis within the dry and barren desert landscapes, and their mouths begin to water under these delicious illusions, giving them the necessary motivation to tough it out on these last stretches of this endless seeming, hellish walk.

Finally the young man stops. In front of them is a shabby looking entrance door within a high and long stone wall that stretches for more than a hundred yards in both directions. The wall is overgrown with ivy and other greenery and looks more than a hundred years old. The group comes to a halt, and everyone wonders what can possibly be behind these walls that makes this young man so sure of himself and prompted him to drag them out here, into the middle of nowhere, it seems, tired and exhausted as they all are, walking for almost one and a half hours of brisk walk, way beyond what anyone thought possible anymore.

The young man takes out a stone from the wall near the entrance, then pulls a string to ring the bell. A soft chime sound begins to fill the air, much to the astonishment of the waiting men and girls who expected a rather sharp bell ring, customary to most homes. A big question mark is written all over everyone's weathered faces, except for that of the young man, who seems well acquainted with the place.

After a short while, approaching steps are heard, and a peephole opens with someone eyeing the young man standing right in front of it. He gesticulates something that seems to convince the person behind the door to open it and let the strangers all in. In the doorframe, an old man with an oil lantern in his hand appears, looking all curious as to who requests entrance at this late hour, but then a smile spreads across his face, and he steps out of the way to let the group members in, one by one. With a feeling of mystery and wonder, the tired nightwalkers follow their young guide into the courtyard. The old man closes the gate again, then walks behind the last one in the group as they follow the young man towards their next destination.

Oil lanterns hanging from poles staked into the ground give off a dim light, which accentuates an apparent garden area and sheds light on the path before them, helping the tired wanderers to find their way in the dark and unknown, for everyone is full of wonder where destiny might have abandoned them. After a few minutes walk, the group is met by three men clad in off-whitish garments, who immediately take it upon themselves to relieve the two exhausted guards from carrying their injured companion, carefully propping up the unconscious guard, to walk off in a slightly different direction. The two guards look at Hyacinthos to see whether it is safe to abandon their companion into the hands of strangers, whereupon Hyacinthos nods, signaling to go have a look where they are bringing him.

The group reaches a more brightly lit, roofed outside sitting area, with a long table and many vacant chairs around it. The old man tells them to please take a seat, as they will serve them some food in a little while, and that after the meal, they will be shown to their nightly quarters. These words sound like balm to the tired souls, and with reignited hope, the four of them sink onto a chair each, glad to drop their belongings to the ground and relax from the day's strain. The old man points towards a well close by, which causes great excitement amongst the visitors, with everyone rushing towards the precious water as if starved from thirst. A bucket is already filled with water, and the wooden ladle is filled and passed around over and over until everyone's burning thirst has been quenched. Then the fun starts, with water being splashed around, faces dunked into the bucket, and the cool, refreshing liquid running down from their dusty bodies to wash off the tiredness and dirt that still reminds of the woes of the day. Finally, they are called to partake of the food that has deliciously been arranged on the table and has the guests astonished as to the generosity of the offering and the quality of the ingredients. A courteous man and a kind-hearted woman welcome the visitors and begin to wait on them, pouring a form of non-alcoholic mead and handing them food from beautifully decorated platters. Hyacinthos, his guard, and the two girls look at each other, for they feel self-conscious to dig into the food before their fellow travelers have come back to join them. And so they sit there for a while, sheepishly pulling out little bits and pieces to slowly but heartily nibble on them until, thank God, the guards appear from the dark to announce joyfully that their buddy is being well taken care of by someone who seems to understand the healing arts. Upon seeing the food, they rejoice even more, which is the welcomed signal for everyone to fall upon the food and not stop eating until their starved bellies are full and their souls satisfied. Halfway through their meal, the young man who has been guiding them to this travelers' paradise situated himself onto the windowsill of a close-by house and began playing the lyre as if his heart was singing hymns to the Gods of eternal friendship, love, and harmony. The travelers begin to feel as if almost at home, deeply reconciled to their testing situation, and grateful they were brought to this hospitable place. Because for whatever reason, the group feels deeply welcomed and wonderfully raised in their spirits; uncanny warmth seems to envelop the whole place, and everyone begins to trust in the goodness of life again.

The nightly gathering slowly comes to a harmonious end, with the old man showing the group to their resting places after everyone had their last plunge in the water. They enter a big barn, which inside is segmented by huge haystacks into several partitions, and in each of these partitions two simple beds made out of wood and straw are placed, offering a bit of privacy to whoever has the fortune to spend the night in this cozy feeling place. Indirali and Hedna sure are glad to have this privacy, for their chest wraps have long begun to hurt, and the wigs feel itchy from all the dust and heat of the day. For even though Indirali trusts the son of Andronikos in regard to her feminine charms, it has become evident to her on many occasions now that traveling as a young man is way less challenging and controversial with regard to the impetuous and sometimes imposing male energies that seem to own the territories of the wild and undiscovered. And so, with a big sigh of relief, the girls sink into their beds, ready to let the realms of the Divine take over, to refresh and recuperate, and to recharge the depleted reservoirs of their bodies and souls.

CHAPTER 15

Indirali sits across from Loriolan, surrounded by the ocean and floating on clouds, breathing in the beauty of his being and exhaling her love for him that knows no bounds, and knows no sorrows. He looks into her eyes, and the cosmos begins to open up, with a multitude of stars tumbling from the skies to shower them with the brilliance of their light, igniting the spark of their love to burst into the fireworks of ecstatic exuberance, their passion entangling and meshing their essences in an endless dance and whirl of unbounded joys and bliss. Floating in the protecting arms of her eternal lover, Indirali begins to heal the most subtle pains of her heart, their eternal love welling from their unified heart center to continuously envelop and energize their combined auras and extended bodies. Time stands still, and there is nothing but indescribable peace and harmony, their soul essences matching on all levels and in all aspects perfectly with one another's, as if one is the other half of the self, and none can live without the other, for it would feel as if the sky could not kiss the ocean, and the inhale could not become the exhale, and vice versa. Caught in this spiral of infinite bliss and ecstasy, Indirali's eyes begin to moisten with feelings of overwhelming energies, with her hoping and wanting this moment to last forever, for nothing comes close to it, and nothing will ever be able to fulfill her in quite the same way as Loriolan's love and attention on her does!

But then the situation assumes a more worldly feel, with them sitting across from each other in a luscious garden, having breakfast within a beautiful and artfully built gazebo, enjoying the pleasures of refined nourishment and alluring scents, the scent of jasmine tea, and the scent of … yummm!

"Mistress! My dear Mistress," Indirali is woken by her servant, "smell these yummy honey baklavas …" She is holding the pastries under Indirali's nose to give her a good whiff of the delicacy.

Indirali has a hard time deciding what smells better, the tea or the pastries.

She would actually like to keep sipping the tea with Loriolan, but her maid just woke her with the temptingly sweet smell of delicious baklava, one of her other secret predilections, and whether she wants it or not, Loriolan begins to fade from her sight, her heart longing for him and crying out his name, for she misses him so terribly much already. But then the situation catches up with her, and with a jolt, she sits up to look around their part of the barn, remembering in one stroke the whole long and arduous journey they have been on, and are still bent on finishing, in order for her to ultimately be with the man of her dreams.

"Mistress, everyone is waiting for us to join them at the breakfast table!" Hedna exclaims excitedly. "These people are super friendly, and our men have been making new friends all morning!" She smiles broadly, in total contrast to the condition she was in yesterday.

"Well, then I better get ready!" Indirali confirms. "I myself can't wait to meet these wondrously hospitable people!" And with that, Indirali jumps to her feet, gets dressed, and joins Hedna in storming out into the daylight to discover more of the extraordinary friendliness they have encountered so far already.

"Hey, look at this!" Kleitos, one of Hyacinthos' guards, shouts at Indirali and Hedna upon seeing them approaching. "This guy is unbelievable!"

"Yeah!" Zotikos, another one of Hyacinthos' men, joins in, pointing at a man clad in a short white outfit, who is standing peacefully on one spot, masterfully avoiding any attacks hurled at him by Kleitos' foot or arm, as if nothing can disturb his equilibrium, and nothing can ever touch him if he doesn't want it to.

"And that's not all!" Zotikos informs. "Look what he is going to do in a moment! … Look!" And with that he joins in the attacks, increasing the speed and amount of the attacking movements, but the white-clad man continues to skillfully evade the attacks, increasing and adjusting his evasive moves according to the impacts coming at him. Getting more and more ambitious and frustrated with their futile attacks, Kleitos and Zotikos finally try throwing themselves full force onto the evading man. But to their amazement, the girls see the attacked man disappear from their sight and turn up at a completely different spot again, as if by magic! Indirali and Hedna shake their heads, for they think they must have experienced a blackout of some sort, or maybe imagined the man showed up in a different place. It was only about two to three yards that the man had changed positions, but it nevertheless was out of the ordinary!

"How …" Hedna stares at the man, dumbfounded as she grapples with what just happened right in front of her eyes.

"Can you please do it again?" Indirali wishes, for she intends to look more closely this time. The men agree, and again, the attacked man changes position by disappearing from the first one completely out of sight and reappearing in the new place, but this time it's about five yards from his first position. Now the girls are convinced that some higher force must be in the game, for no average mortal person can react like this when threatened by violent force.

The men all have a good laugh, and the white-clad man puts his hands on Kleitos' and Zotikos' shoulders, as if to appease their non-understanding selves, who still have a hard time believing what they have been experiencing and trying to come to grips with throughout the morning.

"We still could be in the possession of our wagon and goods if we could have had this guy with us out there on the dirt road!" Zotikos wishes, looking all-regretful, but smiling.

"Everything happens for a reason, my friend," the peaceful warrior reminds him. "We can wish for the best, and let the universe take care of the rest, knowing it will always serve us the best possible outcome for as long as we stay aligned with our Higher Selves!"

Zotikos and Kleitos look at the man as if trying to make sense of his well-meaning remark, but it is Indirali who engages him in a conversation that draws the higher wisdom from him that only few are able to tap into, appreciate, and respond to in a manner that demonstrates a similar level of maturity of soul as the man obviously possesses. Indirali grew up enjoying a very profound, academically and spiritually challenging, holistic education that endowed her with a good sense of higher realities and also with an insatiable hunger for true spiritual knowledge, the kind that helps improve life and empower the individual. Slowly walking towards the dining area, the two of them walk behind the others, exchanging wisdom of the higher spheres, with Indirali quickly being filled in on topics of the relativity of time, and of space curvature, all able to be controlled and manipulated by a strong will, anchored in highest truth and infinite power.

"Photios! You like bursting people's minds, don't you!" A brightly smiling, attractive woman shouts from across the lawn at the man at Indirali's side. "Even on their first day with us you like to dazzle their senses with your hyperspace moves, right?"

Photios smiles back, agreeing with this friendly assessment wholeheartedly and confessing that it provides him much pleasure to see people yanked out of their limited thinking and understanding every time it happens.

Hyacinthos is already sitting at the table with one of his men, enjoying a lively conversation with a beautiful lady who seems to capture the most part of his attention. The dining area is full of people, most of them dressed in ivory garments that express a refined and sophisticated elegance and grace. But there are seats for everyone, and so all the last arriving group members find their appointed chairs, happy to be surrounded by kind-hearted hosts who seem to consider their guests as family already.

And then the atmosphere changes, the lively chatter becomes silent, and a statuesque beauty appears from around the corner, stepping through the rose-entwined, arched gateway to undulate her way towards the sitting area, the air around her vibrating with subtle energy and bliss, as if a Goddess just descended from the heavens to grace her followers in the gardens of her extended aura.

Mouths are gaping and minds are spinning as the group members keep their eyes fixated on the approaching woman, who seems to have everyone mesmerized by her beautiful allurement, bestowing even more bliss on everyone's soul than they have already experienced in this wondrously elevating place.

"Honored guests!" a voice from the table announces. "Meet our group's leader, and source of infinite wisdom and Divine inspiration, Positrona, the direct lineage spiritual heir of our revered forefather and founder Pythagoras!"

All clap, and so do the travelers, acknowledging the extraordinary hospitality and generosity of a group evidently headed by an esteemed, otherworldly, infinitely refined, and powerful leader like her, approaching from her inner worlds to connect with everyone in the outer world, to help bridge the gap between higher and lower levels of existence, and between the light and the darkness. At least these are the thoughts and feelings Indirali can't help but have running through her mind, as she feels humbled in this woman's presence, who, with the utmost simplicity of being, greets the newcomers with a splendid smile, then takes the seat at the head of the table. She looks everyone into their eyes, one after another, presenting them with her dazzling smile, then takes the hands of the two persons next to her, which prompts everyone else to do the same, connecting the people around the table to form a circle of white brother- and sisterhood.

"Let us align ourselves with the Gods of our Ancestors," she begins to attune, her voice vibrating with life and love that has everyone entrained in a Divine resonance field, "with God Kronos and Goddess Gaia, and with the ultimate Source of Life Itself. Let us also call on those Gods and Goddesses of our present times who are still in tune with the Gods and Goddesses that reigned throughout the Golden Age, Divine Beings who still embody their unconditionally loving essence and infinite wisdom, as our beloved Goddess Aphrodite does. Let us thank them for uplifting us with their presence, instilling hope and peace into our hearts, and nourishing us with their unconditional love and limitless mercy to help us connect with the radiant Divine Superbeing within us that we all are."

"In the Divine we trust! Thank you!" everyone agrees quietly and gently, then begins to share the meal with one another. Indirali feels almost as if in a trance, with Positrona's words still resonating in her awareness like a beautiful poem from a higher world, reminding of the glory and bliss of the light-suffused higher dimensions of existence. Her mind would like to follow this stream of highest awareness, allowing her to be carried away and into the innermost, deepest secrets of life. As if outside of her body and looking down at the peaceful scene of eating breakfast with a group of extraordinarily loving people, she sees herself partaking of the delicious, natural food and enjoying every taste of it, as if imbibing Divine ambrosia and nectar, filled to overflowing with the bliss-inducing vibrations of highest ecstasy. The group eats their food quietly and reverently, which turns out to be a blessing for Indirali, for she hovers above the scene and would not have been able to converse with anyone from her physical body and awareness right now — that's how out of her body and above and beyond her usual self she feels.

At some point, however, one of Hyacinthos' guards looks the table over for some meat dish, only to be quietly advised by one of Positrona's people that animal flesh is not ever on their menu, for it contradicts their non-violent stance towards all sentient life. Euthymios, the guard, gazes at the man as if having a hard time understanding his point of view, then looks at his buddies, who all seem to have quietly decided to not raise this issue any further but to be grateful for whatever good food is on the table right this instant. Eyes focused on their food, they continue to bite heartily into it, which makes Euthymios give in and succumb to the group consensus. Witnessing this short interlude of lower, base instincts that aims at devouring animals causes Indirali to slip back into her body, back into the world of lower selves and back to dealing with her issues that still separate her from the ideal higher-worldly life she envisions and hopes to share with Loriolan as soon as possible.

And soon most everyone finishes their meal, pleasurably wiping their mouths with a cloth napkin and starting to put their dishes away and onto a wooden, wheeled service cart standing close by. Two men begin to roll the cart away, ready to take care of the dirty dishes, while others are still enjoying a sip of tea, relaxing into a mood for conversation, ready to see what Positrona has in mind in regard to the visitors.

"A nice urn you carry around with you!" Positrona addresses Hyacinthos, who accidentally brought his piece of pottery with him to the table, positioning it right between his legs. Hyacinthos can't help but blush a bit, for it dawns on him that it must come across as awkward to the others to see the urn with him at all times.

"Are you aware of its symbols? Do you know what they mean?" she inquires.

"My father entrusted this urn to me, making me promise to deliver it safely into the hands of its future owner, the man who ordered this urn from my father in the first place!" Hyacinthos tries to justify his odd seeming behavior, because the other few pieces the group was able to secure from the heist are all neatly and safely stacked in the barn.

Positrona nods understandingly, and it feels to Indirali as if the universe is in accordance with Hyacinthos' reasoning.

"I can't say that I have looked at its symbols closely," Hyacinthos admits. "I just want to make sure to follow my father's wishes."

"I understand!" Positrona comforts him. "May we all have a closer look at it now? Would you like to know what wonderful vessel and message you are safeguarding for your customer?"

"Sure!" Hyacinthos lifts the urn onto the table, and everyone emits a gentle exclamation of surprise and wonder.

A woman looks at Positrona, who nods her agreement, which prompts the woman to begin explaining the depicted scene on the urn, the higher purpose of it all, and the deeper meaning of the symbols woven into the scene in an almost inconspicuous way. Much to Hyacinthos' surprise and to the surprise of everyone else from his group, the scene depicted on the lower half of the urn shows the future owner living in his present life, playing a pandouris, surrounded by other instruments he creates from wood and seemingly sells in his store. The upper half of the urn, on the other hand, depicts his soul living in the beyond, after his death, playing his beloved instrument amongst the angels and Gods, with especially one angel gifting him with her loving attention as she smilingly accompanies his pandouris with the playing of her lyre. They both seem to be much in love, considering the loving gaze they hold between each other. Positrona furthermore points out that the scene on the lower half of the urn is shone on by the moon's light, whereas the upper half scene enjoys the brilliant light rays of the sun.

Hyacinthos and his group members look at the urn carefully to follow the woman's explanations on the basis of the drawings Andronikos' artist had decorated the urn with according to the instructions he received from the customer. Hyacinthos realizes that he always liked looking at the urn, but until this very moment he didn't know why exactly, and how comprehensive and stunning the meaning of the pictures actually are.

"It looks like your customer is an accomplished musician and seems to share a deep, loving bond with one of the angels. Notice the fine line surrounding and connecting the moon and the sun in an eight-like fashion," Positrona takes up the thread, "the infinity sign that connects and unites all opposite and polar values into one unified expression of breath-like movement?!"

Hyacinthos and Indirali try to discern the fine line, and yes, they see it now very clearly! They look at Positrona as if to receive further illumination on the topic.

"And take a look at the musician's heart, both on Earth and in Heaven!" she invites.

"The Flower of Life!" Indirali exclaims joyfully, for she recognizes the symbol one of her tutors once drew for her, saying an old priest once mentioned it to him as being an important spiritual symbol that has its place in most spiritual belief systems of the ancient temples. "What exactly does it mean?" she inquires.

"It is a sacred geometrical figure, a visible manifestation of the underlying order of the invisible, absolute life force of the Divine Source, a symbol in which the macrocosm reflects itself perfectly in the microcosm, a pure and unadulterated passageway for life force to move through and manifest itself into and onto innumerable dimensions of our known universes, the infinitely open light vortex that interconnects and transcends all living systems, a hexagon-based, symmetrical flower-like pattern whose expression reaches from the creation of our worlds to the recreation of the worlds in the next cycles, connecting life as it weaves through all sentient beings, and through all dimensional worlds of existence that our creator force eternally thinks into manifestation, the Akashic Record of all things known and unknown, and the explanation for all of life's deepest mysteries and axiomatic laws of life, nature, and the universe."

Indirali looks at her with open eyes. She wants to understand deeply, but she hungers for more information, more descriptive information that is. How does this universal principle convert into practical reality, and why is the musician on the urn wearing the symbol on his heart?

As if hearing her posing the questions out loud, Positrona continues to elaborate with serene poise: "The Flower of Life is a geometrical figure composed of seven or more evenly spaced, overlapping circles that form a flower-like pattern. It contains many different configurations, all highly symbolic and universally meaningful in themselves. Within its borders, and like a hologram, many deep mysteries of life are contained for the awakened mind to become conscious of and see the universe, the macrocosm, as well as the individual soul, the microcosm, reflected and explained. To study its scope and infinite meaning is like studying the mind of the creator force; it is a profound, transformational experience that leads you from one deep understanding of the intricacies of life to the next, thus compounding the wisdom of all ages and all dimensional locales into one wonderfully perfect symbol of crystalline beauty and transcendental value." Positrona pauses to allow time for integration. The young man who brought the group here, and who played the lyre last night for everyone's soul nourishment, stands demurely a few steps from the table, holding the lyre in his hand. Positrona nods at him, and he takes a seat on a wooden stump and begins to play his instrument gently as if to support Positrona's words of wisdom with a background of refined tunes and atmospheric sounds. The air fills with subtle vibrations, and the revered leader resumes her discourse on the meaning of the symbols displayed on the urn.

"Geometrically, we find within the Flower of Life not only Metatron's Cube, composed of thirteen equal circles with lines from the center of each circle extending out to the other twelve circles, but also the five so-called Platonic Solids, regular convex polyhedrons with each possessing the same amount of congruent faces meeting at each vertex. Some learned minds attributed the five elements of earth, water, air, fire, and ether to these Platonic Solids, studying their properties, angles, and symmetries to tap into life's origin and explain its interconnectedness, and how to achieve balance and transcendence. What really is of interest is that the focus and study on the Flower of Life awakens the mind to higher realities and thus grants it access to higher dimensions of existence. The Flower of Life thus represents a gateway to our multidimensional cosmos, allowing the mind to transcend dualistic and transient states of existence. Within the Flower of Life, we find the Seed of Life, as well as the Tree of Life, all components that serve different spiritual directions to explain the process of Creation in its simplicity and complexity, and when we consider that each basic component of the Seed of Life consists of a sacred geometrical shape called a spherical, or three-dimensional octahedron, then we begin to understand how dimensions are born, lifting us beyond our limited minds and understandings, for each spherically rotating component adds to the unfolding rippling effect of the dynamic, electromagnetic life force in manifestation, accounting for the innumerable appearances, shapes, and forms of the relative worlds our limited senses can only perceive a tiny fraction of."

Hyacinthos' guards become increasingly restless, for the wisdom has its purifying effect on their minds, and they don't know how to deal with it other than wanting to escape from the table and tend to more mind-boggling phenomena along the lines of their expertise and passion: physical training for warfare and self-defense! But for some reason, Hyacinthos is not inclined to dismiss his gang from the table; he sees it as a privilege to share the table with one of the greatest teachers he has ever encountered, and he is not going to destroy the atmosphere by insulting his hostess with the dismissal of his lower-self-oriented men. And so the guards have to swallow their impatience and pride, along with their triggered impurities, and give it another try with assimilating knowledge that seems to have the power to blow their minds.

"Contemplating this most fascinating enigma of all times," Photios explains, telepathically having received the inspiration from Positrona, in order to try easing the guards' minds and help them to open up to her wisdom, "has opened the gateways of understanding for many of us, helping us to integrate the universal laws that, among others, govern the phenomena of time, space, and gravity, and whose integration has empowered us to the extent that we are able to express the supernatural moves you experienced earlier!"

This statement stuns the guards, for here they have something to relate to. With demure faces, they continue to listen, hoping to stumble across a pearl of wisdom that could help them understand and maybe even apply this coveted supernatural craft in their own lives.

"One basic component of the Flower of Life is the so-called Vesica Piscis," Positrona continues, "a sacred geometrical figure consisting of two intersecting circles of the same diameter with the center of each circle being on the circumference of the opposite circle. This simple symbol portrays the powerful first step of the creator's consciousness welling up within the first circle and sphere, and then spilling into manifest creation within the second circle and sphere, deeply intersected, in perfect balance, the mind of the creator hovers over the oceans of his creation, when born from this first dualism, the element of light bursts into existence, electromagnetism begins to enliven and animate the dust of the universes, giving rise to wondrous living phenomena of which our sentient humanity is a tiny part." Positrona looks deep into Indirali's eyes, and all the conveyed wisdom starts to make sense in a very profound, experiential, and practical way, as if an enormous awareness just began to shed its illuminating light through her own mind, allowing her to vibrate and resonate with the highest dimensions of understanding that lie beyond the boundaries of the impure mind, a state of being and existence that knows no boundaries and knows no ignorance.

"When you look closely," Positrona illumines and closes the circle of understanding for those who were able to follow, "the Vesica Piscis symbol portrays the duality of the sun and moon when one of the circles comes to the foreground, overshadowing the area of intersection of the second circle, and thus causing the second circle to look like the moon sickle. The move of one circle to the foreground, and respectively, the other circle to the background, is synonymous with the interdimensional movement of the life force through the light vortexes of sacred geometrical Divine symmetry and orderliness, which, however, gets overshadowed or broken through the introduction of time and space and karma, as these three factors cause spherical rotations and varying facets of the unified essence, or absolute consciousness, splitting it into different aspects and hues of its original purity and power, and thus creating a differential within the unified consciousness of the Divine, one that creates the multitude of appearances and infinite possibilities of Creation. Thus, it occurs that living systems of varying life-force degrees are created, ones that possess greater life force, and ones that possess less of it. Within our solar system, the more energy-rich object is the sun, which exists on a higher vibrational level of existence than the moon, both cosmic bodies representing the duality of life that can be found in any and all particles of life and existence." She pauses and looks at Hyacinthos, "To have the sun and moon connected with the fine line of the infinity sign, the number eight, is a demonstration of high awareness of your buyer, for he knows that throughout infinity, dualism loses its limiting and debasing stronghold over the human soul, gradually — over the course of many higher dimensional stages — turning the soul into the immortal soul it is predestined to be, the only kind of soul form that allows infinite bliss and absolute fulfillment to reign supreme in its awareness, being, and world. Applying duality, the number eight, visually equal to the infinity sign, can be ongoingly divided by 'duo' or two, first into four, then into two, then into one, with one being the nondivisible number of the Absolute, the unified field of the Divine Source of Life. The two circles of the number eight extend themselves into the opposite circle, forming the infinite, self-reflecting sine wave of the unity of life in all its endless dualistic manifestations."

Everyone of Hyacinthos' group, Indirali included, looks at Positrona as if she lost them a while ago. This marks the signal for the spiritual teacher to slow down and wrap it all up into a nice, presentable package of understandable knowledge. "What I mean to say is: Your buyer is a smart man, and I wouldn't be surprised if he is a member of our Pythagorean cult, for not only will the paintings on his urn remind him of the infinity of life in the midst of this highly dualistic world of ours, but his heart is set on exploring and growing into the mysteries of life; thus he is becoming the immortal he knows he ultimately is, and so the urn will never be the resting place for his body's ashes, but rather the glorious reminder that not only is his mind infinite and immortal but also his body is as well. He plays his beautiful music and instrument as an expression of his higher longings and for the delight of his listeners, seeing in them the Divine Angels that they truly and ultimately are, and thus his music becomes the means to connect with the higher realities, with the heavens he so adores!" She smiles a sunshiny smile: "As above, so below, and as below, so above, for the circle of the sun and the circle of the moon are ultimately one and the same, if you can manage to behold them with the eyes of the Divine Creator! Perfect, isn't it?"

Indirali claps her hands, for this discourse moved her to the core of her being, because transcending the limitations and challenges of dualism is exactly what she intends to do in order to unite with her eternal beloved, Loriolan. On top of that, Positrona's voice sounds like an angel's voice to her, even more elevating when floating on the celestial music the young musician is playing for her accompaniment. But immediately she becomes aware of her impetuous clapping, only to shrug off her self-consciousness, and continues to clap anyway, for never has she heard anyone speak the truth of higher concepts in such a reasonable, lofty-minded fashion as this beautiful woman just did. Indirali's eyes are filled with a longing to do exactly what Positrona has been describing about Andronikos' customer, and she would like nothing more than to listen to more of the wise teacher's words and hopefully be given the chance to draw on more of her infinite seeming wisdom for her own journey's benefit.

Hyacinthos has joined in the clapping, feeling all humbled by Positrona's wisdom and presence. His heart feels overwhelmed by her nourishing radiance, and somewhat clumsily, he thanks her for her illuminating speech. Deep within, however, his heart and soul are adjusting to a new reality he didn't even know he was desperately searching for, and for quite some time now too.

"Your father will understand!" Positrona reads his mind. "He won't keep you from your dharma and vocation once you are convinced of it yourself."

Hyacinthos looks around nervously. Positrona's words aim right at his heart, and he is not sure he wants it all disclosed in front of everyone around the table. His guards look at him, wondering what this hint is all about.

Positrona communicates telepathically to one of her men, who immediately stands up and asks Hyacinthos whether it would be okay if his guards would tend to the cleaning up of the barn, exchanging the straw of the beds, and such. Hyacinthos looks at him, relieved, agreeing to it gladly, for speaking any further on matters of the heart in front of his men doesn't feel comfortable anymore. And so the three guards leave, joking with one another to relieve their pent-up stresses, and poking each other in the sides, for they are glad they at least have each other in this way-too-refined environment they find themselves in.

"My people are used to being very discreet," Positrona explains. "All of them were or still are under an oath of silence for the first five years of their novitiate, like Hesiod over there right now is!" She points her head in the direction of the young man who is still playing the lyre in the most beautiful way. "He actually brought you here because he saw the symbols on the urn, convincing him that you all must have some connection to our spiritual lineage, as remote or involved as it might be."

Indirali and Hyacinthos look at each other, wondering whether the other might have this spiritual connection without one knowing about the other. They gaze at each other cluelessly, then turn their heads back to Positrona.

"By the way," Positrona speaks up, "why don't you and your maid come up to me, please!" She addresses Indirali and Hedna, who react surprised at her request, and a bit nervous, for obviously she knows that Hedna is Indirali's female servant. But reverently, the two of them approach the leader, wondering what's in store for them.

Positrona touches the wrap underneath the man's shirt that constricts Indirali's chest, and begins to unravel it slowly, making sure nothing shows to any observer. Then she takes off the man's wig to let Indirali's long beautiful hair fall as it wants. "Here, that's better!" she exclaims joyfully. "You are among friends who accept you as the beautiful girl that you are! No hiding games necessary!" Then she turns to Hedna to perform the same on her, surprising everyone at the table, including Hyacinthos, with the sight of two beautiful ladies they didn't even know existed amongst them.

"In this place, we try to live by the transcendent values as much as possible," Positrona explains. "We consider ourselves androgynous beings who chose to incarnate into either a female or male body, depending on the vocation we want to embody in this particular life, and none of us therefore considers it appropriate to diminish or exalt, disadvantage or prefer, and especially to violate or indulge any specific gender representative we encounter and engage with. For you to feel the need to dress up as a man just so you can feel safe in the streets is a sign of the spiritual winter season or Iron Age we live in, a spiritual-darkness-oriented season throughout which life degenerates in all its many aspects and human vehicles. If a man cannot control his sexual and rapist urges anymore, then the woman becomes subdued to be his slave, an object he can live out his lower-self urges on without minding the long-term consequences of his ultimately self-punishing actions. Because sooner or later, he returns as the victim of a similar crime to learn the lesson he created for himself, and to atone for his violations against the human nature!" And with that, Positrona invites the girls to take a seat again, if they so please.

Indirali and Hedna return to their seats, with Positrona's people, joined by Hyacinthos, clapping and cheering the girls on, as if wanting to help them relax into the wonderful bodies the Angels of Reincarnation have prepared for their exquisite lives and vocations. The girls smile, feeling wonderfully relieved and touched to tears, noticing what a burden the male disguise has actually begun to feel like to them. And so, with a refreshed sense of who they are and where they are going, they sit in their chairs, backs all straight and their minds all clear and receptive for more of Positrona's wonderful knowledge.

"Sorry for the interruption," she apologizes to Hyacinthos. "What I meant to say is that you will most likely keep creating situations that are supposed to prove your point to your father until both of you either get it and act accordingly or you perish from the undealt issues, like a stomach that can't digest a too heavy meal anymore without creating toxic and harmful side effects for the body."

Hyacinthos looks shocked. "What do you mean?"

"The situation you ran into on the road," Positrona enlightens him, "the so-perceived attack on your possessions and guard ..."

"So-perceived?!" Hyacinthos is confused.

"Any situation can be explained from several different angles, depending on the viewpoint of the observer. Let's say we look at it from the viewpoint of your Higher Self, the one who knew this attack would happen the way it did, arranging it in exactly such a way as to reflect back to you the message your lower self needs to hear right now in order to make the right decision for your next life phase."

Hyacinthos looks shocked when hearing his Higher Self might have arranged a situation that almost cost one of his guards his life. What possible importance might such message have for him anyway, he wonders. He knows he secretly covets change in his life, for the way his father has been earning his living is not fulfilling to him at all. But he certainly doesn't want his inner quest to start jeopardizing other people's lives. And so he continues to listen to what Positrona might have to say to this most vulnerable, but essential, point of his life.

"Did it occur to you that you were robbed by an old man who lost his son because he tried to live according to his spiritual and peaceful principles?"

Hyacinthos has a moment of heightened awareness in which it dawns on him that she is right; the situation has some resemblance to his, for he also wants to stray from the path his father has planned out for him, only instead of going to war, his father wants him to overtake the business one day. But Hyacinthos feels drawn in another direction; his ambitions are more spiritual. And so he nods heartily, signaling she is on the right track with him.

"Well, I hope you won't choose to create another situation that has you die in it rather than finally facing your father and letting him know how you truly feel about your life's mission."

Hyacinthos gulps, for all of a sudden he feels like choking. To confront his father on his true ambitions is like facing his worst nightmare, for he loves his father very dearly, and to hurt him would feel like a knife's blade in his own heart. And so he glances downward, trying to keep his tears from forming.

"What Anatolios didn't tell either one of you is the fact that he urged his son very strongly to take up the sword and follow his own warrior example,"

Positrona lets her listeners in on the actual happenings. "Anatolios left for war and was gone for many years, not only leaving his wife and young children to fend for themselves, but also leaving feelings of resentment and condemnation that he harbored against his son, for he could not for the life of him wrap his head around the fact that his son would embarrass him with his — what he considered back then — immature and childish talk and behavior. It was only when he came back, beaten from the last battles and finding his son half-dead and locked up in a despicable dungeon, that he came to his senses, realizing his son had been right about his peaceful ambitions all along and it would have been wiser to have listened to him while there was still time to either move to another place as a family and begin a new life, or find some other solution that would have allowed the family to stay together and fend for their lives as one unified team. Instead, he had to witness his son dying in his arms, a sad and tragic event he now blames himself for, for had he listened to his son, he might still be alive, able to teach his broken father a thing or two. You definitely encountered an old man who has a lot of remorse and regrets to contend with, and you don't want to put your own father in the same position and have him experience a similar fate one day, not if you can help it!" She pauses to allow Hyacinthos to react.

Hyacinthos is mute, and again has to cast his eyes down to assimilate the horrifying, but true message he just heard. Hedna looks lost, for she didn't meet Anatolios nor heard his story. And so Positrona helps her to be at ease with a smile: "You, my angel, did good work on yourself, healing your subtle bodies that had gotten out of alignment with your Higher Self due to the stress of your journey. Without taking this much-needed nap, you might not have made it here."

By now Hyacinthos, Indirali, and Hedna are quite startled at Positrona's uncanny ability to see into their past. And as if reading their minds, one of Positrona's women speaks up, explaining that Positrona indeed is capable of seeing into any person's past, extended present, and even into its future, if the Divine Spirit prompts her to, according to the needs of a particular situation. Astonishment still showing on their faces, the three of them turn their eyes back on Positrona to allow her to continue weaving her magic with everyone.

Positrona, however, waits for another moment, for she sees thoughts forming in Hyacinthos' mind. Finally, he exclaims: "I just don't know any temple in Heraclea anymore that I want to be involved in. They all seem compromised in their spiritual purity and integrity nowadays, succumbing to Roman religious imposition and to the mostly selfish interests of their financial supporters. True spirituality and brotherhood is almost an unknown, and many in our congregations feel terribly lost and have begun to succumb to the immoral tendencies exemplified and proclaimed by our temple elites." His eyes glow with a spark of anger.

Positrona nods, and again, Indirali feels the universe is nodding to Hyacinthos' righteous discontentment. "This is happening all over our planet in this day and age: the once living-word teachings of the Divine Source are disappearing from the temples, and with that, the state of individual and collective beingness is also dropping and diminishing as a result of it. Consciousness is becoming limited when the veils of maya, illusion, fall on mankind during the spiritual winter, thus eclipsing the truth of the unity of life from most people's minds and hearts. It certainly is not a favorable nor beautiful time to experience, but here and there you can still find pockets of bliss, where true spiritual seekers flock together to support each other in their higher and refined aspirations, willing to be models of idealism and Divine virtues, and willing to face, transcend, and transform their lower-self issues to continue to live in their Higher Selves, the way we used to be able to do so easily and loftily throughout the Golden Ages." Positrona stops and, looking around the table, indicates to her people that it is time to resume the curriculum and chores of the day. Everyone agrees, bids the guests a preliminary farewell, then leaves the table to each find their activity for the morning. According to Positrona's inner promptings, only two people stay behind: the lovely lady Hyacinthos had such pleasant conversations with earlier, and a middle-aged man, who looks very sympathetic, as well as strong and gentle all at the same time.

Positrona introduces the woman and the man by their names, telling the guests that her name is Xenia, and his is Sappheiros. Everyone nods their mutual acknowledgment, whereupon Positrona suggests they all take a walk with her through the gardens, which everyone of the small remaining group accepts with pleasure. They begin to stroll along the path, always a reverent step beside or behind Positrona, feeling very relaxed and enamored with her natural grace and ease with which she continues to enchant her guests. Hesiod follows in good distance, lending his celestial music to the sweetness and harmony of the morning stroll.

CHAPTER 16

"Our founding father, Pythagoras, experienced and was aware of the same decline in human spirit and circumstances that we just talked about," Positrona continues her illumining discourse. "He was born on the Greek island of Samos about three hundred years ago, but when he returned after many years from studying abroad in the Egyptian and Babylonian mystery schools, he had to learn that a tyrant had seized power on his beloved island, and because Pythagoras' accumulated wisdom was far superior to the relatively limited knowledge of most of the island's illiterate thinkers, he was mercilessly shunned and ridiculed, which ultimately forced him to leave the oppressive situation behind if he wanted to continue to think independently and be a free man anymore. Thus, he came to Magna Graecia, where he settled in the city of Croton, became politically active there, and founded his spiritually groundbreaking enlightenment school. Anchored in highest truth, Pythagoras was a highly eloquent, convincing speaker, who won much admiration and support from among the citizens of Croton and beyond. His inner circle school exercised the enlightening attitudes and behaviors that many of us followers throughout time are fortunate enough to have inherited from his wealth of wisdom and teachings, and are therefore still practicing them for our own benefit. We live, however, within the transient worlds; change and illusion are an intricate part of our realities, and because of that, our highs are always followed by a low, and vice versa. Every Golden Age has an Iron Age in tow, and every Iron Age eventually gives way to the Golden Age again. It is by studying the highest principles of life, and striding through the spiritual gateways of the Flower of Life that we break through the limiting cycles, and enter those longed-for eternal realms our enlightened ancestors knew and talked about."

She stops to caress and take an intoxicating whiff of a beautiful, peach-colored rose that pokes its head into the path. Everyone stops to become aware of the beauty all around them. Indirali hasn't had time to explore the beautiful sights of her new environment yet since she was the last one to wake up and had to rush to the breakfast table. But now she looks around and is completely overwhelmed and stunned by the lushness of flowers, vegetables, fruit trees, and flower bushes, and with the all-around idyllic sites that surround them. There are fountains, flowerpots on short columns, and statues of Gods and Goddesses, as well as of fairies, elves, and gnomes. Birds are singing and are well taken care of by birdbaths and wooden birdhouses filled with delicacies the feathered friends love to nibble. Small bridges stretch over a narrow creek at several of its bends, and a small, willow-flanked pond inhabited by adorable ducks and swans complete the eye-pleasing sights. No passer-by could, from outside the property, ever anticipate such beauty and natural abundance on this side of the fence. It is mind-boggling, to say the least, and also very refreshing for Indirali, who misses the aesthetic gardens of her parents' palace.

"In those glory-filled golden times," Positrona resumes her speech, and everyone begins walking again, "the human race lived peacefully and harmoniously side by side with all other living beings. There was no sign of wanting to destroy life for the sake of feeding one's own lack of life energy; humans were able to live off the cosmic prana, the cosmic life force that underlies every aspect of life. To smell the fragrance of a beautiful flower was more nourishing for us than any other physical source of nourishment could ever be, for a flower's smell nourishes our soul and spirit, which was the natural focal point of our awareness throughout these bliss-filled times. This ability to bypass the necessity of feeding off physical food substances allowed the body to stay pure, light, and unencumbered, stretching the average earthly inhabitant's life span to encompass well over one or several thousand years of age within one lifetime. Only towards the end of the Golden Age did the humans start to turn their attention towards fruits and nuts as becoming their sustenance in the physical world. And as time progressed into the Silver, Bronze, and Iron Ages, and Earth became more dense, the physical food intake became more dense and predatory, and with that more pronounced and coarse, binding the human soul to the world of decay and death."

A shudder runs through Indirali's veins, for when Positrona speaks, the world around her assumes the quality of her speech. It's as if Indirali is right there, witnessing every facet of the leader's accounts, being exhilarated by the highs and depressed by the lows of her descriptions. Seldom before has Indirali experienced such an intimate connection to a person's presence and words except for her encounter with Goddess Aphrodite, and with the wise and beautiful Oracle of Atina. If only these wonderful, wise souls could all live together in one sacred, blissful place, Indirali wishes. For nothing compares to living with and to being surrounded by enlightened souls: nothing compares to being in the highly radiant and magnetic presence of an awakened soul, one who expresses loving-kindness and a refined sense of justice to the delight of every appreciating individual.

Positrona gifts Indirali with one of her super-radiant and infectious smiles, then continues: "Back in the golden days, friendship and unconditional love between individuals, or between groups of any size, was pretty much the norm, and any form of disharmony and discordance only began popping up when the spiritual atmosphere began to decline, heralding the colder and darker ages of isolation and alienation from the self and others. But in those glorious days, one brother or sister would give their life for one another, being loyal, reliable, supportive, and truth-abiding, and inspiring for each other. These were the days of constant celebrations and exalting creations of life and love, and these were the days we humans still enjoyed the conscious company of the Divine emissaries, and of members from the deva king- and queendoms." She smiles, and Indirali can't help but feel a hint of sadness in her face, for that's how much this beautiful and strong woman evidently yearns for the days of old, and the company of the blessed ones. And Indirali understands her all too well, for she feels similarly, and hopes that by the end of her journey, she will have all the good-hearted, conscious souls reunited in one heavenly king- and queendom, celebrating their friendship the way they used to in those golden times on Earth.

Positrona must have read Indirali's mind, for with renewed optimism she continues: "This Golden Age ideal of love and friendship was the guiding light for our beloved founder Pythagoras, whose followers and inner circle members held each other in highest esteem, and tried to always abide by the universal principles of harmony, balance, and unity. Pythagoras dedicated much of his time to unraveling the mysteries of sacred geometry in different disciplines, like mathematics, astronomy, and music. His findings everywhere confirmed his deep inner knowing that life in all its aspects is founded on unity, harmony, and Divine order, attesting the great realization that love is more powerful than any fragmenting emotion can ever be, and nature-based, timeless beauty outshines any attempt of the human individual to imitate and conceptualize the intricate patterns of nature within the artificialities he considers fashionable at any point in time." She pauses to gently direct their collective gaze towards the sky, where a swarm of birds playfully circles the property, their white bodies and wings glistening in the warm morning sun, as symbols of spirits, elegantly forming different formations to follow the lead of one bird, only to all of a sudden express their frolicking life joy by bursting into a firework-like outpouring from their midst that sends them collecting back into a harmonious pattern and has everyone continuing to follow the lead of their appointed lead bird again.

The group stares at them, fascinated, for Positrona's discourse is just finding its demonstrative example here, harmony and beauty within a group soul that leaves everyone embedded in a higher, more expanded, and unified sense of self.

"Pythagoras taught the principles of friendship to his followers and to anyone who would listen. His influence on the city of Croton was pretty strong and good for a long time. Croton's governing elite, as well as the citizens of Croton, all but functioned in harmony and understanding for each other, for as long as Pythagoras had his say in the political affairs of the time. But the tides were changing, and the principles of the transient worlds and the overshadowing influence of the Iron Age brought the downfall, which constitutes an inherent aspect of any polarity-based society. Many citizens who at first celebrated Pythagoras and his followers as the uplifting influence that they were now turned against them, blaming them for any problems the citizens encountered as a result of their own stress-release actions."

"What happened?" Indirali wants to know.

"Croton got entangled in political problems with its neighboring city Sybaris!" Positrona explains.

Indirali lets out a shout of surprise, for she recognizes the name as the Greek colonial city whose colonists founded the city she was born in, Posidonia, only that Sybaris was destroyed completely before Indirali was able to experience its famed splendor and prosperity for herself. She always felt a little sad when contemplating their founding city's fateful demise. She looks at Positrona with curious eyes, asking her to please continue.

"The dualistic phenomenon of police and criminal, manmade law enforcement and manmade law breaker, is becoming more predominant as the Iron Age progresses, and was a virtually unknown phenomenon throughout the Golden Ages, when humans were still deeply enmeshed in their Higher Selves, able to spontaneously follow and live by high moral and virtuous standards, without anyone having to monitor and control their behavior, and without anyone harming another life," Positrona explains. "And even though humans were able to function well on their own, guidance was always sought and welcomed from spiritually powerful beings who demonstrated higher worldly mastery and life-altering wisdom. One can say that the thirst and hunger for highest truth and ultimate soul liberation were even stronger back then than they are now, because back then, people in their great wisdom realized their non-perfect state in comparison to Divine standards very clearly, and were therefore more strongly interested in devoting their lives to the spiritual awakening process than they currently are. And that is quite paradoxical, for they need it even more nowadays, being spiritually fast asleep as compared to how awake they were during the Golden Age." She pauses to smilingly observe a bumblebee getting all drunk and satisfied from the nectar of an orange poppy flower, dancing around within the half-closed petals as if life is one nourishing, delicious celebration to revel in.

Her entourage follows her gaze, and beholding the same little but meaningful spectacle, they can't help but laugh out loud, for the little critter is absolutely self-absorbed in inhaling as much bliss as it possibly can.

"This is how we feel when imbibing Divine knowledge!" Xenia exclaims, all excited about this timely example of devotion to Divine nectar, the nectar of Divine knowledge, as embodied and taught by someone who mastered the challenges and limitations of Earth's frequency and is therefore able to lead others beyond the soul-crushing boundaries of their limited being and world.

Hyacinthos looks at Xenia with glowing eyes. Never has he experienced a girl as interested in spiritual growth and devotion to the Divine Source as he is. To encounter it in someone who also happens to be as beautiful and attractive as she is seems almost too good to be true.

Positrona notices his affection and, laying her arms around both of them, begins to walk again. "If a person is aligned with her or his Higher Self, she or he acts benevolently towards life. If she or he, however, is misaligned, her or his actions become violations of the laws of nature capable of harming herself or himself and others, as well as the natural environment she or he lives in. A person aligned with Higher Self is able to discern a true master soul, and is willing to learn from her or him. A person who is misaligned, however, is mainly interested in his lower-self interests and needs, often ridiculing, rejecting, and even persecuting a true master soul, for to be reminded of one's lower-self unimportance, and of one's violating behaviors, as thrown back on the lower self by the impeccable mirror of a master soul who is anchored in highest truth, is more than most average-mass-conscious people can bear. And so they would rather blame, curse, and imprison the one who holds the power over one's innate better knowing, hoping to drown out the voice of higher morality, and hoping that by destroying and/or killing this representative of one's own conscience, the problem will go away, and the issue does not need to be dealt with, at least not for the present moment."

"That's what pisses me off in regard to our priesthoods!" Hyacinthos blurts out, only to immediately blush for using a foul word in Positrona's presence. But she looks at him with genuine interest, devoid of any judgment he might have anticipated. Her gaze beckons him to speak his mind, and so he elaborates: "I just hardly can find anyone in our temples anymore that I would entrust my soul to. Everyone seems buyable and corrupt nowadays. And I see that the moral decline is in everyone; people don't give a damn anymore about true spirituality and about living a life of mutual support and appreciation. It just feels hopeless, to the point where I don't want to go to any temple anymore. But what else is there?" He looks vulnerable, because something deep in his heart tells him that he came to the right place to receive his answers.

"We have to consider the times we live in," Positrona reminds him, "and then adjust accordingly, and by that I don't mean to compromise our spiritual values, but to rather withdraw from the public eye, and from places where the masses have their dominion over. For this was exactly what our beloved founder Pythagoras had to do after the same people who saw in him a strong positive influence on society began to turn against him, blaming him for problems that were caused by people's lower-self vices, by greed and envy, rather than overtaking responsibility for their own weaknesses, and allowing Pythagoras to continue exercising his brilliant political and teaching skills that had helped thousands to create better lives for themselves. What happened in his days …" she turns to Indirali to finally answer her question, "is that Sybaris, a city of longstanding great wealth and incredible luxury, began to decline, with the demagogue leader Telys of the so-called democratic party speaking up against the thus far ruling oligarchy, demanding accountability and elimination of the wealthy rulership of the city, manipulating public opinion with demagogic speeches that all but criticized those who administered the city throughout many decades of a prospering economy. Nevertheless, as a collective soul, the city accumulated a fateful karmic load as it ruled over several tribes, and held about twenty-five neighboring cities as subjects. Eventually, Sybaris' citizens turned against their own rulership, seized power, and disowned many of the wealthiest citizens, driving them into exile. These citizens came to Croton to ask for asylum, which they were granted, until Telys and his partisans demanded the extradition of these escapees to further punish and eliminate them. Pythagoras, however, enjoying enough credibility and good reputation within Croton to be listened to at that very moment in time, advised to protect the fugitives, and to not hand them over to their would-be killers. Croton agreed to this bold move, defying the demands of Sybaris. This refusal, however, didn't sit well with the citizens of Sybaris, who, instigated by their revolutionary speakers, prepared for war against Croton, ready to exercise their self-willed judgment and right to extinguish lives. But how fatal did this move prove to be, for not only did they never recapture their fugitives, but their whole city was extinguished by their enemy as well, even though Croton's army was a third smaller than the one of Sybaris. After its complete destruction, Croton redirected the river Crathis to inundate the site of the city, to bury its ruins so as to be never seen again. Some escapees from Sybaris fled to Posidonia and Scidrus, two Greek colonial cities Sybaris had founded, and over the course of several decades, tried to resurrect Sybaris, the once so glorious and magnificent city many had envied for its fabled splendor. Some Greeks consider Sybaris' end the Divine punishment for being so prideful and arrogant, not only in its excessive luxuries, but also for demonstrating its contempt for the Olympic Games, whose main athletes and artists it apparently tried to attract and win over to its own city's games."

Positrona stops, for they have arrived at a beautiful gazebo that she indicates for everyone to take a seat in. Sappheiros courteously offers her the first step in, then rushes to dust off her velvet-cushioned seat. The floor is hewn from precious-looking marble, with a hexagon-shaped pattern artfully arranged in the center of the floor, accentuated with dark stones to contrast the pattern from the light ground. Positrona points at the sitting bench arranged around the inside of the gazebo, and everyone takes a seat as well, to continue listening to her narrative.

"Wow," Indirali goes, "I didn't know the Sybarites were so over the top, and ultimately attracted their own downfall. But I guess that's just how higher justice works. Still sad, that such a great city does not exist anymore."

"If we can take this city's fate as any measure, then maybe there is hope, and the Romans will experience their own judgment day sometime soon, too," Hyacinthos wishes.

"Well, this is all up to the Creator, and to the higher dharma of the oversoul that constitutes this city-state," Positrona balances the hot emotions, "but there certainly is truth to the idea of cause and effect, of excess and rebalancing, for even Croton was overcome with unrest after they had just won against Sybaris, and had stomped it into the ground. This unrest had to do with the distribution of the land of the many killed or exiled wealthy citizens of Sybaris, land that now began to divide the population of Croton, for greed and envy began to escalate, and those who felt treated badly quickly sought and found a scapegoat to blame their discontent on, namely the very people who previously advised to not deliver the refugees from Sybaris to their would-be killers." Positrona takes a moment, for even though all this lies in the distant past, she still feels for her spiritual founder, who tried to bring harmony and peace to the people but was treated with contempt and persecution in the end.

"During the presently reigning Iron Age," Positrona takes up her narrative thread again, "most inhabitants of planet Earth have long lost their connection to their own Higher Selves, and have begun to deteriorate into lower-self vices, blaming and persecuting others for problems they encounter in their own lives, rather than probing into the root cause of those problems, and overtaking responsibility and self-transformative action in order to solve them. A lazy and lethargic mindset is often at the heart of selfishness and self-absorption, and prompts the lazy person to draw the life force out from other living beings and living systems for his own consumption, for lack of being able to provide for his own survival by drawing on his own inner resources. Plus, he tends to find wrong outside of himself, judging others, as well as life and God Himself, in order to prevent having to change his lazy ways and attitudes. Finding wrong in others, however, has one disadvantage for the lazy person, namely that he will encounter another lazy person's instinct for preservation of his lazy lifestyle and outlook on life, which causes friction and possible aggression over the sparse seeming life force the lazy person feels forced to fight over. The natural instinct of this lazy person, therefore, is to go after the life force of a good-hearted soul, who most often is also the more creative and productive material-goods and service provider, the person who adds greatly to the wealth and prosperity of a community and common market. The lazy, life-force-sucking person, often identifying himself as a superior being, an elite member of society, or a politician, advocate, or other self-proclaimed important public figure, and therefore justified robber of life force from people who allow themselves to be subjugated by him, is often in need of a scapegoat for his own constant trespasses against public interests and wellbeing, and for the consequences of his vicious lifestyle, and therefore likes to use people of a minority group, or people who are known for their good-hearted nature, to blame and openly punish them in order to rid himself of any inconvenient public attention on his own lazy, thievish character and self-serving actions. And all this, even though the good-hearted person has nothing to do with the actual problem; he just ends up being the servant to the lower-self nature of the lazy predator person, a welcome distraction from the real problem, which is the lazy predator person himself, along with his competitive, thievish nature. The lazy person's instinct knows, however, that the good-hearted person will not fight back as aggressively and underhandedly as another lazy, selfish person would, but is more likely to surrender his life force willingly for the sake of maintaining peace, harmony, and goodwill amongst the population."

Positrona looks into the round, allowing a moment for the integration of her words. Hyacinthos, Indirali, and Hedna look at her with wide-open eyes, and Indirali can't help but marvel at the uncanny precision with which Positrona dissects the selfish human mind. She, in fact, describes it so well that it becomes crystal clear to Indirali that this phenomenon lies at the bottom of all human evil and suffering, for it is the inclination towards laziness that causes the lazy person to twist and distort reality to suit his lazy aptitude, and support his self-serving, thievish lifestyle. Because of this black-hole nature of the human mind, wars are instigated, persecution and punishments are imposed by violent enforcers, weaker, more gullible humans are taxed and controlled, and the environment exploited and destroyed, all in the name of a higher cause, and all meant to cover up the root cause of the evil and problem: the irresponsible, lower-self-oriented, energy-deflating self of the lazy problem causer.

"So, this lazy mindset is a phenomenon of the Iron Age we live in, and did not exist during the Golden Age?" Indirali tries to understand.

"What I call lazy, my dear friend, is the main quality of a soul who is but the fragment of a once greater soul, who lived throughout the Golden Ages, the spiritually enlightened times, of our physical world. Lazy stands for loss of life energy or life force depletion, due to an inability of the soul to assimilate proper nourishment from the fine ether, from the inner well of life force every soul has available to them from their own Higher Self. As the spiritual frequency of the physical world diminished over time, our soul essence began to retreat to higher realms to stay with the spiritual frequencies that continue to abound on higher levels of existence, causing the earthbound souls to fragment in the same way as a body falls apart whose soul is leaving the body. Death is not a sudden phenomenon as most humans of today assume; it just indicates the final breath a soul takes on this plane of existence, but the dying process begins much sooner in life, and happens in many small increments of dying and choking to death. As the soul gradually leaves the body, the life force leaves with it, and a cruder animation takes over, accounting for the greater multitudes of humans who seem to incarnate on the physical plane during the spiritually dark ages, humans of a less conscious potential, capable of living against their higher knowing, and against their Divine conscience, and with that, they become able to kill and violate life in the many ways that they do." Positrona smiles upon noticing the fervor written all over Indirali's and Hyacinthos' faces, with both wanting to understand and fathom the wisdom offered to them. "But then there are those fortunate humans," she explains, "who were able to maintain their higher integrity to a still large extent throughout the spiritual decline of the physical world, humans whose souls are anchored in the Divine Source of Life, as strong and peaceful as they were in the Golden or Silver Ages, conscious and aware of the universal and natural laws, and of the karmic law of cause and effect, that all gauge their thoughts and actions so life, nature, and the universe will continue to maintain and support them with an infinite reservoir of possibilities and life force. These are the good ones, the light workers, the productive and creative ones, the people who cannot be corrupted by any temptation, and who do not depend on the life force of others, because they are able to draw from their own inner and Higher Selves."

Her listeners cannot help but look at each other, realizing that they all must belong to this fortunate group of spiritually anchored souls, for they certainly don't feel the urge to kill, violate, condemn, judge, verbally or physically attack, control, subjugate, or manipulate their fellow humans. They are quietly in their own ways trying to understand why they feel different from the pack and why it is okay for them to feel good and at peace with who they are. Not eating killed animal flesh comes natural to them and needs no justification. It just feels right and in Divine attunement to preserve life in any shape and form and to not desecrate it for one's own survival urges. A shudder of awe overcomes them, for it is a rarity in these times to be amongst brethren of similar mindset and of high conscious awareness.

"Many non-self-referral, unaccountable people" Positrona continues, "have deteriorated in their ability to discern good from evil, right from wrong, to such an extent that they have come to believe that the opposite to the ultimate truth must be the ultimate truth, namely that darkness is light, and evil is good. Many years, and many lifetimes of gradual descent into the denser atmospheres of this planet, have all but veiled the ultimate truth from the eyes of a person who lives within the illusions of his lethargic, fickle mind, misreading and misinterpreting the events he creates according to his limited understanding. It is therefore understandable that most people throughout the present times are not only unable to relate to their own Higher Selves, but also are unable to discern the Higher Self in others around them, even and especially when they encounter it in a true spiritual master and true leader of a collective group of people, a person so deeply anchored in her or his Divine essence that she or he is able to bring these Divine attributes to everything she or he is doing. But again, her or his goodness and peaceful inclination become a fertile ground for the self-serving, lazy person to trample on, and to use to his own advantage. Throughout the Golden Age, the planetary atmosphere was still saturated with spiritual frequencies, thus supporting spiritually oriented activities and attitudes, and a spiritually anchored leadership able to uphold and foster prosperity and bliss for the good of all mankind. But since the Ages began to degenerate towards the presently reigning

Iron Age, leaders of a more rebellious, disruptive, and ill-intentioned nature have been rising in importance and by the multitudes, heralding the bad times, the times of dissent and of extensive human miseries. Like parasites and bad bacteria trying to finish off the last remaining life in a degenerating body, these kinds of leaders play on the last vestiges of human goodness, and turn everything around to serve the downfall of humanity, dragging the planet's environment in its destructive tow."

Positrona stops to take a breath, then begins to connect her enlightening speech with the life and persona of their spiritual founder: "Pythagoras certainly fell into the category of a spiritually enlightened master, who tried to see, relate, and support the goodness and competence within other ruling members of Croton's city oligarchy. And it was this ability to acknowledge and support the true, benevolent rulership of an established political system that allowed Pythagoras to feel amicable towards the wealthy refugees from Sybaris, as decadent and fallible as many of them had very likely become over time, but these rulers of Sybaris had also for a long time contributed greatly to the glory and luxury of the city's wellbeing, and were at the forefront of creating and maintaining much stability and comfort for all of its citizens, as well as for the citizens of the two Greek colony cities they had founded. It was this ability to govern and provide the communities with everything needed to create and maintain collective prosperity and wellbeing that Pythagoras found close to the ideal of rulership and friendship exercised throughout the Golden Ages, and which he tried to connect with and support in those who demonstrated the natural authority to administer the best social and political interests and benefits for their coinhabitants. Because living in peace and prosperity, and maintaining harmony amongst all human beings and with the natural environment they are surrounded by, is very much at the core of Pythagoras' teachings and code of conduct, for he knew this to be the basis for true health, and for true ultimate fulfillment any soul can aspire to within her or his life. Pythagoras therefore tried to support the ruling class as best he could, assuming that if any citizen ever had anything worthwhile to contribute to the government of the people, or if anyone thought of himself as a more competent, more capable politician and senator, this person would find a peaceful way to bring his suggestions and beneficial contributions to the forefront, always maintaining the peace and harmony between the government and the citizenry.

Of course, much has changed for the worse over the last millennia and centuries, throughout the currently reigning spiritual winter season, as the governing elite is increasingly mirroring the moral degeneration of the masses, and is getting more and more absorbed by the dark force to do the bidding of its dark force leaders, and act unconscientiously to the detriment of all mankind and nature. Pythagoras, however, entrained in higher learning and understanding about the true, spiritual nature of life and the universe we live in, always tried to live by the highest ideal of everything, including politics, and only turned his back on this ideal if no other alternative was available anymore. This principle of harmony and coherence is a universal phenomenon Pythagoras discovered in all spiritual and academic disciplines, and accounts for the precise cyclic routines we can find on the macrocosmic, universal levels, as well as on the microcosmic, subatomic levels, and which comprise the frequencies that in turn constitute the visible and invisible fabrics of life in any and all dimensions of existence. Harmony bridges the gap between any polarities, and thus renders conflict of any kind superfluous and unnecessary. It is therefore that Pythagoras insisted on unconditional friendship and kindness amongst his followers, teaching them the great benefits of a life based on the healing influence of coherence and soul-surrendering loyalty towards each other." Again, Positrona looks into the round, smiling as if to demonstrate her point. Three beautifully colored butterflies flutter into the gazebo, delighting everyone with their scintillating appearances and dance-like chase of each other, then leave the gazebo through the opposite opening.

"That's us here in our small, little paradise!" Sappheiros exclaims, laughing, "First this undisturbed and peaceful environment allowed us to develop our inner strength and beauty, as if in a protective cocoon, and then we were ready to hatch, and under Positrona's guidance become the beautiful, wise, and fun-loving beings we innately are!"

"And several of us had to heal old wounds incurred throughout our upbringing and lives outside of these protective walls," Xenia remarks, "before we were able to fully understand the importance and healing properties of a life shared with other like-minded, peaceful beings, and thus be able to relax into the infinite well of our inner resources and Divine essence!"

Hyacinthos looks at the woman of his adoration, wondering about her refined speech and graceful appearance with which she keeps casting her enchanting magic over his increasingly surrendering self, lifting and turning his yearning heart as if it were the wax in a sculptor's hands. Never has he felt so drawn to another human being; never has his heart felt such swooning at the sight of a woman as beautiful and charming as Xenia strikes him to be with every breath he shares in her presence.

"Pythagoras had to learn, however, that the people of our times don't naturally abide by the laws of unconditional friendship and loyalty," Positrona comes back to her narration, "but rather give in to lower-self traits like greed, anger, and envy. Even among his own followers were some who became corrupted when experiencing the power and influence on people that their political involvement bestowed on them. Brother turned against brother, and Pythagoras felt forced to retreat from political office, and take his closest and more humble followers with him into obscurity. Nevertheless, when the distribution of land left many without what they wanted, Pythagoras and his followers were the next available target on whom to vent their pent-up anger and frustration, blaming them for things gone awry and for the evil character traits of those self-assuming, land- and power-seizing dominators among the elite citizens that no average citizen in their right mind would have wanted to challenge and be at war with, but would rather use a good-hearted group of people instead to discharge their collective stress on, by persecuting and ridiculing them, and making them look wrong from the very beginning. Pythagoras, able to foresee the future to a great extent, chose to leave Croton with his family way before the political unrests against his followers began, but many of his followers did not leave the city they grew up in, and had to pay the heavy consequences inflicted upon them by a raging mob that ended up killing many of them, and forcing the rest into hiding that lasted for quite a long time."

Indirali can't believe the injustice and corruption she is hearing about and, with a mute face, keeps staring at Positrona, as if expecting her to lift the heavy veil of melancholy this story has been evoking in her.

"Pythagoras came to Metapontium, where he founded another enlightenment school. Throughout many generations we have been transmitting his knowledge of the higher principles of life to those who are interested, and who aspire to transcend the limitations of their earthly incarnation. His school underwent several ups and downs in regard to how publicly accepted and open with his teachings it was able to be, to finally, over the last many decades, have his spiritual descendants retreat altogether from any and all public attention so as to not fall prey to and serve as yet another scapegoat for the presently strongly reigning collective resentment against the control-addicted Romans."

"We were fortunate enough to have been donated this very beautiful and fertile land outside of our founding father's last homestead," Sappheiros informs. "A wealthy merchant and his family, God bless them, decreed their land to our group after he died, leaving his wife and children another, equally impressive property at another location, and this one here to the group of people he loved and was a member of himself, a Pythagorean follower whose heart beat according to the blessed rhythms of harmony and friendship, the way our revered Positrona has been describing to us all."

Everyone nods inwardly to acknowledge Sappheiros' information, then turns their attention back to Positrona, whose enriching knowledge seems to flow unendingly, putting everyone right there, into the midst of the historic and spiritual events that shaped the fate of Pythagoras' group over the last few hundred years.

Positrona affirms Sappheiros' comment, adding: "During the Golden Age, nature provided abundantly for all our needs, as we lived in harmony with its laws, observing Mother Earth's, Goddess Gaia's needs and wants as if they were our own, and thus receiving everything from her that our hearts desired. The climate was mild, beneficial, and conducive for life's higher, more refined expressions, the land was lush and green, with an infinite array of plants that satisfied our needs on all levels, and the human race lived in harmony and affluence, without negativities clouding their senses, but rather highest awareness and bliss lifting their spirits to realms of constant celebration and enthusiasm for life. Everyone lived the perfect balance of affluence and modesty, attuned to her or his higher will and best interest for the soul, thus foregoing the negative consequences of a life wasted with superfluous garbage, or a life squashed under the pressures of lack and unfulfilled wanting. Divine attunement of the soul provides just the right mix of polarities to continue energizing the soul with the frequencies of highest bliss and power, to let it dance on the rhythms of cosmic life energy, on the breath in- and exhalations of our Creator." Positrona takes a moment before she continues to draw her spirals of knowledge, all along the thread of her underlying intent of revealing to her guests the special nature and mission of her group.

"Pythagoras emphasized to his followers the enormous benefit of sharing one's own wealth with his spiritual family to make sure one is not exposed to unnecessary cruelty and hardship, but is a vital member of a group who makes ascension its priority, as well as becoming the Divine Superbeings we are predestined to be. It is a known fact to any sensitive person that there is no gain and no joy in experiencing wealth and fortune when your brother or sister is suffering the pain of lack and misery. Likewise, our founder encouraged the striving for wealth and affluence, for it enables a more relaxed and enjoyable lifestyle and outlook on life, for as long as the wealth is not won at the expense of someone else's life force or disadvantage. In fact, Pythagoras fell outside the box of common understanding; his teaching about the right balance between any pair of polar values went beyond the increasingly rigid and lifeless interpretations of reality, and would often trigger the uninitiated to heftily criticize his reasoning and his way of surprising and jolting the average mind out of its fixated ways. His comprehension and teachings indeed were beyond his time, having gleaned his wisdom from enlightened priesthoods initiated into the mysteries of the ancient Hindu Vedas, teachings of the Lord Gautama Buddha from Nepal and India, Babylonian teachings of Zarathustra, and the mystery teachings of the temples of the land of Mizr, or Egypt. Not only did he study astronomy and learn to understand the regular movements and repetitive cycles of our firmament's planets and stars, but he also understood the universe to be mental and spiritual in its nature, the highest conception of the Infinite Living Mind, an endless ocean of consciousness, containing and encompassing within itself the infinite multitudes of individual consciousness and microcosms, the sparks that constantly motivate the individual soul to reconnect with the eternal realm of consciousness, the ultimate source and goal of all of life. Of this eternal ocean of consciousness we all partake, and ultimately influence with our unique flavor of individuality. And it is this all-knowing and all-powerful, infinite ocean of consciousness that radiates ultimate truth and orderliness into all of creation, as an underlying frequency pattern along which individual honesty and integrity allow the highest principles of life to be recognized and lived at all times."

Positrona stands up and takes a few steps towards the gazebo entrance, indicating for Hesiod to come over and let her borrow his lyre for a moment. He smilingly obliges, and Positrona returns to her audience for a short demonstration of a point she wants to illustrate. She begins to play the lyre herself, so beautifully and melodiously that her listeners begin to feel deeply entranced by her musical skill. The rhythm is harmonious, the melody ecstatically soaring in waves of unending bliss and enchantment. Indirali's thoughts begin to drift to her love, to Loriolan, her merman lover. Where might he be, and what might he be going through this very moment? How long still until they will be able to lie in each other's arms? Such are her longings triggered by the hauntingly beautiful melodies Positrona gracefully conjures from the instrument that her eyes become misty and her heart aching with unfulfilled happiness. She notices how even though she enjoys Positrona's presence and discourse very much, as well as everyone else in her present company and environment, a deep void persists in her heart, a void only he can fill, the love of all her lifetimes, her Loriolan!

Positrona's playing settles into a melodious rhythm that keeps repeating itself softly in the background as she begins to speak over it: "From the ancient knowledge system of the Vedas, Pythagoras learned that everything in creation is in its truest essence made of numbers. Everything from the most dense, material composition to the loftiest, most refined, and abstract concepts and essences can be expressed numerically; concepts like abundance or poverty, justice or injustice, can all be expressed in numbers that correspond to their innate nature and highest truth. Our founder was a genius in many ways, but one of his most renowned accomplishments lies in the field of the mathematical theory of music, explaining how the relationship between musical notes can be expressed as numerical ratios. He was an excellent musician himself, playing the lyre like a God, often using his musical playing to heal the sick and weak. He realized that vibrating strings produce harmonious tones when the ratios of the lengths of the strings are whole numbers, and that these ratios can also be extended into other areas of life as well. Thus harmony and wellbeing can easily be evoked, and disharmony and illness can just as easily be avoided, by those who care for the upliftment of all of life! Even in regard to secular interests like land assessment and distribution, or city and drainage planning, the Vedic knowledge of mathematics proved itself an accurate, fair, and just way of dealing with every arising situation and challenge. Much strife and anguish could thus be avoided, for arithmetic and geometry helped with the redistribution and consolidation of the many varieties of land parcels so all involved parties felt fairly treated in regard to the quality of the land, and especially in regard to irrigated land everyone naturally craved for their own prosperity. In the area of city planning, mathematics provided both the small, detailed execution, as well as the big-picture perspective, allowing a higher perception of orderliness to encompass the whole city's layout, guaranteeing precise measurements to add up to a harmonious whole, with certain road types boasting the same fixed widths and angles, and complementary drainage systems working efficiently based on their mathematical implementations. Buildings, the physical and sensual extension of our human bodies, were constructed with the Golden Ratio of numbers in mind to allow the soul to feel expanded and free within the otherwise limiting feeling walls of a house. Attention was given to the fact that life force enters the solid world through the energy vortexes of a transcending mind, which in turn needs a sanctuary in its environment in order to blossom to its fullest extent. The Brahmasthan, or transcendent void, in the center of every building, comprising a certain mathematical fraction of the whole building, provides just that, an open space for the mind to connect with its innermost source, thus bringing enlightenment, harmony, and enrichment to the individual's building and life."

"Wow!" Indirali can't help but exclaim her amazement at the depth and vast scope of the present topic. Because even though she occasionally feels like dreaming and transcending while Positrona speaks and plays the lyre, she still comprehends the illumining nature of her wise words, as if the light of highest understanding tries to brighten any dark corners of her hungering mind, turning misperceptions upside down, and clearing the way for the light of truth to anchor itself into her being and world.

"Isn't it a fascinating topic?!" Sappheiros agrees, clapping his hands together as if to express his own excitement. "I'm just so grateful we have our revered master Positrona in our lives. She understands and lives our founding father's teachings so perfectly and masterfully that we all feel in very good hands with her!"

Xenia nods enthusiastically, smiling broadly, because for some inexplicable reason she feels especially happy today, in the company of these kind-hearted strangers, and right next to Mister Handsome himself!

"Indeed, knowledge is a great purifier," Positrona picks up the sentiment, "and the truth of all things certainly has the power to set us free from our self-imposed bondages, created by our own ignorance and illusions."

"But how can you make sure you can trust someone's words, when they claim to be the representatives of the ultimate truth, and then they don't live by their own words, but rather exhibit selfish little interests and even corruptibility?" Hyacinthos expresses his anguish. For in his world, the temple priests have long developed into the very hypocrites they so relentlessly condemn others to be.

Reading his mind, Positrona answers with the calm and foresight that is her distinct, innate nature: "Know thyself, and you know the universe and everything that is contained in it! If you can trust yourself, you won't be fooled by any hypocrite's words, no matter how magnificently he tries to cover up his contradictable actions and behaviors."

"But how can I get to the point of knowing myself?" Hyacinthos has anguish written all over his face. "By just intellectually studying books on wisdom and all the academic disciplines? Is that really enough to find and enliven my inner connection with the Source of Life?" he really wants to know.

"It can get you to a certain point," she replies, "then the mind collapses onto itself, prompting the immature soul to regard itself as the highest knower of things, irregardless of the fact that the ultimate truth resides beyond his intellectual grasp, and on the other hand prompting the mature soul to surrender to the fact that the ultimate truth exists beyond his intellect, causing him to try to find an embodiment of this highest truth, a true master soul who has the ability to both break open his limited, rigid mindset that tends to regard itself as the ultimate instance of life, and lift him to the refined inner spheres from which rejuvenation and highest truth flow incessantly for his transformation, purification, and ascension. The choice of which path a person wants to follow is all up to her or him, whether to get stuck in lower self arrogance and willfulness, or keep flowing and growing under the nourishing influence of the Higher Self spheres, through the applied attitude of humility and unconditional surrender to the Highest Will of the Divine Super-Mind."

Positrona stops, and Hyacinthos looks at her with big round eyes, trying to fathom her wisdom before he indeed makes a fool of himself, for having the truth thus clearly brought to his attention puts him into high alert to not trespass into a disrespectful attitude, for obviously he has encountered the fortune to have come into the presence of a true master soul, the very guide and teacher he was — on a deep soul level — seeking for all these many last years of his young life.

"You are certainly not the only one wondering about this highly important, albeit often controversial point in a seeker's life," Positrona warmly continues to explain. "After Pythagoras transitioned onto the higher realms of existence, many of his followers, and many late followers who never had the fortune of knowing and living around the master when he was still among the Earth inhabitants, began to alienate themselves from his knowledge, losing their revitalizing connection to the Source of Life — which many were only able to experience through the master anyway — and with that they began to lose sight of the highest truth, quickly diminishing their spiritual powers, and degenerating their level of existence to the level of a compromised person who only possesses partial knowledge, a knowledge that divides and conquers rather than unites and uplifts mankind. The intellectually inclined held on to the logically provable parts of his knowledge, emphasizing mathematics and statistics over the lived experience of higher states of consciousness, and ridiculing those who lost the zest and ability to intellectually explain and describe the vast treasure of knowledge our founding master left behind, whereas the more soul-centered individuals among his followers split into the oral traditionalist categories of firstly the blind believers, who remember Pythagoras' great accomplishments and miraculous doings, but unfortunately have only memories or information to draw from that are not based on any of their own inner self experiences and verifications, which therefore renders them often superstitious and squashed by self-imposed taboos, and secondly those who fall into the category of those few fortunate ones that still live enough of his and the Divine's ultimate truth that they remember with deepest clarity and conviction most of his supernatural powers and wisdom, knowing firsthand the essence of highest truth in his teachings, because it corresponds with their own state of being and consciousness."

"And that's us!" Xenia exclaims, smiling broadly. "Everyone of our mystery school felt attracted to Positrona's grand wisdom and unerring guidance, because life had purified us to the point where her wisdom can help us, can fall onto the fertile ground of our readied and prepared minds, so to say!" Her voice sounds like a joyous dance in Hyacinthos' ears, captivating the young man who evidently can't take his eyes off her radiant countenance.

"The fact, my dear friends, is that Pythagoras is still very much alive to those who are able to lift themselves beyond their physical limitations," Positrona continues to boggle everyone's minds. "Even throughout his lifetime as Pythagoras, he was able to remember and relive his past lifetimes on this planet and on otherworldly planets and planes of existence. Time and space become irrelevant once the mind is able to penetrate and transcend the limitations of one's misdirected focus. The Flower of Life symbol allows the contemplating mind to go beyond these limiting factors, into the worlds of immortality and eternity, to meet up with our brothers and sisters of the light who exist on these elevated levels of existence, including our beloved friend and master Pythagoras. I myself am fortunate enough to be able to communicate on a constant basis with our dear master, who continues to pour his wisdom out for our benefit!"

"Really?" Indirali expresses her heartfelt and growing amazement. "You travel so freely between the dimensions, interacting with beings from higher worlds, able to live and breathe the freedom of unlimited existence?" Her eyes glow as she tries to wrap her head around the fact of this coveted reality. For she herself is on her way to meet the immortals, to meet Goddess Aphrodite and any other God or Goddess who is kind enough to help her on her quest to ultimately and finally unite with her beloved water prince, Loriolan, her eternal soulmate.

"One important and essential part of our purification process, which in turn is the prerequisite for transcending and entering those high vibrational levels of existence, is the adherence to silence over extended periods of time," Positrona illumines her listeners' receptive minds. "Next to meditation, silence allows the mind to settle down to those deep, restful, and rejuvenating levels of consciousness that the busy and distracted mind can only wish for and dream of, but hardly ever gets a glimpse of anymore, for its daily activities just keep thwarting it with their reactive cycles of undigested experiences and the consequent nightly unravelments in restless sleeps. When speaking ceases and the activities become suffused with peace and equanimity, the thoughts and feelings begin to lighten up as well, slowly dissipating into the light of highest truth and all-powerful life energy. Silence allows the soul to step back and begin witnessing the mind's thoughts, to be able to evaluate what kind of thoughts are life and happiness supporting, and which aren't, and then have the freedom and choice to think and create the kind of reality he prefers, thus liberating himself from undesirable attachments, debilitating habits, and self-jeopardizing attitudes. Pythagoras taught those of his followers who were able to understand that silence allows you to see and comprehend those higher realities that constantly permeate our physical reality, but are not perceived by those who are unable to expand their sensory ranges because of their attachments to a limited reality zone. Silence allows the senses to turn to the inner realms, helping to enliven the inner worlds and realities, and opening the channels of higher communication, enabling the voice of the guardian spirit to be heard, and most importantly, the fine voice of the Divine Itself, offering Its impeccable, perfect guidance according to the Will of the Most High for the individual's life, the Will that is able to provide all the right circumstances for the maximum benefit of the individual's and collective life experience. And whosoever is able to hear and follow this highest, purest, and innermost guidance and Will will never err on his path again; he will never fall prey to confusing and debilitating influences, he won't ever be a victim of the black magical power abuse current governing elites apply for their selfish interests, nor will he fall into the traps of manipulation and enslavement, but will instead be able to stand strong in his highest truth, integrity, and Divine power."

"I want all that!" Hyacinthos blurts out. "But how in the world can one person stand against the spiritual darkness currently reigning in our temples? Where can I turn to receive the kind of guidance you are so generously imparting to us, were I not to come and join your group for good?"

"Why don't you?" Xenia can't help but invite him. "If your heart is ready for this kind of commitment, then our beloved master will be ready to accept you as well! At least that has been the experience of everyone else here!" she adds demurely.

Hyacinthos looks at her, a big smile spreading across his face. What beautiful fate might life have in store for him here? But then his sense of obligation towards his father reminds him of his task at hand, and with a trace of anguish in his voice, he reminds everyone: "We should be off to Tarentum soon, and salvage what little I can still get for these few items left to us. My father and mother need this income, and I cannot let them down."

"And you won't have to!" Positrona rises from her seat to return the lyre to Hesiod. "For I will have a boat bring you to Tarentum this very night, close to and along the shore. I have a mutually beneficial agreement with Poseidon that allows me to use this particular coastal water path for our purposes, without being threatened or destroyed by the wrath he harbors against the majority of today's seafaring folks."

The little group of visitors stare at her with eyes wide open, for the thought of leaving this blessed, peaceful place behind rings actually quite horrifyingly in their ears. Positrona's mystery school sure is an oasis within the hostile environments everyone has been encountering, and the thought of not seeing her or any of her loving followers anymore saddens the three visitors.

"You will be traveling throughout the night," Positrona suggests, "for Poseidon is the least of our worries — pirates and the Roman armadas are roaming the sea for possible treasures, and respectively for escapees from the Roman censorship that keeps imposing itself on the Greek population, and rendering the once relatively free people into controlled and accounted-for citizens of the Roman empire."

Hyacinthos and the girls look a bit shocked at hearing this news. Hyacinthos had accompanied his father once before to Tarentum, a year and a half back, but much seems to have changed over this short period of time that has planted the power of control firmly in the hands of the Roman imperialists, much to the dismay of the Greek colonists. He sure is not keen on facing these Romans and letting them get the better of him and his family. But survival needs dictate a certain degree of involvement with the imperialists, if one is not to go down from their punishing and condemning strategies and measures. But if there is something Hyacinthos hates more than the Romans, it is the need to compromise and to sell one's soul out to the most violence-prone, forceful conqueror over one's life. He shudders at the thought and again wishes that there would be a way to stay with Positrona and Xenia, all the while knowing that his parents would be taken good care of.

"Sappheiros will be organizing the boat and crew for your transport tonight," Positrona wants them to know, and addressing Hedna and Indirali, she continues: "and if it is okay with you and your Mistress, Hedna can help out in the kitchen, prepare lunch with the other kitchen staff, and prepare food for the next part of your journey!" She looks at Indirali and Hedna, awaiting their acknowledgement.

Indirali nods at Hedna, and with a big smile, her maidservant rises along with Sappheiros to leave the gazebo with him, glad to be able to be of practical help. Even though she enjoyed Positrona's presence and discourse very much, she has to admit that some of her enormous wisdom simply blew her mind and left her hanging somewhere between spaces, unable to gather her former self back together again. She hopes that some good old work will help her gather her senses and ground her so as to be back in her role of her princess's maidservant, because this is the role she was born into, and this is the job she loves and performs best.

Positrona looks after them with a heartwarming smile, remarking what a lovely, pure-hearted, and devoted young woman Indirali's maidservant is. Indirali smilingly agrees, as another thought begins to absorb her attention, the thought of wanting to help her father find the perfect high priestess for his temple, someone as special and wise as Positrona, if only she could be won for this daunting, yet crucial task and position.

CHAPTER 17

"Thank you very much for helping us to get to Tarentum, very much appreciated!" Hyacinthos remarks, clearing his throat as he tries to hide his emotion.

Positrona turns towards him and smilingly answers: "You are welcome!"

"Yes, thank you so much for all your wonderful help, and especially for your mind-expanding, Divinely-suffused knowledge," Indirali agrees. "I just wish we could dwell in your presence forever, and could have all our loved ones around us, to enjoy each other's company, and grow together into the light of our Higher Beings."

"Your wish is certainly in alignment with the Highest Will," Positrona assents, "for the unification of all unconditionally loving members of our soul family is very much an innate forward momentum of consciousness and life, urging the spiritual aspirants to finish with their separating inclinations and weak focus, to finally come home to our unified, Divine existence, to our richly nourishing Source of Origin."

She takes a step towards the center of the gazebo, extending her arm to direct everyone's attention to the pattern in the marble floor: "This Fruit of Life pattern consists of thirteen circles, as you can see: six on the outside, six on the inside, and one in the center. If by a magic hand this two-dimensional pattern were to erect itself and turn into a three-dimensional sphere …,"

Indirali and Hyacinthos can't believe their eyes because — as Positrona is describing it — the pattern indeed begins to lift from the ground and magically arrange itself into a three-dimensional, cube-like sphere. How can this be, they both think, for there seems to be no physical basis for this kind of phenomenon, no mechanical devices that would explain why these circles begin to rise into the air, becoming three-dimensional spheres, with the six outer spheres staying firmly planted on the center ground.

"… then we would create the Metatron's Cube, a sacred geometrical figure overseen and inspired by the Archangel Metatron, a cumulatively compounded sphere of protection and containment that keeps unwanted and negative entities and demons away from any of the sacred rituals we enlightenment seekers like to perform for the sake of invoking the highest powers to aid us in our soul search and self realizations."

Her two visitors are absolutely stunned, trying to fathom the intricate structure in front of their eyes, as the second layer of six spheres hovers in midair, and the center sphere assumes the tip of the finely vibrating cube that seems to exude a silent, but dynamic liveliness, reminiscent of the invisible, yet powerful presence of a living and breathing being.

"We have come together here for various reasons, all culminating in one grand master plan of our Divine Creator!" Positrona explains, pointing from the bottom spheres all the way up to the top sphere as if to underscore her statement. "As I understand it, Hyacinthos, you have come all the way from Heraclea to lose and to find yourself in your attempt to shake off the outdated practices of a sold-out spiritual temple elite, hoping to find what your searching and yearning heart truly desires, namely true spirituality that has the power to reconnect you with your innermost, Divine Source, thus enabling you to empower yourself to live your life with the joy and happiness only a purified heart and soul can experience. And you, my dear Indirali," she turns towards the Princess, "have tasted the ecstasy of true love, and are now willing to undertake whatever journey and challenges along the way are necessary to unite you with your true love in the most ultimate and eternal way possible. Am I correct?"

Both nod, surprised and overcome by Positrona's supernatural influence on their souls.

"Only that you, Hyacinthos, feel thwarted by your love and devotion for your parents, afraid of what might become of them if their only son decides to leave them and withdraw from worldly life in order to tend to his spiritual aspirations, and thus be no longer available to help support his parents in their upcoming old age. And you, Indirali, have left your parents with a feeling of unease regarding the corruption of Lucania's temple priesthood, as revealed to you and your father during your stay with the Oracle of Atina. It is very much on your mind to help your father find a worthy, spiritually upright, and competent replacement for the High Priesthood of Posidonia's temple." She stops, inviting her guests' reactions.

Again, Indirali and Hyacinthos nod, as if still in a trance. What exactly is going on here, they wonder. How does Positrona know all these things, and why does this Metatron's Cube keep spinning and accelerating its static-looking movements? It feels as if a spinning vortex is radiating its compounding energy outwards, not just encompassing their bodies and the whole of the gazebo, but for some reason the impression of reality seems to have shifted, and both Indirali and Hyacinthos, along with beautiful Positrona and Xenia, find themselves floating within a timeless and spaceless vacuum, devoid of any outer points of reference, and beyond any earthly experience and comprehension they thought they were a part of just a moment ago. Indirali and Hyacinthos have a decision to make, namely whether to freak out from this mysterious and unknown experience or to continue to surrender to its strangely healing effect that seems to overtake them at the same rate as they are able to muster the courage to completely and utterly surrender to the mysterious, magical happenings Positrona obviously is able to conjure from the depths of the infinite cosmos. But being who they are, the decision comes naturally, and both continue to follow Positrona's leads wherever her loving attention directs them to go, into the core issues of their combined lives and into the hearts of their longing souls.

"Your Higher Selves have asked me to expand your conscious horizons so you may make decisions regarding your core issues in life that are based on knowing the whole truth about the matter," Positrona helps them understand, preparing them for what is to come. "If you knew the near future of Heraclea, Hyacinthos, your decisions would certainly take on a different color and nature. You would not leave the decisions up to your unknowing parents, but would take matters into your own hands to ultimately help everyone in the most efficient and best way, ensuring not only your next generation's survival, but also your parents' wellbeing in the meantime."

'What is she talking about?' Hyacinthos wonders, overcome by a strange foreboding. In that moment, however, something outrageously extraordinary happens: the sphere on top of the cube begins to expand like a bubble that continues to grow beyond what one might think it could ever encompass, catapulting Hyacinthos into an altered state of awareness that allows him to take a peek into Heraclea's future, winding the wheel of history forward a few decades, and showing him the city's agonies as it tries to preserve its independence from the Roman dictatorship, only to lose it anyway in the end, around 212 BCE, to Hannibal, the Carthaginian general, who under the guise of wanting to help defend the city, takes it over and uses its resources to finance his insatiable eagerness to vanquish the seemingly unstoppable Romans. 'What a mess!' Hyacinthos realizes, 'what an enormously disturbing mess!' Why would anyone want to tough it out under such oppressive circumstances, and how could he ever let his parents and friends wither away in such hostile environments, people with children and their children's children?! A sense of impotence overcomes him, and helplessly he looks at Positrona's benevolent eyes, eyes that increasingly become the anchor for his confused and aching heart, for knowing this kind of hopeless seeming future does not particularly encourage him to think and act courageously outside the box but rather makes him want to give up and die right here and now under this master's merciful feet.

Positrona touches his forehead, and with one lightning bolt of extrasensory influx of highest energy and clarity, his third eye opens to let another version of his future in, one that he controls and that is according to his Higher Self Will. He sees himself married to Xenia, his beautiful, magnificent soulmate of all times. Together they enrich not only their own lives, but also the lives of all those around them that they are able to guide and touch with their overflowing unconditional love that springs so abundantly from the well of their unified hearts. He sees himself and Xenia leading a temple in the most honorable, highest truth-abiding ways and enjoying splendidly the company of not only his parents and dearest friends but also the many adorable children born to them. This vision makes him happy; this vision he certainly can live with and actually craves to realize for all his dear ones, and for his love, Xenia, if only she will have him.

"We have been expecting your and Indirali's visit," Positrona reveals, "and have been preparing Xenia for her mission as a high priestess, alongside you, Hyacinthos. For the Divine has ordained her to be your eternal soulmate and wife, if only you will have her!"

Hyacinthos can't help but allow tears to fill his eyes. If only he will have her? Of course he will, of course he will! He falls to his knees, and chokingly addresses the woman of his longings; hands laid onto his heart, he asks her — in front of Indirali and Positrona — whether she will have him as her eternal soulmate and husband, for the moment he laid eyes on her, he was smitten by her divine elegance and beauty, by her refined grace and unfathomable magic over his soul, and the thought of leaving her for good feels like a death wish at the moment that he cannot allow himself to harbor. He therefore implores her to consider his feelings, for his life is in her merciful hands, and his soul aches to unite with her beautiful essence, of which he never even knew he was able to dream.

And like the sun caressing the moon with her light, Xenia streams her love onto his soul, nourishing his aching heart, and lifting him from his shadow existence into the light of two suns dancing together in the heavens of eternal love and devotion.

Indirali is deeply influenced by this extraordinary, Divine spectacle; witnessing two true lovers find their way into each other's lives and arms, the way she will be able to very soon as well, she hopes, is overwhelming to her soul, to say the least. Feeling exhilarated because of Hyacinthos' enormous fortune and found love, she joins him in his release of tears, shedding tears of joy and relief that thank the Source of Life for watching out for their destinies and wellbeing, even throughout a time when the soul irrationally fears being utterly abandoned by its Divine Creator.

"Indirali!" Positrona addresses her gently. "Xenia will make an excellent high priestess for your father's temple in Posidonia. And after a few years of receiving teaching and initiations, Hyacinthos will be able to join his wife in her temple duties, as an incorruptible, Divine Truth loving high priest, who will support your father's highest aspirations for his country, two beautiful souls, who will fill the present void in your country's spiritual guidance, two loving beings who will also bring a group of beloved family and friends to Posidonia, willing and able to further support your father's lofty goals and high moral values, throughout Posidonia, and beyond. How does this sound?"

Indirali looks at her as if a shadow just lifted from her soul. This is why she came here! Now it makes total sense! Some part of her would have liked to see Positrona take over her father's temple, but the majority of her being recognizes the Divine organizing power, the Divine plan, of having honorable, kind-hearted Hyacinthos and his magnificently beautiful, spiritually awake Xenia leading the temple, two marvelous souls she is happy to have met and found, and whom she feels very fortunate to be able to bring to her father's attention, with their possible appointment by him. A big smile spreads across her face as she ponders the delightful consequences of this auspicious meeting.

"I myself am deeply entrained in the spiritual spheres, to the point of having only a very diminished interest in this earthly world," Positrona explains to Indirali, reading her mind. "My presence and teachings revolve around a small group of initiates to whom I hope to be able to transfer my knowledge and powers when their minds and souls are open and ready enough. Then, my dear Princess, I intend to join my light sisters and brothers in the higher-dimensional worlds, to continue learning from the grand masters of our universe and beyond, and continue weaving my light magic for the benefit and delight of those who can appreciate it."

"I appreciate it!" Indirali blurts out, still crying. The thought of Positrona not dwelling amongst them anymore is more than she can bear at this moment. "I appreciate you and your infinite knowledge so much!" She lowers her gaze to try and find her center again, that place in her heart and soul that endlessly provides her with a feeling of all is well, and all will be well forever. And hey, she remembers, she will be with the immortals very soon as well, if the Divine wills it so, and keeps supporting her on her way to get there.

"I know you do, I know you do!" Positrona comforts Indirali's sore heart and mind. "And I will be waiting for you in the higher realms, to welcome you to your true state of being, applauding your fervor and heroic courage that help you overcome the most difficult odds and most devious demons of the lower psychic realms. You are an extraordinary young lady, a true princess with the refined senses that allow the Divine Source of Life to be recognized and appreciated in everything you encounter and touch. Many blessings will still flow from your unending will to go and reach the highest goals a human can aspire to, and to unite with a member of the water race in the course of it! Nothing seems to stop you, a soul capable of such deep and vast feelings of love that mountains crumble before you, and oceans dry out so you can step through them unhindered. You will conquer the elements, the lower Gods, the demons, and any hindering objects and beings in your way, for you are chosen to enter the heavenly realms, with all the glory fit for a true princess and queen of the spheres stretching in all four cardinal directions, and into the higher-dimensional directions of the higher queen- and kingdoms."

Indirali's eyes having stopped tearing, her breath almost at a standstill, she hangs on Positrona's every word to let her soul heal and unfold under her nourishing, praising speech and attention.

"Here!" Positrona takes Hyacinthos' hand as well as Xenia's hand, and then puts them together. "The Divine Source has sanctioned and blessed your union. You are both equal and similar in your spiritual bodies, able to inspire and motivate yourselves endlessly and with Divine fervor and support. Go and grow into your beautiful mission, and let others around you be affected by the infinite love and wisdom that pours from your hearts and minds!" She puts her arms around both their shoulders, and thus catalyzes the spark of love between them to take over and have them finally hold hands, their faces blushing, but infinitely happy with the whole situation. Then Positrona turns to Indirali again and, laying her hand around her waist, turns her towards the top sphere of the Metatron's Cube that still keeps spinning in the most alluring and mysterious fashion.

"Now, my dear friend, how about taking a look into the all-seeing eye, the expanded vision of your own Higher Self, to see where your eternal beloved might be at this very moment, to see how Loriolan is doing, and what fate might have befallen him on his journey to meet you, the princess of his heart and all his lifetimes!"

Indirali is stunned to hear Positrona utter these words. Is it really possible to look into Loriolan's life right now, to get a glimpse of what he might be going through? However, her heart feels a big relief hearing Positrona suggest this fantastic sounding offer, and with deepest surrender, she allows the Master to guide her into seeing and perceiving what her soul was secretly wondering and hoping to behold and know, namely, where is he, and how is he? Is he still thinking about her the way she thinks about him every moment of her life; is his love for her still driving him forward and towards the elusive seeming heavens that alone can unite their differences and present them with the infinite love and unity of their souls that they so deserve?

And so, with curiosity and anxious anticipation, Indirali stares into the widening sphere of the spinning and vibrating Metatron's Cube, as it begins to encircle her with its high energetic charge and light-filled luminosity. Positrona gently squeezes her hand, and the gates of perception begin to open up to her.

www.ingramcontent.com/pod-product-compliance
Lightning Source LLC
Chambersburg PA
CBHW080743250626
47162CB00010B/3003

* 9 7 8 1 9 1 0 5 1 8 1 0 6 *